Malignant

Anita Waller

Praise For Anita Waller

"Be prepared to put everything on hold when you pick up this book, for me it was a "one sitting read" a book that I could not put down." **Yvonne Bastian – Me And My Books**

"Thanks for a great read Anita Waller! When is the next one out??" **Rebecca Burton – If Only I Could Read Faster**

"This book has lots of gasp out loud moments and plenty that will make you a little weepy too (it did for me anyway)." **Lorna Cassidy – On The Shelf Reviews**

"This is an engrossing read that I pretty much inhaled." **Philomena Callan – Cheekypee Reads And Reviews**

"Waller has an amazing skill to grab you and keep you interested until the very last page." **Eclectic Ramblings of Author Heather Osborne**

"WOW! ANITA HAS DONE IT AGAIN. What a bloody brilliant, outstanding, captivating story." **Gemma Myers – Between The Pages Book Club**

"This is a very gritty read...Add into the mix, the ruthlessness of the gangsters and you've got a cracking crime thriller." **Claire Knight – A Knight's Reads**

Praise for Captor:

"It has twists and turns, shocks and honestly at times I had no idea what the end would be!" **Donna Maguire – Donnas Book Blog**

"A plot to keep you turning from beginning to end. I really enjoyed this . A captivating read ." **Nicki Murphy – Nicki's Book Blog**

"... a really well written, gripping book with plenty of twists for me!" **Donna Maguire – Donnas Book Blog**

"...building up to a tense, drama packed read. I was literally biting my nails by the end." **Lorna Cassidy – On The Shelf Reviews**

"The author really keeps you on the edge of your seat – the twists made me gasp and she sets the atmosphere absolutely perfectly." **Melisa Broadbent – Broadbean's Books**

"If you are looking for a crime thriller that is somewhat unnerving as it is every mothers worst nightmare, a fast paced page turner that keeps you guessing. Then I definitely recommend Captor!" **Dash Fan Book Reviews**

"Captor will have you gripped from the beginning and won't let you go until you have finished. It is a suspense filled crime thriller that will keep you guessing throughout." **Gemma Myers – Between The Pages Book Club**

"...Waller has definitely done it again and proves herself to be one of the best storytellers in the genre of murder, necessary murder, as she likes to say." **Rebecca Burnton – If Only I Could Read Faster**

"Wow. what an amazing book. To say I couldn't put it down doesn't seem enough." **Jo Turner – Life Of Crime**

"I absolutely loved this story. I was totally gripped. The twists I didn't expect and I didn't guess who the Captor was." **Philomena Callan – Cheekypee Reads And Reviews**

In memory of Alan, my only sibling.
Loved so much.
He would have been seventy
on publication day,
10 October 2018

Alan Havenhand
10.10.1948 – 12.05.2004

In this life we have to make many choices. Some are very important choices. Some are not. Many of our choices are between good and evil. The choices we make, however, determine to a large extent our happiness or our unhappiness, because we have to live with the consequences of our choices.

James E. Faust

Prologue

23 December 2010

The coffin was small and white, the wreath on top heart shaped and pink. Friends and family had packed into the cemetery chapel, all wearing something white in honour of the tiny child inside the coffin. Claudia and James Bell, along with their two other children, Harry and Zoe, followed the coffin down the short aisle, then sat on the left, ushered to their places by the funeral director. Their faces reflected their emotions; horror, disbelief, loss.

The death of the baby had caused family fragmentation. Claudia held onto her husband's arm, struggling to cope. Zoe clung to his other arm, and Harry just stared ahead of him; twenty years of life wasn't long enough to have prepared him for this. Zoe, three years younger than her brother, had fallen apart, unable to comprehend that death could arrive and take someone so young, so tiny. Their plan for a special Christmas with Mum and Dad's brand-new baby was in ruins, and almost without thinking about it, Harry recognised they would never have a good Christmas again. Baby Ella Mae would always be there as a Christmas memory, re-gluing the broken Bell family.

They had asked James if he wanted to carry the coffin, but he accepted it was out of the question. He knew he would be physically holding up his wife and his daughter. The funeral directors had agreed, and one perfectly attired gentleman had walked down the aisle in front of them, carrying the tiny white box with its spray of pink roses atop.

The service was, quite simply, a blur. They heard nothing, remembered nothing, and when told to do so, followed the coffin outside where it was replaced in the hearse and transported to the children's area of the cemetery.

They exited their funeral car, and Claudia noticed other parents tending the graves of their children; she whimpered. This would be the life she would share with them from now on.

'No,' she moaned, and James held her close. She felt the milk leaking from her breasts, milk that hadn't begun to dry up yet. Two days, that was all they had been given with their baby before she slipped away. But Claudia's body didn't know about that, and milk production was in full flow.

They gathered around the empty grave, the Bell family clutching onto their white roses, just as everyone standing around was holding onto theirs. The coffin was lowered; the parents Claudia had noticed earlier stopped what they were doing to pay their respect to the tiny body being laid to rest. In her mind, she acknowledged their thoughtfulness as the tears flowed freely down her cheeks.

Heather, Claudia's friend, stepped forward as the vicar finished his part of the ceremony and read the poem she and Claudia had chosen, amidst many tears. Heather's cheeks were flushed, and all she wanted to do was hold her best friend, hold her until the tears stopped. She began to speak, and the crowd fell silent.

'The world may never notice if a snowdrop doesn't bloom,
Or even pause to wonder if the petals fall too soon.
But every life that ever forms,
Or ever comes to be,
Touches the world in some small way
For all eternity.
The little one we longed for
Was swiftly here and gone.
But the love that was then planted is a light that still shines on.

And though our arms are empty,
Our hearts know what to do.
For every beating of our hearts
Says that we love you.'

Claudia and James, holding hands with their grown-up children, moved forward and threw their roses down onto the coffin. Heather, still standing by the graveside, threw hers down to join them, and slowly the crowd added theirs. The tiny white coffin was smothered in the heady perfume of the roses, and gradually everyone made their way back to their homes and to their own Christmas preparations.

There was no wake; the Bell family returned to their home, and Heather and Owen Gower returned to theirs. The couples had lived next door to each other for many years, but they hadn't had to deal with anything like this before.

The Christmas tree had been taken down in the Bell house; nobody wanted Christmas. The baby had been due on Christmas Day but had arrived a week early on the seventeenth; she had been taken from them two days later.

The tree and cards had already been in place for a couple of weeks, but the evening baby Ella left them, James and Claudia returned to their home and packed away every bit of Christmas.

The house looked as empty as their hearts; all four sat and stared at the flames of the log burner, unaware of whether they felt warm or cold, and grieved for the infant.

Their own Christmas child.

1

Claudia Bell was unsettled, at odds with herself, feeling not quite right. She didn't truly know why she felt as she did; she had a job she enjoyed as office manager at a large haulage company, her social life was as okay as she needed it to be, she didn't look anywhere near forty-four, and her kids were well and happily residing with partners of their own.

And yet she felt out of sorts, a little adrift. She eased her legs out of bed and stretched. Glancing at her bedside clock, Claudia registered that it said 08:10 and she ran to the bathroom. Maybe she shouldn't have given in to the enticing snooze button on her alarm.

Claudia hated having to rush to get to work, and while in the shower reflected that it might have been better if she'd got up when James had, at seven. She was just grateful that she worked in the same area of Sheffield that she lived in and didn't have to do the manic cross-city rush hour thing every morning and evening.

She dried her short dark hair and frowned at her image in the mirror. The hair looked a bit wispy, the make-up a bit sparse. Running repairs would have to be done at work, and not for the first time.

Jumping in the car, carrying a travel mug of coffee and a slice of toast, Claudia arrived with two minutes to spare, breathing a sigh of relief.

'Morning,' she said, and received a chorus of mornings back.

Her small office was in the corner of the main large open-plan space, and she was taking her coat off as she went through the doorway. She winced as the sleeve dragged against a sore spot at the back of her shoulder, and once again vowed to ask James to have a look and see if he could see anything.

She switched on her computer and settled down to work.

As the day wore on, she began to unwind. It was an easy day; there had been no breakdowns, no late loads, and no arguments between colleagues Fiona and Sara. Sara going out with Fiona's ex, one of their drivers, hadn't helped with harmony in the workplace, but it had been a good day. Claudia's equilibrium had gone some way towards being restored.

She gave Sara a lift home, and not a word was mentioned about the magnificent Baz; Claudia thought it best not to say his name, hoping the super-stud would quickly tire of Sara, just as he had tired of Fiona. Peace would then be brokered; Baz could return to being a footloose and fancy-free driver with a girl in every port and loading bay, and his two paramours could renew their lost friendship.

Lights were on at home, and Claudia pulled her car in behind James's Sportage, smiling as she always did at the sight of her Fiesta parked near the back of his much larger vehicle. To her, it looked as though the Sportage had given birth to her little car; both sharing the same colour, a deep navy, created the illusion.

She swung her bag onto her shoulder and winced again as the strap rubbed across the sore spot. She really needed to remember it hurt when touched by anything, she grumbled to herself.

James opened the front door before she got to it. 'I need to go out.'

She sighed. She could do without arguments. 'Okay. I'll move it.'

She put her bag on the doorstep and walked back to her car. Putting it in reverse, she guided it carefully back down the drive, mindful of him probably watching her and preparing his sarcastic comments, and steered the car out onto the road. She parked it by the kerbside, locked it up and headed back to the house.

The door was closed but her bag was still on the doorstep. Again, she sighed. She hoped he was going out soon, and she could settle on the sofa with a book and anything grossly fattening she could find.

She opened the door, and the smell of bacon permeated the house. She took off her coat, careful to avoid the sore spot, and hung it in the cloakroom, then headed for the kitchen.

'Bacon?'

'Yes, just grabbed the first thing I found really,' James said, not bothering to look at her. 'I've got to be in Leeds by seven. If the meeting goes on late, and there's alcohol involved, I'll probably stay over. If not, I'll be home later. I'll let you know.'

'What's the meeting about?'

'The official line is bringing more young people into the party, but as soon as Jeremy became leader, that happened anyway. I think the idea now is to educate the youngsters, let them see what a political career can offer them.'

James worked for the Labour party and took his job seriously. Much more seriously than he took his relationship with his wife, she thought, moving to stand by his side.

'Before you go, can you just have a look at my shoulder, please?'

'Why?'

'Because I'd like you to look at it. It's sore. Is it a rash?'

She heard him tut, and thought he was going to refuse, but he stood, and she peeled back the neckline of her sweater, exposing her upper right arm and shoulder area.

He cast a quick glance. 'Can't see anything.'

'James!'

He had a closer look, and hesitated. 'Yes, there's a sort of blister. It looks like a small grape. A really small grape. It's a bit inflamed around it, but I assume that's your sweater rubbing on it. You want me to put a plaster over it?'

She shook her head. 'No, it's been bothering me for a couple of weeks. I'll make an appointment with the doctor. It probably needs removing.'

He made no further comment, left the kitchen and headed upstairs. Claudia watched him go, then turned and opened the fridge.

It seemed pointless cooking a meal for one, and she too brought out the bacon, with little enthusiasm. The bread bin proved to be empty; James had used the last two breadcakes. She put the bacon back in the fridge, took out a yoghurt, and wandered into the lounge.

She heard him come downstairs, open the front door, and then close it. The next sound was the car engine and she knew that really, their marriage was one huge sham. For years she had ignored the coldness for the sake of the children, but now both Harry and Zoe had left home, Harry to live with his partner Emma, and Zoe to share her life with husband David.

So, what was keeping Claudia here? Not loyalty. She felt she owed him nothing. The bruises were testament to that. Security? She could have security on her own. And it certainly wasn't for conversation; he couldn't even say goodbye as he left the house any more.

Fear. That was keeping her rooted to this house. Fear of his anger, his quickness to raise his hand, whether threatening or hitting her. She shook her head. She would be happy later; she knew he wasn't coming home. There would be alcohol, so he would stay in Leeds; he wouldn't risk his driving licence. To him, his job was too important.

She glanced at the clock, then picked up the telephone handset.

The doctor's receptionist answered quickly, taking Claudia by surprise.

'Oh,' she said, 'I half expected the answer machine.'

'We're here until six now,' she said, her frosty tone indicating she didn't really approve of having to stay an extra half hour.

'Oh, good,' Claudia said. 'Can I have an appointment as soon as possible, please? Preferably with Dr Walker.' She liked Dr Walker; he listened when she needed to talk.

There was a moment of hesitation. 'Friday, 29th April. 9am.'

'What? But it's the first today. I have to wait four weeks?'

'Yes. That's Dr Walker's first available appointment. You can come to the emergency session any day, by ringing at eight, but you won't necessarily get to see him, it could be any of our six doctors.'

Claudia sighed yet again. It seemed to be an evening for sighing. 'So, if I ring Monday morning, I'll be able to see a doctor?'

'If there are any slots left, yes. And if it's an emergency.'

'Thank you.' Claudia put down the phone and stared at it. And she'd thought April Fool's Day had finished at lunchtime. This was no joke. Now she would have to wait until Monday and hope she could get in then.

She wandered back into the lounge, put on some music and picked up her book. She finished off the yoghurt, put her head comfortably on a cushion and began to read. The sore spot was irritating her, and she changed ends so that she wasn't touching anything with her shoulder.

Eventually she gave up and went to find a mirror. She slipped off her sweater and stood with her back to the cheval mirror in the bedroom. She couldn't see anything. Every time she screwed her head round, her body moved as well. She went to find her phone.

The resulting photograph was a waste of time. In the end, she ran a bath, had a soak for an hour, then slipped on a silky nightie, figuring that wouldn't irritate the sore part of her shoulder any more than it already was.

James didn't ring to tell her what he was doing, so she went to bed early, read a couple of chapters, and slept restlessly all night. Every time she turned over she caught the spot, until in the end she got up, had a bowl of cornflakes and mentally prepared herself for the weekend.

Saturday showed promise of being a beautiful day, and Claudia decided to do a bit of tidying in the garden. The borders still had last year's dead foliage on the plants, so she removed it. The spring sunshine was pleasantly warm, and she worked along the long side strip after taking all the dead blooms off the hydrangea; she was halfway along the front edge by the time James pulled onto the drive. She had acquired a large haul of dead matter for the compost heap and was just considering fetching the wheelbarrow from the garage to start moving the brown mound.

She hadn't heard him arrive, and she jumped as she heard his voice. 'I'm back.' Not 'I'm home', but 'I'm back'.

Claudia eased herself off her knees and waved the secateurs at him. 'Thought I'd make a start,' she said.

'I didn't drive back last night.'

'I gathered that.'

He stared at her, then turned and walked into the kitchen.

Moments later, he returned to the back door.

'Can you knock off, please, and make a coffee?'

Claudia placed the secateurs on the kneeling mat and headed for the kitchen. Even his voice made her feel angry. Taking down the cafetière – he didn't like instant coffee – she spooned in the dark blend he preferred. She switched on the kettle, keeping her back to him. If he couldn't speak civilly, then she was damned sure she wasn't going to say anything. James sat at the kitchen table watching her.

'Have you lost weight?'

'No, I don't think so.' Her voice was quiet. She sensed where this was heading. She could hear it in his voice.

'You're looking very fit. Take off your top.'

'What?'

'I said take off your top.'

'I'm making the coffee.' She could hear the quaver in her own voice, so knew he must be able to hear it, sense her fear.

He stood and came behind her, reached around to the buttons, and ripped her shirt open. She heard and saw tiny white buttons bounce on the work surface. He spun her around to face him.

'I could tell you had no bra on,' he said, almost conversationally, staring at her breasts.

She tried to cover herself with the shirt, but he pulled it away from her body again. He placed his hands roughly on her breasts.

'Why no bra? Were you waiting for me to come home?'

'No. The strap on the bra is rubbing against that sore spot on my shoulder. It was comfier to leave it off.'

'Forget the coffee. I've changed my mind.' His tone had altered. 'Upstairs, now.'

'No, James, please...'

He lifted his hand and slapped her across the face. 'I said now.' He spoke quietly, tonelessly, and she left the kitchen, trying to hold in the tears. She felt so alone, and frightened.

2

'Shall we go to Mum's?' Zoe Kenwright leaned over and kissed her man. She liked kissing her man. Very much.

'Will your dad be there?' David, her husband of four months, spoke without opening his eyes. To him, Saturday meant having a lie-in, and that didn't appear to be on the cards. But he did like his woman kissing him.

'I don't know. Why?'

He shrugged, his eyes still closed. 'Your dad's okay when he's okay, sometimes he isn't. S'all I'm saying.'

She remained quiet for a moment. 'So, shall we go?'

He groaned. 'For goodness' sake, woman, don't nag. Was this in the marriage vows?'

'No, and neither was picking up your laundry from the bedroom floor and putting it in the basket, but I seem to do it a lot.'

They swung their legs out at the same time, and Zoe went for the shower. David smiled, and slid back between the sheets. Maybe just a little bit longer...

Claudia, sitting at the kitchen table, heard the front door open.

'Mum?'

''In the kitchen, sweetheart.'

Zoe, closely followed by David, walked over to kiss her mum. 'What's wrong with your face?'

Claudia knew the red mark was clearly visible. 'Your dad hit me.'

'Yeah, right. You've walked into something, haven't you?'

Claudia nodded. 'I left the wardrobe door open and turned around. It's not a good look, but it'll fade.'

'Is Dad here?'

'Yes, he's gone to get the wheelbarrow from the garage for me. I've been doing a bit of tidying in the garden, there's loads of new spring growth coming through. But now we've got a mountain of dead stuff to get onto the compost heap.'

She didn't add 'he's being helpful and nice because he's just hit me and raped me.' It just wasn't the sort of thing one said to a daughter.

David looked at his mother-in-law, at the angry red mark. A wardrobe door? He heard James whistling as he wheeled the barrow around the corner of the house and up onto the back lawn, so he went out to meet him.

'David.'

'James.'

James held out his hand and David briefly shook it. It was their standard greeting.

'Busy?'

James nodded. 'Claudia is. She directs, I fetch and carry.'

'She's got a cracker of a mark on her face. Bathroom cabinet door, she says.'

James nodded again. 'Yes, she hit it with a bit of a wallop. It'll fade.'

'Let's hope she doesn't leave any more doors open, James. Wardrobe or bathroom cabinet doors. Bruises don't suit her.' David turned and walked back to the kitchen, leaving James motionless on the lawn, staring at his son-in-law's back.

David rejoined his wife, sitting with Claudia at the table. A cup of coffee was waiting for him, and he sat, listening to their chatter. This wasn't the first time he'd noticed bruises on Claudia, but she'd always had a good excuse for them. Just like now.

James came through the door and helped himself to a coffee.

Immediately, Claudia stood, and refilled the cafetière. She was jumpy, and she knew it must be obvious. 'Are you staying for lunch?' she asked, her tone a little too bright.

'No, Mum, we're okay thanks. We need to go do some shopping, we're running dangerously low on wine,' Zoe responded with a laugh. 'We'll just finish our drinks, and get off. I just wanted to check you're both okay.'

'Well, we are.' Again, the tone was false.

'Good. You need anything picking up from the supermarket?'

'No, we're fine, thanks.' Claudia smiled at her daughter. With her long blonde hair pulled up into a ponytail, she looked about fifteen. Certainly not old enough for supermarkets to be part of her life. Their matching grey eyes locked on each other, and Zoe returned the smile.

'Love you, Mum,' she said and stood. 'I've got my phone on me, so if you do need anything, give me a call.'

Zoe gave both her parents a kiss, and David bent to kiss Claudia. 'Take care,' he said, briefly touched her hand and followed his wife to the car, paying no attention to James.

David put the car into gear and pulled away from the kerb.

'You don't like my dad?'

'I don't like any man who makes a woman afraid.'

'What?'

'Nothing – forget I said anything.'

'No – you've said it now. What do you mean? Mum's not afraid of Dad.'

David shrugged. 'Okay, I'm listening. But she's always on edge around him. Maybe I'm wrong.' He knew he was keeping the peace.

'You're wrong. I've lived with them for twenty-odd years, and I wouldn't have said she feared him.'

'Let's drop it, Zoe. I'm sure they're fine.'

Zoe said nothing but continued to stare out of the window. She hated discord between them, and this was discord. And to make matters worse, she knew he was right; her mum had been nervous, jittery.

Heather Gower stared out of her back-bedroom window and watched the activity in the garden adjoining hers. She felt deeply for Claudia; they had been the closest of friends for many years, more like sisters than merely friends, and Heather had seen her confidence and joie-de-vivre fade over the past seven years. Losing their child had been something neither of them had ever recovered from, and Heather's heart ached for them.

She knew they must have argued, or even worse, because James was helping move the dead stuff to the compost area. He was obviously sorry for something he'd done, because he would normally be inside working on his crosswords, scouring his newspapers and being waited on by his wife. He was so easy to read.

Heather sighed and turned away from the window. They'd married a right pair of useless lumps, she thought, as she looked at her own husband of twenty-three years, standing in the doorway of the bedroom waving a T-shirt at her.

'I need this one today,' Owen Gower said, and she frowned at him.

'Why?'

'Why?'

'Yes, why?' she repeated. 'Why that one? You must have twenty T-shirts, all perfectly good, and all bloody ironed. So why that one, Owen? It's a sensible question.'

'Because I like this one.' There was now a slightly aggressive tone in his voice, and Heather realised he'd already had a drink. It wasn't yet lunchtime.

'I don't do ironing at the weekends,' she said, and pushed past him. He spun her around.

'I said I want this one.'

'Tough. You know where the ironing board is.'

Heather headed downstairs, and seconds later heard drawers opening and closing as he decided which option to go for in his stash of ironed T-shirts.

She smiled as she reached the kitchen. She knew she'd been optimistic when she'd said you know where the ironing board is. He had no idea where it was.

Switching on the kettle Heather began to prepare a sandwich for them. Lost in her thoughts, she was surprised when he appeared behind her and gave her a quick kiss on the nape of her neck.

'See you later,' he said.

'What?'

'I'm meeting the lads in the pub. Be back around three.'

'I'm just doing us a sandwich.'

'I'll have something at the pub. I don't suppose you'd like to run me down there?'

He looked at her face and answered his own question. 'No, maybe not then. See you later.'

She heard the door close as he left and wondered why she had let her life come to this. He needed help; his alcohol consumption was noticeable to everybody, and he was an embarrassment.

Financially they were struggling. Alcoholism came at a cost, and she knew she would have to go cap in hand to see her employer soon, to ask for more hours. She wasn't sure Michael would say yes; the small clothes shop she managed part-time didn't have a huge turnover, and she felt sure he would say he couldn't do it.

Heather hated the thought that she might have to leave the job she loved and search for something with more pay, but she knew that was rapidly becoming an option.

She went out into the back garden, quite surprised by the warmth of the sun, they were so ready for nicer weather. Leaning on the fence she watched her friend as she loaded the barrow, oblivious to everything, focused on what she was doing.

'Claudia!'

Claudia jumped, and turned around with a smile.

'Hiya. You startled me.'

'What's wrong with your face?'

She shrugged, and Heather had her answer.

'Want a hug?' she asked softly.

'No, a gun.'

Heather smiled. 'Make that two.'

'He's drinking?'

Heather nodded. 'He is. Says he'll be back around three, but that means maybe six. And I don't know what to do.'

'Do we really need a gun each? Will one gun do for both?' Claudia said the words gently, and Heather laughed.

'We'd manage,' she said. 'What's the red mark for, this time?'

'I said no.'

Heather drew in a quick breath. 'No to…?'

'Sex.'

For once Heather had no words. This was a new development in the Bells' relationship.

'And before you ask, yep, I gave in. I didn't want a red mark on the other side of my face. It was partly my fault; he noticed I didn't have on a bra.'

And then Heather found words. 'It was not your fault, not partly, not wholly, not ever. If you say no, then it's bloody no.'

'Well, I've got a bra on now, even if it is making life uncomfortable. I'll not make that mistake again.'

'For God's sake, Claudia! It should be your decision whether to wear a bra or not… It's nothing to do with him. Is he in?'

'Please, just leave it, Heather. It will only make things worse if he thinks I've told you.'

The two women stared at each other, and Heather gave a reluctant nod. 'This can't carry on though, Claud, he'll really hurt you one day.'

'I know. I'd reached that decision this morning, before this happened. Now I know I've got to do something. I'll wait until after Monday, get the doctor out of the way, and then do some proper planning.'

'Doctor?'

Claudia slipped her top off her shoulder. 'This is why I wasn't wearing a bra. The strap is rubbing on it, and it makes it sore.'

Heather examined it closely. 'Is it a mole?'

'No idea,' Claudia said with a laugh. 'I can't see it. What's it like?'

'It's almost like a little pearl. You're right though, it's in the wrong place for your strap. They'll remove it for you, but I don't reckon it will be at this appointment. You'll have to wait till the minor ops surgery.'

'I don't care as long as they do something eventually. So – we were killing Owen at the start of this gossip…'

'I might have to kill him before he bankrupts us.' Heather shook her head, despair etched on her face. 'I'm going to try to get more hours at work, but I can't see that happening.'

'Things haven't improved then… it seems as though both have reached middle age and gone on a downward spiral. James has always had a quick temper, but it's more than that now. He's become controlling, downright nasty, and far too handy with his fists. One day the kids will realise, if they haven't already, and then it will become so much worse. I think David has already clicked on, he gave my hand a squeeze when they left today. And Owen's drinking has obviously gone up a notch.'

'More than a notch,' Heather said. 'I suppose I'm lucky that he becomes daft, rather than violent, but it's mostly about the money. He's the one that buys rounds for everybody. And then he comes home, collapses on the settee, and that's the end of my evening.'

'We could leave together…' Claudia's smile was wide.

'We could. Can you imagine what they'd say then? It wouldn't be their fault we'd left, it would be because we were lesbians.'

'Well, I'm not. Are you?'

Heather grinned at her friend. 'Not bloody likely. We could always move two fellers in to prove we're fine with men.'

'I might not be a lesbian, but I'm never taking another man into my life. No thanks. I'm not that stupid.'

'So, where is he? Big, brave James.'

'No idea. He was helping me, but then he went inside. I'm happier on my own. Wonder what his bosses would think if they knew what he'd done today…'

'Would you tell them?'

'Definitely not. They'd probably sack him, and then he'd be at home all the time. I won't tell them unless circumstances say I have to, but the time has come for me to go, I think.' Claudia looked at her friend. 'Will you help?'

'Of course. You don't need to ask. And get a two-bedroom place, will you? One day I might have to join you.' There was no hint of a smile.

'Are you serious?' Claudia leaned against the fence. 'Surely you can sort it? I know he's always liked a drink, but he knew when to stop. What's changed? What the hell has turned him from being a perfectly normal, likeable bloke, into one who prefers being in the pub to being at home?'

'It must be me.'

'Whoa, hang on there a minute. Didn't you just tell me it wasn't my fault I was raped and beaten? How can you be to blame for him being drunk all the time? Come on, Heather, answer me.'

Heather thought Claudia looked like an avenging angel, standing with her feet apart, her hands on her hips.

'Touché,' she said, a huge grin on her face. 'Have they got other women?'

Claudia returned the smile. 'I have no idea, but if James has, I hope he treats her better than he treats me.'

Heather reached across the fence and put her arms around her friend. She felt Claudia stiffen. 'Oh my God, Claud, I'm sorry. I caught that spot, didn't I?'

Claudia gave another wry smile. 'Don't worry about it. It's nothing compared to a smack in the face, is it? And I needed the hug. And even if you have to sleep on a sofa, there'll always be somewhere to lay your head while I'm alive.'

Claudia moved away from the fence. 'Of course, any decent friend would have been round here and emptied this barrow...'

'Yeah, right.'

'Or even made a cuppa,' Claudia added as she grasped the handles and wheeled the barrow to the top end of the garden.

'Two minutes,' Heather said, walking towards her own kitchen.

Claudia tipped the barrow and picked up the rake. She moved all the brown foliage to the top of the pile then covered it with the old carpet.

She paused for a moment to ease her aching back. Time to stop, she figured. She took the barrow and the other tools back to the garage and returned to the fence to take the mug of tea from Heather's hand.

'Thank you, you're a good friend,' she said.

'Cheers,' Heather responded, and they clinked mugs. 'And now leave the gardening alone, you'll be knackered. Turn around and let me put this dressing on that sore bit.'

Claudia lay back in the bath and let her thoughts drift around inside her head. Now she had made the decision to leave, she wanted to be gone. The previous seven years hadn't been good for either of them; the loss of Ella had been devastating. They had been shocked initially when the pregnancy was confirmed, but so happy to be having a new baby.

The cruelty of losing Ella had destroyed them. All of them. She knew James had found it difficult to express his feelings, couldn't interact with Harry and Zoe, and wanted no comfort from his wife.

But eventually they had survived; everyone except James. He had changed beyond all recognition.

She sighed, pulled the plug and climbed out of the bath. She didn't want to go downstairs; she didn't want to talk. And she didn't want a conversation about the activities of the morning.

She did her hair with considerably more care than she had the previous morning when racing to get to work, but she knew it was only because she was killing time.

The dressing on her back had come off in the bath, and she decided she couldn't have another plaster; she didn't want James to touch her. She slipped on a silky top and jeans and lay on the bed for a brief time to let her mind ease.

James heard his phone buzz and took it out of his pocket. He smiled when he saw the sender.

Missing you. Loving you. You having a good day? Can you stay over Tuesday night?

James deleted the text then responded.

Day been good, and I can stay Tuesday night. Warm the bed. Love you.

He once again deleted after sending and smiled. His unhappiness was slowly dissipating after years of emotional trauma, and he had one person to thank for that. He wanted Monday to be there already, and not a day away.

Claudia finally walked downstairs and past the lounge. She could see James lying on the sofa, so went through to the kitchen. She made a hot chocolate and sat at the table reading. He didn't wake until seven, and they decided to have a pizza.

Neither spoke; there was very little of interest on television, so both read. Claudia went to bed around ten and left James downstairs. She decided if she wasn't asleep by the time he came up, she would pretend to be. She wanted nothing more to do with him.

James sat on the sofa and took out his phone.

3

D r Walker looked up with a smile. 'Claudia. Good to see you.'

He waited until she sat down. 'What can I do for you?'

'There's something really irritating on the back of my shoulder. It's right where my bra strap is, and it hurts. I'd like it removing if I can, please.'

He stood. 'Show me.'

She dropped the shoulder of her loose-fitting jumper and felt his hands on her back.

'I'm pretty sure it's nothing to worry about, but you're right, it couldn't be in a more awkward place. I'll refer you to the Hallamshire, and they'll remove it for you. We don't have a minor ops day scheduled for about six weeks, so it will be removed quicker with a referral. If you pop along to the nurse, she'll put a dressing on it, give you a bit of protection from the bra strap.'

'How long will I have to wait?'

'Not long. They're always quick with the easy stuff. Probably about a week.'

He pulled a piece of paper towards him and wrote. 'Take this to reception and they'll fit you in within the next twenty minutes or so for a dressing to be applied.' Without lifting his eyes from the paper, he continued. 'What happened to your face?'

She involuntarily touched her cheekbone. 'Wardrobe door. I forgot I'd left it open and turned around.'

Now he did lift his head. 'Really?'

'Really.'

He signed his name and handed her the piece of paper. 'I'll send the referral letter today. With a bit of luck, the spot will be gone in a week or so. Take care, Claudia.'

'Thank you.' She left his surgery and walked around to reception.

Within five minutes, she was in with the nurse, who applied a dressing and handed her four more. Claudia was told to keep it covered until it was removed, and she went straight to work.

She could sense there was a minor panic in the office as she walked through the door. It soon transpired that one of the drivers had overturned his lorry, and she quickly took charge of organising having the load collected, the lorry transported to a garage, and the driver's family informed.

Claudia missed lunch, and by mid-afternoon she needed food.

'I'll be back in ten minutes,' she called to nobody in particular as she walked out the door, and several hands were held up in acknowledgement.

The canteen was quiet. She picked up a cheese and pickle sandwich and made a coffee at the machine.

The table had a small vase of four daffodils on it, and she smiled. There were around fifteen tables, each holding a few bright yellow flowers, and it brought the place to life.

'Your idea?' she called across to Betty, the woman who had controlled her drivers for many years.

'Look nice, don't they,' she responded. 'How's Tony? Have you heard anything?'

'He's in hospital in Penrith. Broken leg, so he'll be off for a bit. His wife and two kids are on their way. We'll get him brought back to Sheffield as soon as he's fit to travel.'

'Poor lad,' Betty responded. 'That'll stop his football for a bit.'

'It certainly will. And it seems it was all because of a dog. He was driving past a lay-by when a car door opened, and a dog shot out and across in front of Tony's truck. He swerved, hit the brakes, and the lorry went. He couldn't get control back, and it tipped.'

'Bless him,' Betty said, and sat down opposite Claudia. She placed her cup of tea down carefully and gave a deep sigh. 'I hate it when any of my lads have accidents. It puts a proper downer on everything. And is that your lunch? You're late.'

Claudia laughed. Betty mothered everybody, including her. 'I've been sorting stuff out for the accident and for Tony. I didn't get here until eleven, had a doctor's appointment first.'

Betty nodded. 'That's okay then. You want something else?'

'No, I'm fine thanks. The sandwich was enough. I'll just finish my drink and get back.'

They chatted for a few more minutes, then Claudia returned to her office. Her phone was ringing, and she answered it before sitting down.

'Claudia Bell.'

'It's James.'

'Oh.' She felt quite shocked. He very rarely rang her on her company phone. 'Did you want something?'

'To see how you went on at the doctors. I thought you might ring me.'

'I haven't had time, I walked into a major issue when I finally got into work. One of our drivers has had an accident, and I've had lots of sorting out to do.'

'And the doctors?'

'He's told me to keep a dressing on it, and he's sending me to the Hallamshire to have it removed. It's nothing to worry about, he says, but he wants to get it off because it's in an awkward place.'

'Okay. That's good. I'll see you later then?'

'Yes. What time will you be home?'

'About seven. I'm in Manchester. Depends on the Woodhead traffic. I'm... er... I'm sorry about Saturday. I shouldn't have hit you.'

She felt her anger escalate. Shouldn't have hit her? Didn't the rape count then? Wasn't it rape if the two people were married?

'No, you shouldn't,' she said stiffly. 'I've got to go, there's another call coming through. I'll see you later.' She put down the receiver clenching her fists angrily. He hadn't said a word about it the previous day, he had waited until she was at work and wouldn't be able to respond.

She sat at her desk and pulled her keyboard towards her.

Half an hour later she had a list of six potential properties that were all to let. She had specified a minimum of two bedrooms in her search, and she was pleased with the properties that search had delivered to her.

Tony's wife, Donna, rang her just before five, to say that Tony was comfortable, his leg wasn't too badly broken, and she and the girls would be staying the night in Penrith to be near to him.

Claudia told her the company would cover her expenses and to submit all receipts when she got back, then disconnected. She sat for a few minutes watching as the evening shift took over from the daytime people, then saw Frank Allen approaching her own office as he arrived to take on his duties as night manager.

'Hi, Frank,' she said. 'Have you heard about Tony?'

'Silly bugger should have just hit the dog,' Frank said, in his usual forthright way. 'Now he's going to be off work for weeks, and a young family to keep.'

Claudia smiled at him. 'Stop being so grumpy. At least he's alive. The truck's a wreck, it could have been so much worse. Anyway, his wife has just contacted me, he's doing well.'

'Oh, that makes it all okay then.' The growl was still in his voice. 'And let's hope the bloody dog's doing well, and its bloody owners.'

'Oh, shut up, you narky old man,' Claudia laughed. 'Right, these are my hand over notes, no problems apart from Tony. I sent Adam up with the DAF to rescue the load, and he's bringing it back here. We don't know if any of that got damaged. He should be back by eight.'

'We collecting for the lad?'

She nodded towards a cardboard box on her desk, that had a crudely cut slit on the top. 'There's a notice in the canteen telling everybody, so quite a few drivers have been by and put in something.'

Frank took out his wallet and withdrew two twenty-pound notes. He stuffed them in the top of the box and once again Claudia laughed.

'Bit of a softy, then, Frank?'

'Get off home and let me sit down.'

She stood and waited for him to sit in her chair, then planted a kiss on his head. 'See you tomorrow.'

He rubbed the top of his head. 'Get off me, that's sexual harassment in the workplace, that is.'

'And you love it,' she called, as she exited into the central office.

She drove home, switching her mind off from work issues. She really wanted to spend an hour with Heather, going through the list of properties, but if James didn't arrive home until seven, that wouldn't be possible. She didn't expect James would be going out again, so the evening would be spent keeping the peace, maybe watching some crime series at nine, and bed at ten. The list would have to wait until she knew James was going to be away.

Over dinner, he explained he would be away Tuesday and Wednesday night, the first night in Leeds and the second in Newcastle. She nodded and tried not to let the inner 'whoopee' show on her face.

They watched Silent Witness and almost before the show ended, James stood and said goodnight. 'Early start tomorrow,' he explained, 'I'll be getting up at six. Will you be up to do breakfast?'

She quickly counted to ten and said yes.

She blew out the candles and locked everything up, but before locking the back door she stepped out into the garden. The work she had done over the weekend showed, and with the exterior light on it looked to be a sanctuary. She stayed for five minutes, aware of shouting coming from Heather's house, and then heard a crash of glass. It was followed by silence, and Claudia had no idea what to do.

She moved back inside, locked and bolted the door and headed into the lounge. She picked up her phone and texted.

You okay? xx

It was ten minutes before she received the reply.

I'm fine. He's a drunk dickhead. xx

Donna called early Tuesday morning to say Tony was doing well, and they were hoping to get him home sometime Wednesday, so she and the girls would be staying an extra night to save having to drive home then back again.

Claudia chatted with her for a while, then put down the phone with a smile. That had been good news, and an earlier phone call to Heather had led them to agreeing to a wine night at Claudia's, so today life was good.

It proved to be a day of lorry drivers being where they should be, loads not being contaminated, and no delays at Dover, so there was very little on the handover sheet for Frank.

She called at the supermarket on the way home, picked up some nibbles and Prosecco, then headed home. She lit the fire and the candles and took out the printed sheets she had hidden in her laptop case. She truly didn't want James getting any idea that she might be wanting to move out; he must have no sight of these documents.

She was glancing through them for the third time when Heather pushed open the back door. 'It's me,' she called. 'Shall I lock it now?'

'Yes, please. And bring the wine, it's in the fridge.'

Heather entered waving the bottle of wine and wearing pink pyjamas.

Claudia laughed. 'God, we're so predictable.' Her own pyjamas were tartan. 'Comfort first, glamour second. Where's Owen?'

Heather opened the wine and poured them a glass each. 'You'll only need one guess. So. Let's see the properties then. I've been looking forward to this all day – how sad is that?'

Claudia held up her hand. 'Tell me about last night, first. I was worried about you. I was in the back garden, just having five minutes before going to bed. Your argument was pretty vocal, and then I heard a glass smash. It's why I texted you. What happened?'

'It was about money. The bank hasn't made our mortgage payment. Not enough funds, they said. When I checked, it would have taken us £20 overdrawn. He took £40 out the day before. If he hadn't done that, everything would have been fine. I tried to talk sensibly, but because it was a serious matter and he was drunk again – and probably feeling guilty – he turned nasty.'

Heather lifted her head and showed Claudia the red mark on her neck. 'He tried to strangle me, except he didn't really. I only had to push him off. He wasn't capable of killing anybody. But just to show him I was, I smashed a glass and held the jagged end up to his neck. God, I was so close, Claud, so close.'

'Oh my God! Heather, he needs help!'

'He's gone for it – to the Blue Bell.'

'Shit… you want to stay here?'

'No, he'll only show off and come to find me. It's ultimatum time though. Tomorrow, when we're both sober, and before he starts drinking again, I'm going to spell it out for him. No alcohol, or I go. There's no cutting down on the drink clause in that, either. It's total abstinence and attending an AA group. I've always managed to pay bills before, but the mortgage… that's a whole new ball game.'

Claudia nodded. 'Certainly is. You want to borrow some money?'

'No, I'll be fine. If I'd realised he'd virtually cleared out the account, I would have transferred some – I've savings from my wages he isn't aware of. If he was, he'd have them as well. We're going into the bank tomorrow to talk to them. He doesn't know this yet. I'm going to tell them the situation and set up an account just for him, and get him off the joint account, the one we pay the bills with. I know he'll be embarrassed, feel he's being shown up, but I don't care. Again, this is an ultimatum. And the mortgage payment will be there when they re-apply for it, I'll just have to accept the bank charges. If he can't agree, or wants to prevaricate about the accounts, then I'm gone. I can't live like this. I'll walk away from everything, Claud, leave him with the house that will be repossessed because he's spent all his money on booze, and I won't care.'

They sipped at their Prosecco and stared at the fire. The flames flickering around the logs were magnetic, soothing. The music playing softly in the background was soporific, and both women immersed themselves in their thoughts.

Claudia roused herself. 'So, these are the properties I printed off yesterday. Have a look and see what you think.'

Heather picked them up and initially did a quick scan through them. Then she looked closely.

'You need to go and see them. Want some company?'

Claudia nodded. 'When is it your day off?'

'Friday, but I've also got Saturday off this week. Did a swap to suit Glenys, she needed next Saturday off.'

'Okay,' Claudia said, 'I'll book a day's holiday for Friday, and we'll go and check them out. If any look okay from the outside, we'll see about getting keys. And we'll go and have something to eat, be proper ladies what lunch, yes?'

'That sounds so good. I never seem to do anything other than worry these days, but I'm taking control now. And if Owen doesn't agree to all my demands, we'll be looking at the three-bedroomed properties. We can afford those rents between us.' For the first time in weeks, both women began to feel optimistic.

Claudia laughed. 'I almost hope he doesn't agree. Have you stopped loving him?'

There was a moment of hesitation. 'I don't honestly know. I don't want to live with him any longer, because it's getting to the stage where its unbearable, but I suppose some small part of me will always love the man I married. I was crazy for him at the beginning, but we've both changed and it's simply not working. If the drinking stopped, I believe we could get back what we had, but there's no chance if he doesn't follow my rules. No chance at all. Maybe if we'd had children it would have been different...'

Claudia stared into the fire, knowing she could feel no love for James. One bruise too many had killed it. She was thankful her friend hadn't had to suffer violence; with alcohol the scenario could have been so different.

'Look, let's leave it like this. There are two three-bedroomed properties. I don't think it's fair that I take up a family-size property, so although I like both of them, I wouldn't consider them, with hindsight. The two-bedroomed are ideal, if it's just for me. So, we have time for decisions after your day with Owen tomorrow. If things don't work out, we'll see about getting keys, or meeting up with the estate agents, for the three-bed houses. Plan, pal?' She held up her hand for a high five, and Heather responded.

'Plan, pal,' she said. There was a pause. 'When did the violence start, Claud?'

Claudia gave a slight laugh. 'Long before anyone was aware of it. It started that Christmas when we lost Ella. He hit me for the first time on Christmas Day. I hid it for ages – you noticed the bruises before anyone else. But it stops now. He's never forced me to have sex before, and that made me feel dirty. I don't love him, I don't want him, and there's nothing keeping me here now Harry and Zoe have gone. Whatever you decide after tomorrow, I'm leaving anyway.'

Heather didn't say anything; she was focused on the properties. 'I like this one.' She handed a sheet back to Claudia. 'It's above a shop, which means no garden, and it's massive, three huge bedrooms. There's only one entrance door, and that's at the bottom of the stairs leading from the street up to the flat. In other words, it's secure. He's not going to take kindly to you leaving, you know. He's going to hunt you down. You need to feel safe as well as be safe.'

4

Owen had a headache. And right at that moment he couldn't have cared less about his bloody wife. The nasty cow.

'Mr and Mrs Gower, I'm sorry to have kept you waiting.' Katherine Jones smiled at her first appointment of the day, and hoped it was going to be an easy chat. She was feeling just a little fragile after the girly night the previous evening.

She sat opposite them and switched on her computer. 'Now, how can we help you?'

Heather leaned forward in her chair. 'My husband is an alcoholic, and we're here to sort out our banking so that he can't take any more money out of our joint account.'

Katherine sighed. This sort of conversation usually happened on Mondays after errant husbands had spent everything on the weekend bender, not Wednesdays. And it certainly wasn't going to help her own hangover that had just escalated.

'Do you have your account number?' she asked, keeping the smile fixed firmly. Mr Gower was looking extremely unhappy, and Mrs Gower had the most determined expression Katherine had ever seen on anyone. 'Perhaps you'd both like to tell me what you want to change.'

And Heather began to talk.

Owen Gower was a very unhappy man. For a start, the park bench was cold underneath his bum, and secondly, he had until five to come up with answers. He had felt a little bit rattled when he had rung his boss earlier to explain he needed a day off to take care of some personal business, and his boss had laughed and mentioned hangover in his remarks. Was that how everyone saw him?

He sat forward on the bench and rested his head in his hands. He could see the roundness of his stomach. Shit! When had that happened? He quickly sat upright, and breathed in.

It seemed his good times had been well and truly cancelled. He had an allowance in his own account of £100 every month, and their joint account required two signatures to withdraw money in branch, with no debit card in his name. That nice lass, Katherine, had obligingly cancelled the bank charges on the recent mortgage hiccup, and had made the instructions on the account fixed for five years.

He couldn't blame Heather for being honest at the bank, she needed their help, but he'd felt about a metre tall when they'd finally exited.

Her suggestion of going for a coffee before she had to leave him to go to work had seemed a promising idea, even if he would have preferred a pint. Once in there, things had rapidly become worse.

Owen took out the piece of paper she had handed over in the coffee bar. It showed the AA headquarters in Sheffield. She had spoken very clearly and slowly when she had said no AA, no marriage. And she wanted proof by the time she got home from work that he had made arrangements to attend a meeting.

He took out his wallet, checked how much was in it, and stood. He'd get the proof later. For now, he needed a drink.

Heather was physically at work but mentally nowhere near it. She had seen from Owen's face in the coffee shop that he wouldn't be able to accept her terms; and it was the AA meetings that he couldn't handle.

She would give him the benefit of the doubt until she arrived home, trust him to do the right thing, and they would take it from there. Nobody would ever willingly give up on twenty-odd years of marriage, and if it could be salvaged, that would be for the best.

If it couldn't…

Claudia went out in her lunch break and drove to the flat that had caught Heather's eye. Claudia knew her friend had been correct when she had spoken of her needing to feel safe; James would track her down, she just had to make sure he couldn't physically get to her.

The flat extended over two shop fronts. It had large windows and was clearly empty; there were no blinds or curtains to be seen. The shops underneath were a bakery and a charity shop, and the area, at first glance, appeared to be a good one.

She walked into the bakery, with the somewhat quirky name of Breadline on the signage, thinking to buy a sandwich for her lunch; there was a small queue, and she guessed the sandwiches must be pretty special. She waited patiently.

Placing an order for a turkey salad and a huge vanilla slice, she handed over money that to her didn't seem exorbitant.

'Do you know anything about the flat upstairs?' she asked, while the attractive dark-haired lady made up the sandwich.

'I certainly do,' she answered with a smile. 'I have a key for viewings, but I can't take you up there now, it's my busiest time.'

'What time do you open?'

'Nine on the dot, eight on Saturdays.' She handed over the sandwich and placed a vanilla slice in a small cardboard tray.

'So, if I came eight thirty on Friday morning, would that be any good?' Claudia asked, popping the sandwich into her bag.

'That would be fine. I won't be in the shop – if I'm in, people will expect to be served,' she said with a laugh. 'I'll wait in the flat. That white door at the side of the shop is the flat's entrance. I'll leave it open for you. My name's Michelle, Michelle Baldwin.' She handed over the vanilla slice.

Claudia thanked her, and assured her that she would definitely be there, and would be accompanied by a friend.

She got back in the car and sat for a moment looking up at the flat. Heather was right, it would be ideal. Claudia hoped the interior was just as good as her mind was imagining. From the outside the windows looked clean, the entrance door was new.

She didn't want to wait until Friday; she felt like a child on her first day at school, excited for what was to happen next in her life.

She drove back to work, hoping she would be able to chat with Heather later, find out what had happened at the bank and the AA meetings. She prayed Heather would get what she wanted from taking this uncompromising stance with Owen; she doubted it. Could Owen really stop drinking at a minute's notice?

Heather inserted her key in the front door and pushed it open. The house felt empty. No heating on, despite the coolness of the day, and no Owen waiting to tell her everything was going to be all right.

She put her bag on the kitchen table and switched on the heating. She was moving mechanically. Crossing to the freezer she took out fish for dinner, then began to peel potatoes. Decisions, decisions; chips or mash?

Her brain told her chips; they would be quicker to make once Owen turned up. She felt tears in her eyes. She wanted to believe he was at the AA place, discussing what happens next. What she really thought was that he was in a pub somewhere, fondly imagining he could talk his wife around.

She slammed the small knife down onto the wooden chopping board and dropped her head. Her tears were flowing, and she grabbed a piece of kitchen roll, dabbing at her face as she dried them.

She heard Owen's key as he attempted to line it up with the keyhole and knew.

She waited until he came into the kitchen and turned to him.

'I thought you would have been home.' Her tone was stiff, unyielding.

He grinned. 'I got chatting to Eric, you know what it's like.'

'I do. Where were you when you did this chatting?'

'In...' He hesitated. 'In the Blue Bell. But it's the last time. Definitely the last time.'

'You have appointments for AA meetings?'

'Not yet. I'll sort it.'

'When?'

'Tomorrow.'

'You don't seem to understand the concept of ultimatums, Owen. When I said we were over if you hadn't sorted yourself out with an AA meeting by five, I meant by five. Not by tomorrow, maybe. And when I said you'd had your last drink, I didn't mean your last drink except for what you could neck this afternoon. And now I'm going to tell you something that you'd better understand. I am going. I'll pack tonight, and I'll be gone tomorrow.'

He moved towards her, holding out his arms. She pushed him away and headed upstairs. Time to sort out suitcases. Time to talk to Claudia. Time for a new life.

Heather sat on the bed and took her phone out of her pocket.
Make the search three-bedroomed x

Claudia heard the text come through as she was driving home. She'd stayed a little later at work, chatting on the phone to the newly returned Tony. He was comfortably at home being waited on by his family. The collection box had been emptied once and was slowly filling up as different drivers returned to base.

She pulled onto her road feeling insanely happy that James was on his second night out. If everything looked to be okay on Friday, she could quite easily be in her new home by Monday. Before getting out of her car, she took the phone out of her bag.

She felt sick for her best friend; the text told her that Owen had been stupid and not believed the 'do it or else' seriousness of the situation he had quite deliberately put himself in over the last few years.

With a sigh that seemed to come from her toes, Claudia got out of the car and headed inside. It felt cooler that night, and she lit the fire before doing anything else. The phone in the hall rung, and she closed the doors of the wood burner and went to answer it.

'Mrs Bell?'

'Yes.' She was wary. Too many PPI companies appeared to be able to get names with ease.

'Hi, Mrs Bell. It's the Hallamshire Hospital. Can I just check a couple of details with you, please?'

Claudia went on to confirm date of birth and her address, and then was surprised to hear that a cancellation meant she could have an appointment for Friday.

'Thank you,' she said fervently. 'It's become really sore. It's right where my bra strap rests.'

'It's a very quick operation, done with local anaesthetic. Takes about a quarter of an hour at the most. I'll confirm by text, because you'll be here before a letter reaches you. I'll book you in for two o'clock.'

The confirmation text came through as she was replacing the receiver. Things seemed to be working out well after her horrible weekend, and maybe Heather could go with her, after they had viewed the flat and had some lunch.

She was surprised when, only minutes later, Heather tapped on the back door.

'You have a spare bed, pal?'

'Always.' Claudia held open her arms. 'Come here.'

Heather laid her head on Claudia's shoulder; the tears came again.

Eventually they separated, and Heather sat at the kitchen table. She reached across and removed an orange from the fruit bowl. She rolled it backwards and forwards, and Claudia watched her with some amusement.

'Don't smash that down. It's not Owen's head. You ready to talk? And do you want a drink? Tea? Coffee? Wine? Or maybe champagne?' she said with a smile.

'I'll just have a tea, thanks. I need soothing, not winding up, I think.'

Claudia made the drinks without speaking, then handed a mug of tea to her friend.

'He didn't stick to the rules, then?'

'Not at all. I think he thought it was enough having the bank take away his booze money, leaving him with what he sees as peanuts. I went back to work saying I'd be home just after five, and I expected him to have sorted out the AA meeting he was going to attend.' She paused and looked down into the mug. 'He went to the pub. Had a lovely afternoon drinking and chatting with Eric.'

'You've left?'

'I've told him I'm sleeping here tonight. I might stab him if I stay there. Tomorrow, after he's gone to work, I'll go and get my stuff. I'll stay in a Travelodge until we find a place. I don't want to stay here. He'll eventually get around to blaming you for me leaving him, and that's not fair.'

'I think you're right. If you stay here and he makes a nuisance of himself, it'll wind James up and he might just click on I'm going as well. He won't be quite so accepting as Owen. James will use his fists.'

'Hopefully we'll find something Friday. You are still okay with sharing?'

'More than okay,' Claudia said. 'And I have news on that front. Remember the flat you said looked safe and secure? It's not too far from where I work, so I had a run out in my lunch hour. It was more to look at the area than to look at the flat. The shop that's next to the flat's front door is a bakery, so I nipped in for a sandwich. It seems the lady who owns the bakery has a key for the flat, so she can show people around it. I've arranged for us to go at half past eight on Friday morning.'

'Good lord – you don't hang around, do you? Is the area okay then?'

'It's quiet, clean. Think we'll be okay there. I liked the fact that there is only one door to the property, which does mean we'll be safer. I've not been in it, just looked at the outside. Nice big windows, and there's a bakery underneath it! That has to be a plus. There's something else as well. The hospital rang. I'm having this thing on my back removed on Friday afternoon. Will you be able to come with me? I may need you to drive me back.'

'Wow! That's quick! Of course I'll go with you. I won't be taking our car when I leave, though. He can have it, I never liked it.'

'I'll be taking mine. We can car share until we get organised. I'll sort out the insurance tomorrow for you driving my car.' Claudia paused for a moment. 'It's a whole new world for us, isn't it?'

Heather nodded, sipping thoughtfully at her drink. 'It feels a bit like a whirlwind's gone through my life. And it's all been brought to a head by a missed mortgage repayment. The funny thing is I'm now going to have to go back to the bank and reverse everything I've done today. Ms Katherine Jones is going to love me.'

They laughed, tears now forgotten, and clicked their mugs. 'Cheers, friend,' Claudia said. 'To new lives. And whatever lives our husbands decide they want, is up to them. James and Owen, you're history, and we didn't need to buy the gun.'

James completed his second lengthy meeting of the day in Newcastle and drove back to his hotel for the night. He ordered room service and spread his notes out on the desk in the corner of the room. Sorting them into order took some time and after eating, he took out his laptop.

He began to transcribe his hurriedly written notes and ideas and by eight he was finished. He could relax.

He picked up the laptop and moved across to the bed. The pillows were carefully stacked up so that he would be comfortable with the laptop on his knees, and he opened Messenger. He clicked on the name that said Marilyn M. The connection rang out and he waited patiently for someone to answer.

The blonde hair was visible first, as the recipient leaned in to answer the call. James smiled. He now felt at peace.

'Hi,' he said. 'My own Marilyn.'

'Well, hello, Mr President, is it your birthday again?' came the whispered response. And then the song. 'Happy birthday to you, happy birthday to you, happy birthday, Mr President, happy birthday to you.'

James laughed loudly. 'My God, you crease me. I felt like it was my birthday last night. I love you, my sweet Marilyn. It's a pity you couldn't have been a bit nearer to Newcastle, two nights with you would have been brilliant.'

'Maybe we'll be able to get together next week. You in Leeds again?'

'Yes, probably. I'll try to work it so that I am.'

They chatted for half an hour and then said goodnight, finger kissing each other's lips at the end of the conversation.

James closed the laptop, and finally got around to scanning the newspaper. He took further notes on items on the political pages and made himself a hot drink before settling down for the night.

He felt as though he had lived in a vacuum for too many years; the death of baby Ella had affected all the family, but his wife had fallen apart and withdrawn into a shell that he hadn't been able to penetrate. He remembered the first time he had hit her.

Christmas morning, just a couple of days after the funeral, and he had tried to hold her, to show his support and share what she was going through. Her words 'don't touch me' had been vitriolic, and in his grief, he had done the unthinkable; he had hit her back hard enough to knock her over and smash her head on the coffee table. Neither Zoe nor Harry had been there; they were both still in bed trying to ignore Christmas.

And so it had begun. But now he had two loves; Claudia he would always love for all they shared, but he had found a new love in his Marilyn.

5

Claudia collected Heather from the hotel at eight and they were outside, looking up at the flat windows by quarter past. It was a grey morning, heavy with the threat of rain, and the lights in the flat were glowing.

'Definitely needs curtains or blinds,' Heather said with a laugh. She could feel excitement building in her.

They squeezed each other's hand and climbed out of the car.

As promised, the bottom door leading up to the flat had been left unlocked, and Claudia called, 'It's only us, Michelle,' as they went in.

They stepped into the entrance hall, onto a thick grey carpet that made them take off their shoes. This carpet was new.

They climbed the stairs and Michelle met them at the top.

She smiled. 'I've put coffee on, but there's tea if you would prefer.'

Claudia and Heather both assured her coffee was good, and they followed her down the corridor to the tiny kitchen.

'This is the only room in the flat that's not enormous,' Michelle explained, 'but it's fine. I lived here for five years and never had a problem with it, and now everything in it is brand new.'

'It all feels and smells new.' Claudia stared around her.

Michelle laughed. 'It is. My hubby and I have bought a house around the corner, but when we bought the bakery, this flat came with it, so it made sense to live here. My husband's been hankering after a garden and a man cave and stuff, so we've decided to move out as the business has really taken off. We've had this completely refurbished for rental, nobody has lived here yet.'

They placed their mugs on the kitchen work surface and moved to inspect the other rooms. The bathroom, spectacular in its newly refurbished state of white tiles edged with turquoise, was impressive. The toilet was a tiny separate room next door, perfectly adequate. They moved onto the bedrooms and lounge.

'This is the small bedroom,' Michelle said, opening the door and stepping back. The grey carpet continued all the way through the flat, and Heather entered first, followed by Claudia.

'This is the small room?' Heather asked.

Michelle laughed. 'I said it was a big flat.'

It looked out onto an overgrown grassed area at the back of the shops. 'Are you going to be the gardener, Claud?' Heather asked.

'Fortunately,' Michelle explained, 'that land belongs to the council, and runs underneath the patio. It's nothing to do with this flat, you'll be pleased to know. You'll understand more when we get to the main bedroom.'

They crossed the corridor to the next bedroom. It overlooked the shop frontage. The windows had appeared to be large from outside, but from inside they were huge. They stretched almost the full length of the exterior wall.

'Wow. Will this be mine?' Heather's eyes were shining. 'I love it!'

They laughed at her enthusiasm and moved to the room adjoining. It was the lounge and it was massive. It had a fireplace that was plain and functional, and fitted in perfectly with the ambience of the room.

Claudia stared around her. 'This is amazing. I live in a four-bed house, and I think there's more room here than I have.'

'You're selling up?' Michelle asked.

'Moving out. Had enough,' was Claudia's response.

'Moved out, had enough,' was Heather's response.

'So you would both be moving in?'

'Is that a problem?' Claudia felt sick. She wanted this flat, and she didn't want Heather being a joint tenant with her to be an obstacle.

'Not at all. It's a big place for one person, and there are no neighbours. It could be very lonely for one person. I'm happier there are the two of you. It'll take some furnishing, though.'

'We'll manage.' Heather's voice was firm. She moved across to look out of the window.

'You see that row of garages across the road? The second one from this end is yours, the one with the red door. You can't see from here, but it's got a number two on it. And there's no junk in it, it's empty if you actually want to put your car in it,' Michelle laughed. 'And now let me show you the best part, the third bedroom.'

They reached the end of the corridor, with one last door to go through.

The bedroom was the same size as the lounge but had patio doors instead of a window. Outside was a large patio, fenced with metal railings, and some considerable height above the unkempt grassed area.

'This is really private, and a wonderful suntrap. You're not over looked, and,' she raised her arm, 'over there are some houses, but you can't see much, and neither can they. As an extra safety feature, that box fastened to the brickwork contains a rope ladder. If, heaven forbid, there should be a fire that cuts you off from the downstairs door, that rope ladder hooks securely onto the top of the railing, and you'll be able to get out. I had it made specially when we moved in, just to be on the safe side. When it was fitted, my husband tried it out. It's never been used since, but we did check it was still good, and it is.'

'We'll take it,' Claudia said. 'How soon can we move in? It's urgent,' she added. 'And all I would ask is you don't tell anyone we're here, anyone at all.'

Michelle looked at them both. 'Is violence involved?'

They nodded, hoping she wouldn't change her mind about letting to them.

'Then we'll have a special arrangement. I have been advised to ask for a month's rent as a returnable deposit, a month's rent for the first month, and a half-year minimum let. In view of what you've said, I'll waive the minimum let. We'll make it four weeks. You may need to move quickly. Having said that, it will be a half-year rolling let from my side.'

Claudia and Heather looked at each other then back at Michelle. 'Thank you. That's brilliant,' Claudia said. 'I'll pay all tenancy costs today. You're a star.'

'Then your letting starts now. Here are the keys, and I hope you have safety and security here. And happiness. Move in whenever you're ready. And I understand what you're both going through. I wasn't always married to the man I'm with now. I had another one…'

Michelle left them to wander around and even provided them with a tape measure for taking measurements; she opened her shop, knowing she'd done the right thing. Her first job was to ring another lady and tell her the flat had been taken, and then she switched on the ovens. The bread delivery arrived, and her day officially began.

Claudia and Heather drove into Sheffield city centre, parked in an impossibly difficult multi-story car park, and headed for a coffee.

Celebrations were in order, and they clinked mugs.

'We done good, girl,' Heather said.

'We done excellent,' Claudia responded.

'Are you going to tell Zoe and Harry?'

'Not till I've left. Don't forget, they don't know about the violence, so they're quite likely to tell their dad, in some misguided effort at keeping me with him. And that's not going to happen. No, I'll wait until we're in our new place, and then ring them. I'm not going to tell them where we are, either, because if they need me, they can always ring.'

Claudia took a notebook out of her bag. 'We need to make a list. Essential stuff that we need before Monday.'

The list was long. Claudia put ticks against things she could bring with her, and Heather put crosses against her contributions. By the time they'd reached the end, it was clear their main requirements were furniture. They could cover almost everything else.

'He's going to be so mad at you, Claud,' Heather said thoughtfully. 'Don't take any risks. Don't move anything out of that house that he might notice is gone, not while you're still there. We can do it Monday, after he's gone to work.'

Claudia nodded. 'I won't. I've booked all next week off, because he's going to turn up at work, I know he is. He'll not show off there, but he will try to find out where I am.' She glanced at her watch. 'It's time we were heading up to the hospital. The sooner this is sorted, the better. And I think you should drive up there, get used to the car.' She handed Heather the keys. 'And don't damage it.'

'As if I'd dare,' Heather scoffed. 'This attitude change, this confident woman is pretty scary, you know. Come on, let's pay the bill and get going. We need to get it over with, I hate hospitals.'

Claudia laughed. 'It's me they're operating on, so you don't need to worry.' She placed her card on the saucer, and the waitress brought across the card reader.

Ten minutes later, Heather was manoeuvring, with curses, down the long curving exit of the car park. 'Next time we'll park on a flat piece of ground,' she grumbled, and Claudia smiled. Heather hadn't really needed to practice, it was simply that Claudia didn't want to drive down the exit road.

Claudia lay on her side, felt the needle go into her back, and the coldness of the anaesthetic.

'Okay, Mrs Bell?'

'I'm fine.'

She lay quietly while the registrar moved around the room, waiting for the numbing effect to kick in. Claudia's mind was reflecting how good it had felt to give them her new address at the reception desk.

'I'm almost certain it's nothing to worry about, Mrs Bell, and we'll be sending it off for testing just to make sure. You'll hear from us in about three weeks, confirming we don't need to see you for further check-ups. We'll soon have you able to wear a bra without pain again,' he said with a smile. He touched her back with a pointed object. 'Can you feel that?'

'No, not at all.'

She was aware of pressure on her back as he began to cut out the mole, but no discomfort, and she tried to relax and not flinch at imaginary pain. It seemed to be over very quickly, and the doctor explained he was putting in a couple of stitches, but they were soluble and would come out on their own. The nurse then dressed the wound, handed Claudia a leaflet explaining the procedure she had undergone, and escorted her to the door.

Five minutes later, she was dressed and heading back to Heather in the waiting room.

'All done,' she said. 'How many magazines have you read?'

'Three. And all about home décor,' she said with a laugh. 'You okay?'

'I'm fine, but it is still numb. I've to take paracetamol later.'

They drove back to Heather's hotel and pulled up outside.

'You know, I could do with moving in before Monday,' Heather said. 'It would save money.'

'But there's nothing there. No beds, no anything.'

'There's a fridge, and a cooker. And it would be cheaper to buy a single blow-up bed and some bedding than spend another three nights here. In fact, I need to get back into my house, because I've lots of spare bedding there. I'd only need a blow-up bed.'

'I've got one. We've had one for ages, used to use it when the kids had friends over for sleepovers. You want to go in and cancel for tonight?'

Ten minutes later, Heather was back in the car and her suitcase was in the boot. 'All done. My God, Claud, this is really happening. I just need to get in our house now and get some stuff without world war three breaking out.'

'You worried?'

'Nah, he'll not go for me. It's the verbal bit. He'll want me back. I don't really think he'll be there; it's Friday afternoon and he finishes at lunchtime. He'll be in the pub.'

'Right, here's what we'll do. We'll go back to mine and get the bed put in the car. James isn't due home until about eight, he said. Leeds again. He seems to nearly live there these days. Then you go across the gardens and in your back door and get whatever you need. Didn't you say you'd some curtains that would fit your bedroom? Bring them as well as bedding, you can't sleep with bare windows. It's good that Michelle left all the curtain poles in place. Bring everything around to mine, and if you reverse the car up the drive when we get there, we can load it without anybody seeing what's going on. I've moaned about that high privet hedge for years, but it's now going to come in useful. Then we'll drive you down to the flat. While you're sorting stuff, I'll message Michelle and tell her you're moving in tonight, and why. Don't want her thinking she's got burglars when she turns up for work tomorrow.'

'You're okay to drive?' There was concern on Heather's face.

'I'm fine. I can steer one-handed. Thank heavens it's an automatic. And I'll only be doing the return journey from the flat, you can drive the rest of the time.'

Heather drove them back to Claudia's, reversing the car up the drive as instructed. Claudia went to find the single bed, and packed a large bag with tea towels, washing-up liquid and anything else she could fit in it that would help make it not quite so spartan for her friend.

Heather had disappeared out of the kitchen door and around to her own house.

Heather let herself in and closed the door quietly. She stood and listened, but knew the house was empty. 'And which pub are you in?' she muttered, then walked down the hallway and climbed the stairs.

The linen cupboard at the top of the stairs held almost everything she needed. She took a suitcase from the spare room, placed it on the bed and filled it with curtains, a double duvet and two sets of bedding, extra clothes that she needed, towels, everything she could pack in, she did. She closed down the top, leaned all her weight on it, and began to pull the zip closed. It wasn't easy, and she dragged it off the bed, and winced as it landed with a thud on the bedroom floor. The two pillows had proved to be almost the sticking point.

She sat for a moment to catch her breath, then stood and grabbed the handle of the suitcase. She felt as though she was going off on a camping trip. It was heavy, but she didn't care. She could bump it down the stairs; she didn't think she could carry it down. She would have to roll it into the boot; an incapacitated Claudia wouldn't be able to help.

Heather wheeled it to the top of the stairs, and then went back to close the doors of the main bedroom and the spare room. She didn't really want Owen knowing she had been there, if she could help it.

Before closing the main bedroom door, she went in the room and paused for a moment. She glanced around and let her mind drift to the early days of their life there, the laughter they had shared in that room, the love they had enjoyed. All gone.

She sighed, closed the door, and turned around to head to the top of the stairs. On the third step from the top was a furious Owen.

'What the fuck...?' he roared, and she saw him sway. His speech was slurred, and she knew she was in trouble.

For a moment she froze, then felt the sob begin to build inside her. She moved fast.

Pulling the suitcase to block the top of the stairs would give her precious negotiating seconds, time to calm him down. She grabbed hold of the handle and tugged. So did Owen. She opened her fingers and allowed it to fall.

It was almost slow motion; the suitcase tipped towards an already staggering Owen, and his balance went completely. The overweight case tumbled down the stairs taking him with it. He tried, to no avail, to hold onto spindles as he bounced on every stair, cracking his head with a very loud thud as he hit the newel post at the bottom.

Heather stared, unable to move. It seemed from where she was standing that the suitcase had survived the fall, but Owen hadn't. Her legs trembled, and she had to drop to the floor.

Slowly her brain began to surface. 'Ambulance,' she muttered. 'Need an ambulance.' She reached into her jeans pocket for her phone, then remembered it was in her handbag, in Claudia's kitchen. House phone. Hallway. Downstairs. Past Owen.

Heather stood, her legs still shaking so badly she didn't think she could get downstairs. She walked slowly, clinging onto the banister.

Owen wasn't moving. The suitcase was on its side, about two metres away from him. Heather wanted to scream, wanted to do anything except touch her husband. She stopped, still three stairs up, and looked at him. His eyes were open, staring.

She knew she had to pass him to get to the phone but didn't know if she could do it. Slowly she moved down one more step, then another, until she was near his head. She bent down and felt for a pulse. She had no idea where to place her fingers, so tried in several places. Nothing, she couldn't feel anything.

Claudia would know. Claudia was her company's designated first aider. She would know what she was doing.

Heather skirted around his head, her eyes never leaving him. Stumbling, she walked down the hall and through the kitchen, opening the back door to let in some fresh air; she breathed it in. She went through the small gate into Claudia's garden, and walked to her back door.

'Claud,' she said, and Claudia looked up to see her friend clutching onto the door jamb.

'It's Owen,' she said. 'He's drunk, and...'

'And what?' There was anguish on Claudia's face as she could see something had happened to Heather.

'And I think I've killed him,' she said, and vomited all over the kitchen floor.

6

Claudia knelt and placed her fingers on Owen's neck. Nothing. She shook her head. 'Sorry, Heather, but he's gone. We need to think.'

'Don't we need to send for an ambulance?' There were tears running down Heather's cheeks.

'No, I've a feeling that's the last thing we need to do. Grab that suitcase and let's get out of here. There's nothing that says you've been here, is there?'

Heather shook her head, not trusting herself to speak.

'Right, let's go back to mine and take time out. We need to decide what to do next. And we need to get that bloody suitcase in the car. James has just rung, he's staying overnight in Leeds, so we don't have him to worry about.'

Heather edged around Owen's inert body and heaved the suitcase upright. The wheels ran over his splayed fingers as she tried to manoeuvre it around him, and she thought she was going to be sick again. Claudia held doors open for her to pass through them, and she tugged the suitcase behind her.

Two minutes later, it was stowed in the car and they sat at Claudia's kitchen table. She handed Heather a glass of water.

'Drink that, and don't faint on me. We have to think now. If we send for the police, they're going to take you in. I don't think there's any doubt about that. You've left him because of his drinking, and there's proof that is an issue because you've changed your bank accounts, so he can't keep taking your money, and when they do the tox screen it's going to show up exactly how much alcohol is in him. They'll say you pushed him. And if you pushed him, it's murder. They're never going to believe it's accidental.'

She hesitated, trying to grasp at something, anything that could help.

'I think we have to say you've not been here this afternoon. We'll head off to the flat in a minute with you on the floor in the back, and me driving. We have to put your house out of our minds. Let's face it, was he drunk enough to have fallen downstairs anyway, without your help?'

'Oh he was. He was staggering, slurring his words. It's why he grabbed hold of the suitcase, he needed help to balance. Problem was, it moved, and both him and the suitcase tumbled down the stairs together. I heard the bang as his head collided with that newel at the bottom of the stairs. God, it was awful, Claud, awful.'

'Then we have to leave him. It could be days before someone finds him, and then the time of death will be much harder to accurately predict. Especially if we turn up the heating.'

'You mean I've to carry on as if this hasn't happened?' Heather looked shaken.

'You have if you don't want prison. You're already dodgy – you didn't send for an ambulance straight away. Now come on, let's get to the flat. It will all seem much brighter when we're away from the house.' Claudia winced as she stood. The numbing effects of the anaesthetic were wearing off. She took two painkillers and pulled on her coat.

She locked the kitchen door and they walked towards the front of the house. Claudia exited first and checked there was no one around, then opened the rear door on the passenger side. Heather ducked down and climbed inside the car, getting as flat as she could on the floor. Claudia threw a blanket over her and climbed into the driver's seat. She pulled out onto the road, indicated left and waved at Irene Patterson, a neighbour from two doors down. Claudia pulled up alongside her and asked if she was all right. Irene assured her she was fine, and they said goodbye. Claudia wanted Irene to be able to say there was nobody in the passenger seat, should it ever be necessary to say anything on the subject.

On reaching the flat, she was relieved to see that the bakery was closed. She held open the rear door, and a stiff Heather climbed out.

Heather dragged the heavy suitcase upstairs, one painful step at a time, and then went down to bring the bag that Claudia had packed, and her own suitcase from the hotel. She sank onto the floor in the lounge and leaned her head back against the wall.

'What are we doing, Claud?'

'We're keeping you safe. Now, we, or should I say you 'cos I don't think I can do it, are going to blow up this bed, sort out some bedding for you, and get you set up for the night. Tomorrow I am going to organise the delivery of two double beds, so I'll need you to stay here to take them in. I'm also going to buy a couple of reclining loungers for the patio that we can use in here until we can organise furniture. At least we'll be able to sit down. You have to put your positive head on, Heather, because sooner or later the police are going to turn up here.'

Heather wailed. 'And how do we get around that? Nobody knows we are here. Who can tell them where I am? They are going to immediately assume I had something to do with his death and I've legged it.'

'But you haven't. They'll check Owen's phone, and they'll ring you. That's when you tell them you've left him, and you left Wednesday night, sleeping at mine. You have proof you were in the hotel Thursday night, proof we were here getting this flat today, proof we were at the hospital before cancelling your hotel, and then I dropped you off here. You haven't seen Owen, Heather, you haven't seen or spoken to him. And you didn't want to see him, but you didn't want him to be so drunk that he fell down the stairs.'

Heather nodded miserably. 'You're so logical, Claudia, you'd have made a brilliant criminal.'

Claudia laughed. 'Thank you. I kinda think that's a compliment, but I'm not sure.'

Heather eventually slept. Many times during the night she relived the bang as Owen's head hit the newel; she had an awful feeling if that hadn't happened, he would have survived the fall.

The inflatable bed was reasonably comfortable and when she clambered out to face a bright sunny Saturday, she felt rested. She was very grateful that a kettle had been part of the kitchen's fixtures and fittings, and she made a cup of coffee which she took back to bed with her.

The sunlight had woken her; her first job had to be getting the curtains up. There had been a text from Claudia the previous night saying that the beds would be arriving between noon and two; under normal circumstances this would have been greeted with excitement. Nothing would ever be normal again.

She finished the coffee, shook out the curtains and laid them on the floor while she attempted to free a screw with a knife. Eventually it loosened, and she managed to slide the curtain pole off. She had nothing to stand on and at full stretch she could just about manage to hang them, she figured.

Half an hour later she stepped back to admire them. They were a little bit creased, but she guessed the creases would eventually drop out. She hoped so – they didn't have an iron.

James arrived home shortly after eleven, tired after spending the night with Marilyn, an unexpected bonus that had ended his week nicely. He could tell that Claudia was a little stiff when she moved her right arm, but she seemed to be okay.

He took his overnight bag upstairs and emptied it, then went down to rejoin his wife.

'It went well, yesterday?'

'It did. They said there's nothing to worry about, and I'll get a letter in about three weeks discharging me. It's a bit sore, but not enough to merit painkillers, so that's good.'

'Right, so do you want to know my itinerary for next week?' He didn't wait for her answer. 'Monday and Tuesday, I'm in Leeds,

Tuesday evening back home, Wednesday, Thursday and Friday, Doncaster.'

'Busy week then. Things seem to be stepping up.' She tried to inject some enthusiasm into her voice, but it was difficult.

'You're okay with me being away so much?'

'Yes, I'm fine. Missing Heather, though.'

'Missing Heather? Why? Where is she?'

'She's gone, left Owen. Couldn't take the drinking any more. And he wouldn't do anything about it, so she went. She's in a hotel but looking for somewhere to rent until things are sorted.'

'What? You serious? I'd best go see Owen, see how he's handling it. He'll fall apart without her.'

Claudia felt nauseous. This wasn't supposed to happen. Where had this caring James surfaced from, and was it permanent? She hoped not, and somehow, she needed to stop him going next door.

'He's not here. He said he was going to his brother's place for a few days, asked me to keep an eye on the house.' She held her breath while James digested the information.

He nodded. 'Probably the best thing he could do, I'll see him when he gets back.'

She waited, but he made no mention of Heather. To him, it was obviously all Heather's fault.

Claudia breathed a sigh of relief that one more crisis had been averted. She didn't want anyone in that house for a couple of days. It had been awful having to go back in and turn up the heating, but the more fudging they could do to timelines the better. And it had been at the last second that she had thought to pull a tissue from her pocket before touching the thermostat dial; anyone would expect her fingerprints to be in her best friend's house, but not on the thermostat dial.

He stood. 'I'm going in the office. Got some stuff to type, spreadsheets to update, that sort of thing. You'll be okay?'

She didn't know who this stranger was. Or why he was being considerate. That person had stopped existing a long time ago.

'I'll be fine. I'm taking some flowers over to the cemetery later. I'll do us some lunch before I go.'

He looked at her without speaking, then nodded.

He had only been to Ella's tiny grave one time, the week after they buried her. His collapse had been spectacular, his grief finally becoming visible. After keeping strong for his wife, Harry and Zoe, throughout the dreadful week following the baby's birth, suddenly James had given in.

Claudia had had to drive them away from the graveside, an inconsolable James by her side; they reached home, and he told her he would never go again. She never understood his stance on it. She took comfort from telling her tiny daughter about her brother and sister, and everything they did as a family.

That day, her trip to the cemetery would disguise her trip to see Heather.

The text from Heather came at almost exactly midday and told Claudia of the arrival of two new beds. It also added that she needed two further pillows – they had enough bedding in the stuff she had brought the previous night, but had only had two spare ones in the house. She responded immediately. **Will bring everything Monday. James here atm. Won't take risk of him seeing me carrying pillows. You need anything else? Calling round to see you about two.**

Claudia was making a sandwich to take upstairs to James when she heard the sound of laughter. Harry, Emma his partner, along with Zoe and David, all piled in through the back door.

'Hey, it's lunchtime,' Harry said, before bending to kiss his mum's head. At six feet four, Harry tended to bend down to everyone.

Emma grinned. 'I can't believe you're actually part of this family, nobody else is tall.'

'Hey,' Zoe joined in, 'I am five feet one, you know.' They laughed and patted her on her head. She was by far the smallest in the room.

'So, are you all here for lunch?'

'No, Mum, don't panic. We've called to tell you something.' Harry smiled, and pulled Emma towards him. 'I've asked Emma to marry me. I think she said yes.'

Emma held out her left hand; the diamond sparkled as she wiggled her finger.

'You only think she said yes?' Claudia laughed.

'She burst out crying. I assumed she meant yes so I put the ring on her finger.' Harry's smile creased his face. 'No wedding plans yet, but probably this time next year.'

Claudia pulled Emma to her and hugged her. 'That's wonderful news. Let me go tell Harry's father.'

James, aware of the laughter and commotion in the kitchen, was already half way down the stairs.

'James, Harry has some good news.'

James said nothing, merely walked into the kitchen, ignoring his wife.

He instantly became the life and soul of the party, kissing both Emma and Zoe, and shaking hands with Harry and David. David moved to Claudia's side.

'Everything okay?' he asked quietly. 'No more doors to walk into?'

'I'm fine, thank you, David,' she said. 'It's been a quiet week. Are you two good?'

'Very good. As you know so very well, I love the bones of your daughter. I hope Harry and Emma will be as happy as we are.'

'I'm sure they will.' Claudia sighed. 'It doesn't seem two minutes since they were little kids, creating havoc. And now look at them.'

There was a loud pop as James opened a bottle of champagne and poured into the six glasses he had lined up on the kitchen side. He handed them around and raised his own glass.

'To Harry and Emma, congratulations and many happy years together.'

They all echoed 'Harry and Emma' and Claudia returned her glass to the work surface. She was going to be driving in another hour or so and didn't want alcohol stopping her doing that.

'Do you have any plans, yet?' James asked.

'None. We told Emma's parents this morning, then called around to tell Zoe and David before bringing them here with us to tell you. However, one plan we do have is to invite all of you, plus Emma's parents, to a meal next Saturday. I'll have to tell you the venue later, when we know we can get a table.'

Claudia felt sick. By the following Saturday she wouldn't be there, and she couldn't see James wanting to go on his own.

'That will be good,' James said, saving Claudia from having to say anything on the subject.

'And what are you doing now?' Claudia asked, her voice slightly too raised, her eyes slightly too bright.

'We've tickets for the match, so we're off to Hillsborough. Perfect way to celebrate our engagement,' Harry said, taking hold of Emma's hand. 'Couple of beers first, then football. Can't beat it.'

They finished their champagne, and ten minutes later the house was in recovery mode, peaceful, calming once more. Claudia finished the lunch she had made and took it upstairs to James before telling him she was heading off to the cemetery.

His eyes didn't leave the computer screen. 'Thanks. You okay?'

'I'm fine,' she said. 'I can hardly feel it now. Thank you for not telling the kids. They didn't need to know about it, and it would have put the focus on me instead of on the engagement.'

He shrugged. 'Don't be too late back. See you later.'

She closed the office door, and almost ran downstairs. She picked up the small white teddy ornament she had found in a garden centre and dropped it into her bag. A packet of baby wipes followed it – she liked to keep the headstone clean – and she put on her coat, right arm carefully.

Her first stop was to pick up some flowers and she chose pink carnations and gypsophila, with one beautiful white rose.

It was a large cemetery, but the children's area was quite close to the entrance gates. Over the years, Claudia had got to know one or two of the bereaved mums, but that day the sector was empty of parents. She walked up the slight incline to Ella's grave and stood for a moment, before kneeling. She took out the old flowers, then wrapped them in the paper the fresh ones had been in.

She walked over to the rubbish cage, threw them in and filled the vase with water. Arranging the flowers always gave her pleasure; she could do nothing else for her tiny daughter.

Claudia quickly wiped down the headstone, and then sat on the marble base. She placed the new little ornament centrally at the base of the headstone, then spoke of her love, her heartache; she told Ella her brother was now engaged to be married, and he was happy. She said Daddy sends his love. She always said Daddy sends his love, but privately thought it was a pity Daddy couldn't deliver that message himself.

And then she told Ella that Mummy didn't love Daddy anymore because Daddy kept hitting Mummy, but it didn't matter because Mummy had a nice new home to go to, and she would be living in it with Aunty Heather.

Claudia stayed half an hour, then stood and pressed her kissed fingers to the headstone. 'Love you, baby,' she said, and wondered if it would ever get any easier. She suspected not.

She gave a backward glance as she drove away, then wiped the tears from her cheeks. All these tiny graves, all these teddies, birthday cards that were laminated to protect them from the weather, flowers everywhere, some blue, some pink. Gifts for angels.

7

Heather was standing at the lounge window when Claudia pulled up. She had been crying. Despite everything, she would not have wanted Owen dead, and all she could see was his body at the bottom of the stairs, his eyes open. And to make matters worse, she now regretted not calling the police and ambulance at the time. Unfortunately, it was too late for that; she would either have to return to the house and find him or hope someone else did.

The door banged, and Claudia called her name.

'I'm in the lounge!' Heather responded.

Claudia dumped two pillows on the floor. 'I called at Tesco and picked these up. I can't stay long, because I don't want James thinking I'm in contact with you. He's going to work early Monday, so I'll get up when he does and shoot straight across here. What I can do over the weekend is do an online shop for delivery early Monday morning – between seven and nine okay?'

Heather nodded. 'That's fine. If nothing's happened with Owen before Monday, I think I might have to go over there and discover him.'

'No!' Claudia looked shocked. 'James knows you've left him, and when I go as well, James is going to go and find Owen, to see if we're together. Don't forget we have a key for yours. He'll find him. The police will find your mobile number, either on Owen's phone or they'll get it from James, and for heaven's sake, be shattered by it when they ring. He's in Leeds Monday and Tuesday. He'll be home Tuesday evening, so I guess it will all start to kick off after that. In the meantime, we set this place up, act perfectly normal. Heather, you didn't kill him, it was an accident.'

Claudia picked up the pillows and headed for her bedroom. The bed had been put in place and the headboard attached, but only had a bottom sheet on the mattress. There was a duvet cover and pillowcases on the bed, ready for use, and Claudia put the pillowcases on her new pillows.

'There's no duvet,' Heather called. 'I forgot to mention it.' She walked through to Claudia and looked around. 'You okay in here?'

Claudia smiled. 'I'm okay with everything in this flat. I'll add a duvet to the online shop, so I'll be okay for my first night here on Monday. Did you sleep okay?'

'Surprisingly well. It's years since I've slept on an inflatable bed. I've deflated it now and put it in that broom cupboard thing at the end of the hall. There's a Hoover in there, by the way, and it works.'

'That's good. And will you be okay tonight and tomorrow night? You'll be on your own, and we can't really communicate. I don't want James getting any inkling of this. I want him going to work Monday morning a married man, and coming home Tuesday evening separated.'

Heather sat on the bed. 'I'm widowed.' Her tone was bleak.

Claudia had no idea what to say. Owen and Heather's relationship had been complex. It had been alcohol, and only alcohol, that had driven the wedge into the marriage; they hadn't stopped caring for each other, it simply became impossible to live together.

Claudia moved to sit by her side and placed her left arm around her friend's shoulders. 'It's a one-armed hug,' she joked.

Heather gave a weak smile and sighed. 'The sooner Owen is found, the better. What was I thinking of, not ringing 999 immediately? I hadn't done anything, he over-balanced.'

'And that's what will show when he is found, but you would have been taken in for questioning, all the stuff with the bank would have surfaced, and his drinking could have been seen as your reason for helping him down those stairs. Trust me, we've done this right.'

Heather turned her head to look at Claudia's face, seeking the truth. 'And you believe I didn't push him?'

'Of course I believe you,' Claudia scoffed. 'I've known you for many years, and you haven't got a bad thought in you.'

Heather gave a huge sigh. 'Then I have to just sit it out. Wait for somebody to find him.'

'Ring him,' Claudia said. 'And when he doesn't answer, leave a voicemail. Tell him you're okay, but you meant it when you said it was over unless he stopped drinking completely. That will reinforce the problem when they find the alcohol in him, they'll know he fell downstairs because he couldn't maintain his balance.'

'You're probably right. And I will ring his phone and ask him to ring me back. I'll say I can't tell him where I am, not yet, but I will when I'm properly settled. Then what? We sit back and wait for the police to contact me?'

'That's about all we can do. And when the police arrive, we ask them to respect our privacy. Nobody must know where we are.'

Heather was silent for a moment, deep in thought.

'You okay?' Claudia squeezed her hand.

'I will be. But I want you to go home now. Don't give him any excuse to go for you, you've only to get through two more nights and you're free.'

Claudia heard James's phone ringing as she went in, and saw it vibrating its way towards the edge of the coffee table. James was nowhere to be seen, so she glanced at the screen.

Marilyn. The ringtone stopped abruptly. Marilyn? She hadn't heard James speak of anyone with that name before. The sound of the toilet flush alerted her to her husband's whereabouts, and she headed for the kitchen.

She sat at the table and looked around her. This kitchen was easily three times the size of the one in the flat, and she didn't care that she was giving it up. She wouldn't be living in fear of getting a battering that went a step too far; the coldness of the relationship would be gone, and she could relax. She wanted desperately to be herself, not Mrs Bell, wife of Mr Bell and subordinate to him. Afraid to have an opinion. Scared every time she heard him put his key in the lock when he returned from work.

She stood to take off her coat and felt a twinge in her shoulder. At least that was one problem sorted. She swallowed a couple of painkillers, not wanting the twinge to become any more than that and took two steaks out of the freezer. She fancied she might just take the other four with her when she left on Monday. She'd leave James with the shepherd's pies. The thought brought a smile to her face.

'Oh, you're back.' James stood framed by the kitchen doorway. 'I didn't hear you come in.'

'You were in the bathroom. Your mobile was ringing, someone called Marilyn, but it stopped before I could answer it.'

James nodded and moved towards the lounge. Claudia waited a few seconds and followed him. He had the phone held to his ear without speaking; Marilyn had clearly left a voicemail.

'I've not heard you speak of a Marilyn before.'

He put the phone into his back pocket. 'No, she's part of the Leeds staff. She's not been there long, and that's the reason she rings me. She double checks before she does anything. She'll be fine when her confidence builds.'

Claudia smiled. 'Just like Sara at work. She's improving now, but for the first six months she brought everything to me before actioning it. There's one in every office, isn't there?' Claudia returned to her meal planning, knowing the husband she had lived with for twenty-eight years was lying to her.

James switched on the television. He felt a bit of football might be in order, maybe cool him down. The voicemail had made him tingle and he was thankful Claudia hadn't listened to it. *Hi, Mr President, it's your Marilyn, and I only wanted you to know that I would love to be stroking your beautiful cock right now. It seems a long time until Monday night. Love you.*

He watched the football that appeared on screen without knowing what was going on. He didn't listen to the commentators, figuring they knew nothing anyway, and let his mind go forward to Monday night. He would finish his workday early, so that he could get his reports emailed quickly, then he would head for the Travelodge he used whenever he stayed in Leeds. Marilyn was an accident; he hadn't meant it to happen, but it had, and now he was finding it almost impossible to keep the affair to himself. He wanted to tell the world, but a wife and two kids, albeit adult kids, stopped that. Especially after the surprise announcement of Harry and Emma's engagement – he needed to be the loving family man for a while yet.

It would decimate his family; Marilyn understood and accepted that James came with baggage, but he had slowly come to the realisation that he couldn't go on like this. What had happened the previous Saturday with Claudia was unforgivable, and something that happened far too regularly, but he didn't know how to put it right. He didn't even know if he had the energy or the willingness to make things better.

And to add to his woes, it was obvious David knew the mark on Claudia's face wasn't caused by walking into a door. If he told Zoe…

The ball went in the back of the net, and he raised his head to watch the replay. Things seemed to have improved at Manchester United with the advent of Mourinho, and he had no doubt that the goal would prove to be the winner with only five minutes left to go. With a sigh, he picked up the remote control and switched it off. He would try to be a bit nicer to Claudia, she didn't deserve his constant criticism and bitchiness.

He walked into the kitchen and took out a bottle of wine. He poured them both a drink and smiled at her. She reacted with a look of shock.

'To Harry and Emma,' he said, raising his glass.

She repeated the gesture and wondered why he was being so nice. Something was amiss. Usually, when she had been to the cemetery, he became so wound up she always tried to avoid being in the same room as him. She wouldn't let it stop her visiting her daughter's grave, but she always knew what to expect when she returned home.

That day appeared to be different. Had he forgotten where she had been? She mentally shrugged and turned towards the food preparation. Two more evening meals, and she would be free... And she could visit Ella without feeling she needed to apologise for loving her tiny daughter.

Sunday was a long day. The sun shone, although not with any strength, but nevertheless Claudia sat out on the patio for quite some time, drinking tea and reading. She had completed the online shopping order and hoped she hadn't missed anything. She booked the delivery slot for lunchtime instead of the early slot she had said to Heather, then closed down her laptop. Claudia noticed an absence of pain; she hadn't had to take any painkillers, so assumed the wound was healing well. It was such a relief that the mole had now gone.

She wanted to start packing but knew she couldn't. James had been upstairs working on the computer for most of the morning, and she was damn sure she wasn't going to do any housework. If he queried why she hadn't cleaned the bathroom, the chore she usually reserved for Sunday morning, she would simply say it would have to stay as it was, her shoulder was too sore, and she didn't want to burst any stitches.

What she really wanted to say was 'Clean it yourself, you idle manipulative piece of shit', but knew the resultant beating wouldn't be good.

But James said nothing. He even loaded the dishwasher after their evening meal, and she began to worry that he had picked up on the great escape.

James's mind was in another city, and that overrode everything. Even loading the dishwasher had been a pleasant chore; his mind could go where it wanted to go, to the Travelodge in Leeds.

His phone vibrated every few minutes as he chatted with his blonde temptress, and he didn't mind at all. They spoke of love, of lust, of plans for the week ahead; they did not speak of any issues surrounding James having a family.

Around nine, James sent his final text of the evening. He said goodnight and see you tomorrow.

He did it with a smile and Claudia noticed.

She frowned slightly. James had said he was in the middle of a discussion with one of the Leeds councillors, regarding a development in the city centre. She had listened to the everlasting pings all evening long but tried to ignore them as she became lost in her book.

And then James made a mistake. He sent that final text and smiled. He fucking smiled. Claudia knew he wasn't texting any old councillor, he was texting a female councillor, one he was happy to be texting. Possibly one he was happy to be doing other things with as well.

Claudia put down her book. 'I'm going to bed, James.'

He looked across at her. 'You okay?' There was still a half smile on his lips.

'I'm fine. My back's feeling a little sore, so I'm taking some tablets and going to try to sleep. Don't wake me when you come up, will you?'

He stood. 'I'll get you the tablets.'

'Make sure they're not arsenic, won't you?' She gripped her book. Had she really just said that?

'I'll have a rummage around the drawer and make sure they're paracetamol,' he said, and winked at her.

She was in shock. Who was this stranger? A stranger she would be saying goodbye to in eight hours, and it would be goodbye for ever. For over six years he had been a bully, a wife-beater, a sarcastic thug of a man, and then on their last night together he develops a new personality? She wasn't buying any of it.

'Thank you.' She eased herself up from the sofa and stood her book on the bookshelf. It briefly occurred to her that these books would have to go with her; he would destroy them if they didn't. He hated her ability to lose herself in a story, and constantly carped about her ignoring him in favour of a novel.

She heard him go into the bedroom with her painkillers while she was brushing her teeth, so she brushed for a little longer.

'Night, God bless,' he called as he went back downstairs, and she rinsed her mouth. She splashed a little water on her face and left the bathroom.

The tablets were on her bedside table, and she picked up the glass of water to facilitate them going down her throat.

Ten minutes later she was asleep, drifting off in the middle of planning in her head what she could get in the car the next morning.

James opened up his laptop and logged onto the Leeds City Council website. He read through Marilyn's page, and wondered if they would ever have the courage to be together properly. James had felt happy all day; the previous week had been good, and they had shared several nights, but he thought next week might only be Monday night for them. He had other meetings in various parts of the country that he had to attend, and his job had to come first.

He finger-kissed the photo on the screen and closed the lid after logging off. They would speak in the morning while he was driving up to Leeds, and once again the thought put a smile on his face.

He switched off all the lights and slowly climbed the stairs. He needed to sleep; an early start was essential.

The rain was coming down heavily as James wheeled his small suitcase out to the car. He put it into the boot, along with his laptop, then sprinted back into the house to collect his dark blue suit.

He bent to kiss Claudia, and she recoiled. 'I'm not going to hit you, woman,' he growled. 'I'll see you tomorrow night. Don't forget to check that everything is okay next door. You heard from either of them?'

'I've heard from Heather, but not Owen.'

'Well, check the house. Bye.'

He turned and went towards his car. 'See you tomorrow.'

'Not if I've got anything to do with it,' she murmured, and closed the door.

Within a couple of minutes she had two large suitcases open on the bed, and she was packing. She filled the cases with all her clothes, then moved them to the top of the stairs ready for transporting them out to the car.

Having to lay her back seat flat caused her some shoulder pain and she knew she had to be careful; it took her until nearly eleven to get the little car packed. Almost every part of it was heaving with stuff, and she was aware she would have to make a return journey, but she would come on her own. She didn't want Heather anywhere near her old home until she had no choice but to be there.

Claudia got out of the car, and Heather ran across the wide pavement to meet her. They hugged each other, and slowly carried everything up the stairs. The flat was warm and welcoming, and they stood, staring at the disaster that Claudia's belongings were creating. It resembled a car boot sale in the middle of the lounge.

'You're not travelling light, then,' Heather said drily. 'There can't be anything left in that house. He's not hinted that he suspected anything?'

'Nope. And I've one more trip to make, then I'll never go back there again. Part two of our lives starts now. I've already left the letter proudly propped up against the kettle, so it will be there to welcome him home Tuesday night.'

8

The online delivery arrived on time and included with the groceries were two sun loungers. Heather set them up in the living room, facing the tiny television set that used to live in Claudia and James's bedroom. She hoped James would miss it.

By five, everything was sorted, and they opened a bottle of wine Michelle had delivered, along with a coffee and walnut cake, as she finished for the day.

Claudia grinned. 'As far as I can see, the only drawback to living here is we're going to get very fat, very quickly.'

'That cake's heavenly,' Heather groaned. She paused for a moment. 'This has all happened very fast, hasn't it? And I know you say I didn't kill Owen, and you're right, but if I hadn't walked out of that life, he'd still be alive.'

'Do you regret it now?'

'No.' She shook her head emphatically. 'I regret losing Owen, we've been together a long time, but this drinking stuff – it stopped the love.'

Claudia sipped at her wine. 'There's something I haven't had a chance to tell you. I think James has another woman. Marilyn something. He says she's one of the Labour party workers, but I've a feeling she's a Leeds councillor.'

Heather stared at her friend. 'My God! Let's hope he treats her better than he treats you. You bothered by it, if it's true?'

'Not in the slightest. In fact, it'll be easier to tell Harry and Zoe that he's screwing around, rather than he's a wife-beater. Makes me look like a strong woman because I didn't put up with it, rather than the wimp who's tolerated violence for years.'

Claudia heard her phone peal out, and she looked around. 'Well, I can hear it, but I can't see it,' she laughed.

'Bedroom?'

'Could be.' She stood and moved into what she had already deemed her sanctuary. The phone was on her bedside table and as she bent to retrieve it, it stopped. She picked it up and went back into the lounge, staring at the screen.

'It's the hospital,' she said. 'They'll ring back if they want me.' She placed it on the upturned plastic box they were using as a coffee table and topped up both their glasses. She was taking a sip out of the newly filled glass when her phone rang again.

'Hello?'

She listened for a moment, then spoke her date of birth, followed by her post code.

There was a period of silence, and finally Claudia spoke. 'I'll be there for half past nine. Thank you for ringing.'

She disconnected and stared at Heather. 'They want to see me again. Tomorrow morning.'

'You want me to go with you?'

'Yes, please, if you can. It's lucky we both booked this week off, isn't it? That nurse, or whoever she was, has just told me to bring someone with me.'

'Didn't she give you any clues?'

'No, she said the doctor would talk to me tomorrow.'

They were parked in the hospital's multi-storey car park before half past eight and went in search of the coffee shop. Claudia was quiet, and Heather tried to keep her entertained; she picked out male maids they could invite to stay with them, just for board and lodging, and she bought a couple of doughnuts.

Claudia couldn't eat hers; worry was etched into her face.

'Why do they want me back so quickly, Heather?'

'Could be any number of reasons, Claud. Stop the panic. We'll find out very shortly, and whatever it is, we'll deal with it. Now… if you're not going to eat that doughnut…'

Claudia gave a weak half-smile and pushed the cake across the table. 'Who says we need Michelle to help us get fat?' Claudia glanced at her watch. 'Can you eat and walk? We should be going.'

'I can eat while doing most things,' Heather responded. 'That's the problem in a nutshell.'

They found the clinic easily, and checked in. They hardly had time to sit down before a nurse appeared to lead them to a smaller waiting area; she asked them to sit and wait. 'Mr Robson will be out for you very shortly.'

'Is that who did your op?' Heather asked.

'No, they did tell me his name, but I can't remember it. He was a doctor. This chap must be the consultant if he's a mister.'

Heather wanted to respond with 'shit' but allowed the word to fester in her brain instead. Now was not the time to speak of worries.

Mr Robson proved to be a tall slim man; Claudia judged him to be around her own age. He glanced down briefly at her notes, and then his grey eyes locked onto her own.

'Mrs Bell, I've called you back in quickly because we have the results of your biopsy from the mole we removed last week. It is showing that it is malignant melanoma.'

He paused for a moment, and Claudia switched off. She heard the rest of his words through a haze, answering whenever she felt she should, and hoping that Heather was taking everything in.

'I need you to come in as an inpatient; I will be taking a much larger area than the one we took on Friday, to make sure we remove every single part of the cancer.' He stood. 'Can you just come with me into the examination room, Mrs Bell?'

She followed him into the next room, leaving Heather to look through one of the leaflets he had given Claudia.

Claudia removed her top and waited patiently while Robson examined her back. He then checked her armpits and asked her to get dressed and return to his office.

Pulling the file towards him, he began to make notes. Heather stood as Claudia walked through and pulled her into her arms. They hugged for a moment, then Claudia retook her seat. She held on to Heather's hand, and they waited.

'Let me start with reassurance, Mrs Bell. Malignant melanoma is the most curable of all cancers. We don't treat it with either radio or chemotherapy, it is removed by surgery. As I said, I will be removing a much bigger area, and this will necessitate a skin graft. If I don't do that, you will find that your right arm won't have full movement. The skin will be removed from your leg. I will also be taking lymph nodes from under your arm. You have obvious swellings there, and we'll take no chances. These swellings can indicate that the cancer has spread, but it can also mean that it is indicative of your body fighting back from the minor surgery you had on Friday, and it is trying to heal you. Is everything clear so far?'

Claudia nodded, still not able to speak. Heather squeezed her hand.

'So, I need you to come in on Thursday. We'll go through everything then, do any checks we need to do, and the anaesthetist will have a chat with you. You'll be first on my list Friday morning. Do you have any questions?'

Suddenly, Claudia's head cleared. 'Does it have to be this week?'

Heather answered before Robson could. 'Yes, it does. This is our priority, Claud, whatever else this week throws at us.' She looked at the consultant. 'She'll be there, Thursday. What time?'

'Around ten will be fine. We'll have you settled into the ward, and I'll come around in the afternoon to have a chat with you.'

Claudia nodded in acknowledgement.

'Thank you, Mr Robson.' Again, it was Heather speaking. 'Is that everything?' She was scooping up the leaflets Claudia had been given and putting them in her bag. 'I think Claudia needs a cup of tea.'

Robson smiled. 'Then go and have one. And try not to worry. We have a very high success rate with this cancer. You'll be uncomfortable for maybe three weeks, but then you'll start to feel better. I suggest six weeks off work and then we'll discuss whether you are fit to return.'

The coffee shop was bustling. Claudia found a small table for two nestled in a corner and sat down while Heather went for their drinks.

'It's bloody cancer,' Claudia hissed, as Heather placed the tray on the table. 'Cancer!'

'Curable cancer,' Heather responded. 'It's not lung, pancreas, liver, blood, it's melanoma.'

'Malignant. The very word makes me want to cry. I need to go home and find out every damn thing about it. And six weeks off work! I'll ring Raymond this afternoon, tell him the unwelcome news.'

'Raymond's a good boss,' Heather said firmly. 'He'll tell you to take as long as you need. You know he will.'

There were tears in Claudia's eyes. 'Why now? Just when we are sorting ourselves out...'

'We'll get over it. I'm going in to see my boss after... well, after Owen is found, and ask for a few weeks off, so it's all working out. I'll be able to look after you until you're back on your feet properly.'

They sat for a few minutes, drinking their tea and flicking through the leaflets.

Claudia was quiet; the diagnosis was slowly sinking in. 'Let's drink up. I need to go home and think through what all this means, who I need to tell, that sort of thing.'

Heather nodded. 'I know, but you also needed something to combat the shock. You're going nowhere until that tea is drunk.'

Claudia raised a tremulous smile. 'I don't know what I'd do without you.' She picked up her cup and sipped at the hot drink. 'I'm not telling James. I'll tell the kids, but I'll ask them not to tell their father.'

'That's unfair.'

'I know. But he's hardly been fair for the last six or seven years, has he.'

Heather hesitated. 'I mean it's not fair asking the kids to keep secrets from their father. It might be better not to tell them anything. Then they're not being asked to lie for you, and you're not passing the worry onto their shoulders. He said you'd be uncomfortable for three weeks, and then you'll be back to normal. It might be easier for you all if you don't tell them. You had decided not to give out your new address yet, anyway, and if you tell the kids about this, they're going to want to come and see you.'

'Oh what a tangled web we weave, when first we practise to deceive,' Claudia sighed. 'You're right.' She put down her cup. 'Come on, let's go home and have a couple of hours respite – I reckon the police will be ringing you later.'

James frowned as he approached the drive – his wife's car wasn't there. She hadn't said she had plans to go out. He parked and took his suitcase and laptop out of the boot. The alarm was swiftly dealt with and he bent and picked up the mail. Holding it in his hand, he stood for a moment in the hallway. Everything felt strangely empty.

He hung his coat on the newel post and walked through to the kitchen. Throwing the post on the table, he turned to switch on the kettle. That was when he saw the envelope.

He quickly read the contents, then ran from the kitchen and up the stairs. Everything of Claudia's had gone. Her wardrobes were empty, as was her bedside table and chest of drawers.

He sat on the bed with a thud.

'Bitch. Absolute fucking bitch. Didn't have the guts to tell me face-to-face, bitch?'

Heather. She'd know something about this. He ran down the stairs, and towards the back door, cursing when he realised it was locked. He returned to the hallway to get his keys and then unlocked it, heading around to the Gowers', feeling fury overwhelm him. He banged on their door, and when nobody answered quickly enough to appease his temper, he used the same bunch of keys to gain access to their kitchen.

'Heather!' he roared. 'Owen, you two here? I know somebody's here, your bloody car's out front!'

The heat in the house was overwhelming, and James became aware of a strange smell. He passed through the kitchen still calling Heather's name. Owen was at the bottom of the stairs; the smell made James gag, and that was the moment he remembered Claudia telling him that Heather had left.

He staggered back into the kitchen, then through to the back garden. Calling 999, he briefly explained the problem, assured them the man was dead, and went to sit on the front doorstep, to wait for the police to arrive.

It didn't take them long. Everything happened in a blur; a forensics team donned their white suits before moving into the hall, and crime scene tape was placed around the driveway entrance.

Two constables stayed with James in his own kitchen, making him the coffee he had thought about having before this nightmare of an evening began, and he told them that Heather no longer lived there. She was, it seemed, living with his wife.

He passed Heather's phone number to them, saying he had no idea where the two women were living; until his arrival home from work he had been a married man. Now it appeared he wasn't.

'So, your neighbour left her husband last week?'

'Yes. From what I can remember, she gave him an ultimatum. Stop drinking or that's it. Owen was a heavy drinker, a very heavy drinker, and I guess she'd had enough. I think she walked out Thursday morning, but you'll have to ask her, I'm not really sure. And now it seems my wife has joined her.'

It was an age before anything further happened, and then a police officer, clearly senior in rank to the two young men who had kept James company, popped his head around the kitchen door.

'Mr Bell? I'm DS Liam Norwood.'

James stood.

'Sit down, please, sir. Just a couple of questions, and I want to fill you in on what's happening.' He waited until James was seated. 'You're friends with your neighbours?'

'Very close friends,' James said. 'Have been for years.'

'Then I'm sorry for your loss, sir. We have removed Mr Gower's body, and there will be a post-mortem, but initial observations from our forensics people suggest it is a tragic accident. The angle he has fallen at leads to thoughts that he lost his balance, and it happened some time Friday afternoon, although that time is a bit vague because he must have turned up the heating, possibly to get the house warmed up quickly.'

'He would have been drunk,' James said.

'Would he?'

'Oh, yes. That's without doubt. It was a Friday, and Owen's Friday lunchtime session tended to last until Sunday evening. You don't have to look far to find out why he fell down the stairs. Heather, his wife, will be gutted.'

'I'm going to call her, find out where she's living, so we can give her the news.'

'Will you tell me, please?'

'What?' DS Norwood looked surprised.

'My wife left me yesterday. I've only just found out, and she says she is with Heather. I'd like to know where that is.'

'If your wife says I can tell you, sir, then I will. But if she's left you and not told you, I think it's highly unlikely she'll allow me to pass that information to you or anybody else.' The bloke's attitude stank, and Norwood had no intentions of pandering to him with information of any kind.

Shock was etched on James's face. In his world, he gave orders and they were obeyed.

Norwood stood and shook James's hand. 'Thank you for your assistance. I'm sure Mrs Gower will be back at the house at some point. I would suggest you leave her alone. We don't want any problems, do we, sir?'

The two constables followed him out, and James slumped at the table, his head whirling. Harry and Zoe. He needed to get them over, see what they knew. Zoe was particularly close to her mum, she'd know even if Harry didn't.

But they would want to see Claudia's letter; the letter that made it very clear why she had left. And the hint that she suspected him of adultery had caused the most anger in him. He had been so careful to hide his relationship – how the fuck had she cottoned on to that?

He knew he couldn't speak to his children yet, not until he'd covered his tracks a bit more; not until he'd worked out how to either get Claudia back or... he didn't know what the 'or' was, not yet.

But he would.

Neither of the women wanted anything to eat; both had knife edges of differing sorts hovering over them, and things were coming to a head. They sat on their garden chairs in the lounge, occasionally holding hands when their private thoughts threatened to overwhelm them, randomly getting up to make yet another cup of tea.

It was while Heather was making them a hot chocolate, just for the sake of having something different, that her phone rang.

Claudia leaned forward and checked the screen as Heather rushed back into the lounge.

'Strange number,' Claudia said, and quickly passed her the phone.

Heather had no time to think, to consider not answering. She pressed the accept button.

'Hello? Who's calling, please?'

There was a momentary lull in the conversation, and then Heather spoke.

'Yes, I'm Mrs Heather Gower. What's the matter?'

This time the silence was longer.

'Yes, of course you can. I will have to ring Moss Way to check who you say you are, though, because there are two husbands out there who would dearly love this address, and you could be anybody. I'll ring you back in two minutes.'

She switched off, checked the police station number, then verified the caller was genuine. She had known he was genuine. She was just being a bloody good actress.

'DS Norwood? I'm sorry about that. I have to be careful. Can you tell me what this is about? I don't think I've broken the law.'

After listening to Norwood's response, she dictated her address and disconnected.

'They'll be here in ten minutes,' she said, fear etched onto her face. 'It's happening, Claud. It's happening.'

9

Heather sat in one of the loungers; Claudia stood behind her, a hand on her friend's shoulder. DS Norwood, at Claudia's insistence, sat on the other lounger.

He was explaining the circumstances surrounding Owen's death, when Heather got up and ran to the toilet. She almost knocked over the young policewoman accompanying Norwood as she exited the kitchen; she watched as Heather hurtled down the corridor to the toilet.

'I'll go to her,' Claudia said.

Norwood stopped her. 'Leave her. I imagine she's thinking he would still be alive if she hadn't left him. Just give her a hug when she comes back.' He looked around the room. 'You've only just moved in?'

'Heather last Friday afternoon. Me yesterday. We've had to carefully co-ordinate my move for when my husband was away. He can't know this address, DS Norwood.'

'He's already asked for it,' he said with a smile. 'Don't worry, I've said not without your permission, and you've withheld that. If he does find out where you are, it won't be from us.'

'Thank you.'

Heather was grey when she returned to them. PC Yaxley, the fresh-faced PC who had made drinks, handed her a mug of tea, and Heather sank back onto the lounger. She turned to Norwood.

'Did Owen die immediately? I would hate to think…'

'That he was in pain? The doctor at the scene said he thought it was instant, but we'll know more after the post-mortem. The time of death will, of necessity, be a little vague. Your husband had put the heating on high, probably to get a quick boost, before he fell. The house was like an oven when we walked in.'

'I arrived back home around half past three,' Claudia said, 'and his car wasn't there then. I collected an inflatable bed and some bedding and other bits to bring down here to Heather, because she'd decided to stop wasting money on the hotel bill and move in as soon as we had confirmation the flat was ours. I was at home about a quarter of an hour, but I'll be honest, I didn't notice when I came away if Owen's car was there then.'

'It's looking as though he arrived home drunk and simply lost his balance. I'm so sorry for your loss, Mrs Gower.' He handed her a card. 'This is my number, if you need to get in touch about anything. Please leave it a couple of days before going back to the house – and I have warned Mr Bell that he isn't to harass you for this address. We will need you to identify your husband formally, but I'll contact you when it's time for that.'

Claudia escorted them down to the car, then locked and bolted the exterior door.

Heather was sobbing, deep, gut-churning sobs, when she walked back into the lounge. Claudia put her arms around her and held her close.

'Come on, think we need more than tea, don't you?'

Wednesday morning was grey, with a strong hint of the rain that was promised for later in the day. Surprisingly, both women had slept well, putting it down to the relief of the discovery of Owen's body.

Claudia nipped down to the shop, devoid of customers temporarily, and bought bacon sandwiches for their breakfast. While she was waiting for them, Michelle asked if everything was okay.

'No,' Claudia conceded. 'Not really. We found out last night that Heather's husband died sometime Friday afternoon or evening. Remember we told you he had a massive drink problem? That it was why Heather left? According to the police, it seems he lost his balance at the top of the stairs and crashed back down. They're doing a post-mortem to establish actual cause of death, but Heather's devastated. I think they would have got back together, once he saw the sense in giving up the booze. It won't happen now.'

Michelle looked shocked. 'Oh my Lord! Is there anything I can do to help?'

'No, we're fine, thanks, Michelle. I'm just praying we're not going to end up with my husband on the doorstep because of all this.'

The shop bell tinkled as Michelle handed over the sandwiches. 'Look, we can't talk here. Please, tell Heather I'm really sorry...'

'Come upstairs when you close, and have a cup of tea with us, unless you've something else to do.'

'You're on. I'm closing at two today.'

'We'll be in unless something crops up with the police, but we're not expecting anything. I'll let you know if it does. Can you bring a chair?'

They enjoyed the bacon sandwiches, neither speaking, each of them lost in their own thoughts. Those thoughts led Claudia on to the quickly arranged visit.

'We're having a guest for afternoon tea,' she said with a laugh. 'This should be good – our guest is bringing her own chair. Michelle's coming up.'

'I'll sit on the floor if she doesn't, she might have thought it was a joke,' Heather said. 'And don't go getting all heroic on me, saying you will, because you're poorly.'

'I'm not.'

'You are. Haven't you read those leaflets?'

'I don't feel poorly.'

'Claudia Bell, you're a stubborn old cow...'

'Less of the old,' Claudia hit back.

They grinned at each other. 'Right,' Heather said, 'we have phone calls to make. You need to ring Raymond and tell him you're having an operation and won't be in for six weeks at least, and I'm going to ring work and tell them about Owen. Michael doesn't know I've left him, so I'm assuming he'll say have whatever time you need.'

Claudia nodded. 'I'll take my cuppa into the bedroom, and ring now. You ring from here. And thank you, Heather. You're organising me. I'm a bit woolly-headed at the moment, can't really comprehend all this.'

'Anytime, best friend, anytime.'

Heather waited until she heard Claudia's muted tones, and then rang through to Michael, the dress shop owner. She explained succinctly what had happened, and he immediately said take all the time you need, as she had known he would.

She breathed a sigh of relief that the phone call was out of the way and listened to see if Claudia was still talking. She was, but her tone suggested it wasn't the same conversation she had initially gone to make.

'Yes,' Heather heard. 'I can confirm that Heather was with me every bit of Friday. We left about 7.45am to view our new flat, and the only time she wasn't with me till about nine in the evening was the very brief quarter of an hour I was at home getting her some bedding and a bed. She was in our flat for that time, without transport because I had the car.'

Heather pushed open the bedroom door and tilted her head to one side in query.

'No problem, DS Norwood. Happy to help.' There was a momentary pause. 'She's okay. I know she didn't sleep much. We were both awake at three this morning, having a hot chocolate. She keeps mopping up tears, asking me if he would still be alive if she hadn't left him. In short, she's devastated at how things have turned out. Please be gentle if you have to speak with her, she's definitely fragile.'

Claudia put down her phone. 'Just checking your alibi, Heather, don't worry. I don't think he was seriously doing it anyway, it felt more like a tick box exercise to me. He's going to ring you, organise getting you to identify Owen. I'll be with you, don't worry.'

'You'll only be with me if it happens today,' Heather said.

'I know. You think maybe you should ring him and see if it's possible to do it today? I don't mind if you explain why, as long as he keeps it to himself.'

'And work? Was Raymond okay with the amount of time you need off?'

'Very caring. I'm scared, Heather. Really scared. Mr Robson spent a long time checking out this right armpit, and although I wasn't aware when he was doing it, you can definitely feel the lumps.'

'Now you're being negative.' Heather was firm. 'He explained it could be your immune system fighting the invasion of the surgery you had last week.'

'I know. It's the word malignant, isn't it? Such a massive word.'

Claudia's phone pealed out and she glanced at the screen.

'Zoe,' she said quietly.

'Then answer it. Just don't tell her where you are.'

Claudia took a deep breath and connected with her daughter.

'Mum...' Zoe was obviously crying. 'Mum, Dad's told us about Owen. And you've left home.'

'Hey, come on, sweetheart. Owen wouldn't want you to cry. He had a terrible accident...'

'But you,' she wailed. 'Why have you left home?'

'I haven't left home, I've left your dad.'

'But why?' Again the wail.

'This isn't the time or place to talk about it, sweetheart. We'll meet up in a couple of weeks...'

'A couple of weeks? Why not today? I've taken the day off work to meet you.'

Claudia laughed. 'Then maybe you should have checked with me first. Honestly, Zoe, I'm fine. Devastated by Owen's death, but I'm with Heather so I'm not alone. We only found out about

Owen last night; we're supporting each other. I promise I'll keep in touch, but I can't tell you where I am. Is David with you?'

'No, I said I was okay, and he'd to go to work. He didn't seem surprised that you'd disappeared. Has Dad got somebody else?' Zoe's question was abrupt and unexpected.

'I have no idea,' Claudia said. 'What makes you ask that?'

'Something David said.' Zoe was calming down. 'He said this break up won't be your mum's fault. Don't go laying the blame at her feet.'

'You don't need to worry, Zoe. I'm fine, and if you have to tell Dad you've spoken to me, that's okay, too. Does Harry know?'

'Yes, I imagine he does. Dad rang me this morning. I can't get my head into gear with this, Owen wasn't old.'

'Owen was drunk.' Her tone was sharper than she wanted, and she tried to soften it. 'They're doing a post-mortem to rule anything else out, but the police said last night that it looks as though he climbed the stairs and lost his balance. You can imagine how Heather is feeling. She's wracked with guilt because she keeps saying if she hadn't left him, he'd still be alive. It's simply not true. Heather could have been in the kitchen while he climbed those stairs. She couldn't have done anything.'

Zoe sighed. 'I hate this, Mum. We were so happy last Saturday, when we came with Harry and Emma. Now it's all falling apart. Are you going to talk to Dad?'

'Maybe on the phone, but there will be no physical contact between us.'

'Mum...'

'Zoe, stop it. I'll never go back.'

'Then will you let me know when we have details of Owen's funeral, please? We'll all be going.'

Claudia felt a chill envelop her. Owen's funeral. James would be there.

'Of course I will. Speak to you soon, sweetheart, and stop worrying, because I'm absolutely fine.' *Apart from having cancer.*

They said they loved each other and disconnected.

Heather dropped onto the bed by Claudia's side, and they sat there in silence.

Finally, Heather spoke. 'Last Wednesday evening, just a week ago, we sat in your house getting tipsy on Prosecco, making plans for the rest of our lives as free women. No violence, no alcohol, self-reliant… What the hell went wrong? I feel as though I've been hit by a whirlwind. Is Zoe okay?'

'Not really. She was crying at the beginning, but I think I've calmed her.' Claudia turned to face Heather. 'What on earth do we do about the funeral?'

Heather's face lost any bit of colour it had. Funeral. She hadn't even thought about that. Her thoughts seemed incessantly to focus on Owen's face, as he had lain at the bottom of those damn stairs. That image filled her mind all the time, and she couldn't contemplate that final goodbye of a funeral.

'What do you mean? I'll have to sort it when they say I can have the body, won't I?'

'I didn't mean that. I meant James, Zoe and Harry, David and Emma will all want to be there. And me. And I may be not too good. He said it takes about three weeks before I'll feel more myself.'

'Shit.'

'Exactly.'

'This is all bloody Owen's fault.' Heather stood and walked to the lounge window. Her mind flashed to the way she had opened her fingers as his hand had tugged on the suitcase, and she leaned her head against the windowpane.

'Michelle is just locking up. And she's carrying a small garden chair. Let's forget our worries for an hour if we can and have a cuppa and cake.'

Claudia nodded. 'I'll go down and let her in. You put the kettle on.'

The bell rang out and Claudia headed downstairs, then kissed their guest on the cheek as she came through the door.

Michelle handed over a box full of goodies.

'Brilliant,' Claudia said. 'But I'm going to pay for them.'

'No, you're not. They're just what's left, and I wouldn't have put them on sale tomorrow. I must say, though, I don't normally have to take my own chair with me when I go to visit friends.'

'Just be thankful we've got enough mugs to be able to give you a drink,' Claudia laughed.

She handed the box to Heather and led Michelle up the stairs and through to the lounge.

'Put your chair wherever you want,' Claudia said. 'Apologies for the coffee table, but we've not had time to think about furniture beyond making sure we both have a bed.'

'I'm impressed. It takes some sort of genius to think of upturning an old plastic box. Recycling gone mad.' Michelle unfolded her chair and placed it between the other two.

Heather brought in the drinks and went back for the plate of goodies.

'Is Heather okay?' Michelle kept her voice low.

Claudia shook her head. 'No, it's been a rubbish few days for us. I think we're both thinking six months ahead, when everything will look better.'

'Your husband knows you've gone now?'

Claudia nodded, as Heather joined them. It was Heather who answered. 'We've asked the police not to disclose our address. The last thing we want is hassle from James. There wouldn't have been any danger of him finding out where we lived, but then Owen…'

Michelle touched her hand. 'I know. You don't need to talk about it. But I think you're fooling yourselves if you're thinking that he won't track you down, because he will. My ex never leaves me alone, and I have to keep hiding it from Steve. If Steve knew…'

'And how long have you been split up?' Claudia looked concerned.

'Five years. It was okay for about a week, but then he started. He followed me everywhere, and then one day he beat me up.

Badly. He did an eighteen-month stretch in prison because of it. I almost lived a normal life for the time he was away.' Michelle took a deep breath, unhappy with her memories.

'Even the night I met Steve he knew about it. We got engaged and planned our wedding, but George found out and cancelled our venue. I only knew about it because the hotel rang me to ask if they'd done anything wrong to cause the cancellation. Of course, I knew nothing about it. I thought Steve was going to kill him. He absolutely hammered him, and things quietened down for a bit. I keep seeing him now and again, and I know he's following me.'

'You've told the police?'

'I did, but there's nothing they can do. He's not attacked me or anything since Steve sorted him out, even though I know from experience that he could. He's the reason I gave you this flat immediately. I could see strain in both of you, and I've been there, done that.'

Claudia felt tears prick her eyes. She was starting to think she couldn't take any more. She reached across to take one of the buns and tried to hide how distressed she felt.

'These are delicious.'

And then she began to cry. Michelle stood first and moved across to hug Claudia. She flinched as Michelle caught the operation site, and Michelle moved back. 'I'm sorry,' she said, 'did I hurt you?'

'Not really,' Claudia responded. 'It's just a bit tender still. I had a minor op on it on Friday after we left you. It's getting better. And thank you for the hug. It does help.' She wiped her eyes and picked up the mug of tea.

Heather watched her closely. Claudia was definitely on the edge, and she decided that tonight they would google malignant melanoma, get as many facts about it as they could, and then have a proper discussion.

Michelle stayed a couple of hours, and then said she had to go, Steve would think she'd left him.

Heather went downstairs with her to make sure the door was locked and bolted, and as they reached the bottom Michelle hugged her.

'If either of you want anything, at any time, you have my number now. Just call me. I mean it, Heather.'

Heather nodded and kissed Michelle's cheek. 'Thank you, Michelle. We will, I promise.'

10

Claudia sat in the plastic-covered armchair by the side of the bed and opened her book. Heather had dropped her off at the entrance with a promise to visit later, then had rushed off to identify Owen formally, leaving Claudia to spend money in the hospital shops before making her way to the ward. It occurred to Claudia that she had had better Thursdays; her worries felt as if they were overwhelming her.

She had been reading for around two minutes when the first nurse arrived to do blood pressure checks.

Five minutes later, another nurse arrived to take blood samples and then the tea trolley came around. It briefly occurred to her that there was no time to be bored.

It was during the hour's rest period after lunch and before visitors that the anaesthetist arrived, spoke quietly and confidently with her, then left her to speak quietly and confidently to his next victim. It was when Mr Robson arrived that she began to feel a little bit scared. He explained in detail what he was going to do, that she would wake up with a drain in that would remain in situ for around four days, a bandage on her upper thigh where he would have removed the skin for the graft, and a dressing on the actual operation site.

'You won't be in pain when you first wake up, but by about the third day you will be. You will be given suitable painkillers to take home. The pain, of course, comes from everything starting to settle back down, not from anything going wrong. I suggest you take it easy for a couple of weeks, then start to resume your normal routines. Do you have any questions?'

'Yes.' She smiled. 'When do I get the results?'

'Saturday morning. Whatever I remove tomorrow will go straight to the lab. The email will be waiting for me when I arrive Saturday. Is there anything else?'

'No, I don't think so. If there is, I'll ask a nurse. I just want it over with, it's a scary word, malignant.'

'It is,' Robson conceded, 'but a lot of progress has been made in the treatment of cancer, and particularly with melanoma. Just trust me, I'll do everything I can for you. And the follow-up care lasts for about seven years.'

'Seven years!' There was shock in her voice.

'Yes, initially we give you two appointments three months apart, then we give you six-month appointments to take you to the two-year mark. After that it is annual until we feel all danger is gone. That's usually an additional five years, but if there's any concern you come back immediately. For oncology patients, it's a kind of open house.'

Claudia leaned back in the chair and smiled. 'Thank you. I feel a bit more at ease now I've spoken to you. I hadn't a clue what you'd said when we left the other day. Luckily Heather, my friend who was there, remembered most of it. We did a bit of research yesterday, but it's better from the horse's mouth, isn't it?'

Robson stood. 'You'll be fine. We'll take good care of you. I'll see you in the morning. You're first on my list, eight o'clock.'

'Thank you.' Claudia stood and shook his hand. 'I won't say this hasn't been a shock, but I feel as though I'm in safe hands.'

A quarter of an hour later, Heather was with her. She looked pale and unhappy.

Claudia stood and pulled her into her arms. 'Okay?' she whispered.

'No.'

'Come on, let's go for a coffee while I'm still able to escape.' Claudia grabbed her purse, and they walked down the corridor to the bank of lifts.

Once seated, and cradling cardboard cups of coffee, Heather insisted on knowing what Robson had said. Claudia repeated as much as she could recall but added that she now felt better about the whole thing.

'And Owen? Talk to me, Heather, don't hide it.'

'It wasn't him. I mean, of course it was him, but it didn't look like my Owen. His face was bloated and completely white. They have confirmed accidental death, and I can now organise the funeral. I've already contacted the funeral director, because I don't want Owen to be in that awful place any longer than he has to. They're going to collect him this afternoon. I've now got the death certificate, so tomorrow morning I'll contact the insurance companies. I'm going to the funeral director's Tuesday, but I want you back to normal so I'm delaying it for a couple of weeks.'

'Insurance companies?'

'Yes, we're both well insured. I'll certainly be able to pay off the mortgage, which is a massive relief.'

'Will you go back to the house?'

'What, and live next door to your apology for a husband?' She smiled at Claudia. 'Not an earthly. He'd never leave me alone. Besides, I kinda like living in our flat, it's comfortable, warm, cosy. And nobody knows we're there. Suits me.'

'You selling it then… the house?'

'Don't know yet. I tried to think about it when I was in bed last night, but I'm not good at big decisions. I'm seriously considering keeping it for my pension pot. I could let it out fully furnished, but we need stuff, don't we?'

Claudia grinned. 'Choose your tenants wisely. A bunch of teenagers all sharing the rent, and all being allowed to bring their own music systems should do nicely. And we can afford to buy a suite. Leave yours in your house, or else we'll be reminded of Owen's death every time we look at it. I'll miss him too, you know. He was funny. And when James and Owen got together and began clowning around, I used to cry with laughter. Remember the holiday in Crete with those ridiculous hats they bought? That was pre-Ella…'

There was a moment of silence as each of them let their minds remember the tiny baby. With her birth and death, so much had changed.

Claudia shook her head. 'Enough. Let's get this damn operation over with and start our new life. I've been thinking about that small bedroom. We could put a couple of desks in there, make it our office. Get some shelving in it – you've seen all my books.'

'I sort of like the idea of books in the lounge. It's a massive room and can certainly take some posh bookshelves, and then we can pretend to be knowledgeable smart-arses because we read!'

Claudia laughed. 'Whatever. As long as they've something to stand on, I don't care. What do you think to the office idea?'

'I think it's great. We both use computers a lot, and if we're setting it up properly, I want a desktop.'

They continued to discuss plans, and eventually headed back up to the ward, Claudia reassured that Heather had cheered up somewhat. She had tasked her with getting two desks and matching filing cabinets, then sent her home just after five with instructions to call at Ikea and organise them.

Heather blew her a kiss from the ward entrance, and Claudia climbed on to the bed for the first time. She felt tired; it occurred to her it was more than tiredness, it was exhaustion. Her eyes closed, and a nurse appeared to take her blood pressure.

'A little high,' she said, 'but that's probably because of tomorrow. Now make sure you eat all your evening meal, because after that you're nil by mouth. Sips of water only after six.'

High blood pressure? Cancer? It had certainly been a rough week as far as her health was concerned, and she wondered just how James would have reacted if she'd told him.

Claudia and Heather had looked on the Leeds City Council website the previous evening, searching for a councillor called Marilyn, but it was a fruitless mission. There had been nobody. Maybe Marilyn was the young helper who needed constant reassurance as James had explained; but she didn't think so, her instincts told her otherwise.

The evening meal arrived, and Claudia looked at it knowing she had to eat it. It was almost too much effort, and she was truly grateful when the last spoonful of ice cream disappeared.

She took out her book and within two minutes was asleep.

At eight, they woke her, checked her blood pressure and gave her a sleeping pill.

She showered quickly, slipped on her pyjamas and settled down for the night. Her blood pressure, still slightly raised but not enough to cause concern, was checked twice through the night; she was aware but too tired to care.

Half past six came, and her eyes slowly opened. Once again, her blood pressure was checked, and her pre-med given to her. She was beautifully drowsy by the time she was transported to theatre an hour later.

The nurse held the bowl under her mouth as she was violently sick. She finally laid her head back and smiled weakly.

'That's the third time. Is everybody like this?'

'No, my love, you're just unlucky. I'm going to give you something now that will settle it.'

'Thank you,' Claudia whispered.

'Are you in pain?'

'No, just a bit uncomfortable. I don't need pain relief yet.'

'I'll bring you some.'

If Claudia had had the energy, she would have shaken her head in disbelief. Why bother asking if they were going to give it anyway?

She glanced at the ward clock and was surprised to see it was nearly three. She had half expected to see Heather waiting for her but realised she didn't know if anything had cropped up in the Owen situation. Her eyes began to close, and suddenly Heather was there.

She placed the little blue plastic chair by Claudia's side, leaned over and kissed her. 'You smell of sick.'

'Not surprised.' Claudia smiled at her friend.

'You okay?'

'No. Been sick three times. Why are you late?'

'I rang to check you were back from theatre about one, and they said no. You were still in recovery because you hadn't come around properly from the anaesthetic. They advised waiting a couple of hours, so here I am. You moaning at me?'

'Yes.'

'Oh, okay. So, how are you?'

'Sick. Not in pain though. I've just had something to stop the sickness, and some painkillers. Feel drowsy, so I'm sorry if I nod off. You brought me some grapes?'

'Yes.' Heather bent down and retrieved a tub of melon and grapes from her bag. 'Thought you might like these if you can't manage a meal yet.'

'You're a star.' Claudia's voice faded away, and Heather smiled.

'Close your eyes. I'll just sit here and read. I promise I'll still be here when you wake.'

Claudia nodded, and seconds later had drifted into sleep.

Heather put the fruit in her locker, and settled down with her book, feeling glad that she'd thought to collect a coffee as she came through the hospital.

There were a couple of moans from Claudia as she slept, caused by her attempting to move in her sleep, and Heather stood each time. She'd never seen her friend wiped out like this; it had been bad when Ella had died, and they had cried in each other's arms so many times, but this was different. This was illness, serious illness. She prayed it would all have been taken care of, and that they could get on with rebuilding their lives.

Claudia woke once; she stayed awake for ten minutes and then drifted off again. One of the nurses checked her blood pressure and suggested Heather go home.

'She'll be like this all day. Come back tomorrow, she'll be a lot livelier, and she'll have her results.'

'I'll leave her a note – make sure she gets it, will you, please?'

'Leave it on her bed table. I'll see to it.'

She scribbled a few words, then headed down the ward. Time to go home and erect the second desk.

James was angry. He'd had to fend off questions from Zoe and Harry, both wanting to know what their mother had given as her reasons for leaving him, and he hadn't been able to show them the note. Claudia hadn't pulled any punches with her words; in fact, she had referred to punches several times.

They wanted to know if she had another man; he had said no, but she appeared to have another woman. They had been quite scathing in their reply to that one, saying they knew exactly why Heather had walked away and it wasn't because she was having an affair with their mother.

James had no idea where his errant wife had settled. He needed to speak to her and she was ignoring all his calls. Heather, likewise, was blanking him. He needed to spot Claudia's car; they must be using that, because the Gower car was still on their drive where Owen had drunkenly parked it.

He took out the pizza and looked at it. Singularly unappetising. He had one slice and threw the rest in the bin. Grabbing his coat, he stormed out of the front door, his anger increasing by the second. Bloody woman. He'd find her and let her know just how unacceptable her actions were – before he dragged her home.

He drove around the area, up and down every little street; he found only one car in deep blue, a Renault, and then it began to get too dark to see the colours.

'Fuck, fuck, fuck,' he said, and hit the steering wheel. This wasn't the way. He'd find her somehow… and then he remembered the funeral. She would be there; he would force himself to be pleasant, to ask her to go for a drink with him and talk things through. He had stopped on a side road to think through his next move; it was to put on his right indicator and to pull away, then head for home.

As he turned left at the end of the road, he didn't notice the little blue car that entered the road from the other end, nor did he notice Heather getting out of it after parking up.

'Your dad's an angry man,' David said, and pulled Zoe towards him. She sank into the warmth of his body and nodded.

'I know. Is there something we're not aware of that's happened between them?' She lifted her face to his.

'There's a lot wrong in the relationship,' he said. 'I worry that you're too close to see it. Your mum has too many bruises, and you can see fear on her face, can sense it when you walk in the house. And yet...' he hesitated, 'I was still surprised that she left. I see it every day in my job, Zoe, women just like your mum. But most of them are women who are scared to stand up for themselves, brow-beaten by life, by too many children, by drugs. Your mum doesn't fit into any of these categories.'

Zoe was staring at him. 'What are you saying? That Dad beats her? That's utter rubbish. He's never lifted a finger to me...'

'That's you, sweetheart. Your mum had a corker of a bruise coming, when we called round the other Saturday. She didn't walk into any door, yet another door by the way, and she knew I knew. He hits her, and she's had enough. I reckon that's the top and bottom of this.'

'No...' Zoe's cry was drawn out and full of anguish.

'When we find her, you ask her. And don't pussyfoot around, ask her the question. Did my dad hit you? That's all you need to say. And you'll know from her face. Even if she denies it, you'll know the truth.'

'But why has she never said anything? You think Heather knew?'

David could sense Zoe was coming around to his thinking. 'Yes, Heather was her best friend. She would know. And they're off somewhere safe together now. Heather will protect her until she recovers from everything, but unfortunately Heather won't be in a good place, either. She left Owen, but I suspect if he'd stopped drinking, they wouldn't have split up. And now it's too late.'

'Does Harry know? Have you said anything to him?'

'No. I've only spoken to you. I'm not sure how Harry would take it. I knew you would recognise that I'm right. I see so many domestic abuse cases, Zoe, that they're really easy to spot. And the women never fight back. We could prosecute, but they rarely want to take that step. I don't know whether it's from fear, or whether they can't live without the dickhead who's hit them. They see our police car turn up, and they panic. It's serious when we appear, and they chicken out of even making a statement.'

'Poor Mum. If only we'd known. Harry would have done something...'

'What? What could he have done? It's not easy interfering in a marriage, don't forget. I let your mum know that if she needed us, we were there for her, in a couple of little ways. Maybe it's the reason she left, the fact that I'd recognised she had problems. We'll know when we find her.'

'Somebody knows where she is.' Zoe spoke slowly.

'Who?'

'Whoever attended the Gower house when Dad discovered Owen. They must have gone to wherever Mum and Heather are, to tell Heather. They wouldn't tell her over the phone, would they?'

'No, they definitely wouldn't. I'm not risking my job for this, but I'll see if I can find out anything at work. Now come on, it's time for bed. And we'll talk to Harry and Emma tomorrow, when we see them. It'll be strange without your mum and dad there, but we're celebrating, with or without them.'

11

'Mrs Bell?'

Claudia turned her head slightly and saw Robson. She moved the sick bowl away from her, hoping it wouldn't be necessary any more. The anti-sickness medication clearly hadn't worked, and to make matters worse, she was now in considerable discomfort – not screaming pain, but she guessed it could very soon become that.

'Mr Robson.' Claudia knew she looked a mess, but she couldn't have cared less. It was his fault she looked like this anyway.

He stood by the side of the bed and waited while his registrar pulled the curtains around to give them a bit more privacy. She thought it was a joke, she'd heard everything that was going on at the other beds on Thursday.

'Okay,' he said. 'There's a problem. The cancer has spread, it was present in the lymph nodes we took. We're now going to refer you to the oncology hospital at Weston Park. They will do scans and x-rays to see if it has remained in the lymph glands or if it has spread elsewhere.'

She looked at both men, then at the nurse standing at the end of the bed. 'What? I have cancer?'

'Not necessarily,' Robson's soothing tones cut in. 'We may have removed it all by taking the sensible step of excising the lymph nodes, in which case you will need no further treatment. The fact that it had spread that far means that we must check everywhere to ensure it hasn't moved on. Weston Park is the specialist hospital, as you know, and they will check with everything at their disposal to make sure you are cancer free. We check for cancer, but we also check for freedom from cancer.'

As he asked if she had any more questions, she looked at the nurse. 'Yes, I do. Can I have some more pain relief, please?'

Heather looked stunned. Nothing could have prepared her for this. That tiny little grape-like protuberance could potentially kill Claudia?

'I'm not sure how long I can stay awake,' Claudia said.

Heather squeezed her hand. 'Then sleep. I'll sit here and read and fend off nurses with blood pressure machines, if I can.'

She opened her book but couldn't follow the words. She was having difficulty thinking and wished with all her heart that she had been here for the early morning consultant round. Even if Claudia hadn't asked questions, she would have.

Around four o'clock, Claudia woke, demanded more pain relief and drifted off again. Heather kissed her and said she was going home via the cemetery and would be back the following day. Claudia gave a weak smile and slept.

'She'll be at the bloody cemetery,' James mumbled. After all, he wasn't speaking to anyone, just himself. He checked his watch. She normally went Saturday afternoon, so he reckoned if he went around half past twelve, waited in the top car park that looked down onto the children's area, he would see her car arrive and head for the small parking spots down the hill, closest to the graves.

He filled a flask with coffee and fifteen minutes later was pulling in to the cemetery. He had a perfect view of the lower parking area and hoped she would be there sooner rather than later. He took out his phone, clicked on Marilyn in Messenger, and chatted for half an hour, his eyes never leaving the cars entering and exiting.

After disconnecting, he poured out a coffee. 'Come on, woman,' he growled. 'Where the hell are you? Any other Saturday you'd be here by now...' And his voice faded away as he realised she was going to come later, precisely because she knew what time he would be waiting for her.

He laughed aloud. He could wait just as long as it took. He opened the car window, rested his head against the doorframe and settled in for a potentially long wait.

The irritation set in around half past three, and when the little dark blue car pulled into the car park he raised the window and left his vehicle. His view of the lower area was obscured as he walked down the curving road, but he knew she was always there for at least half an hour. He wasn't sure of the exact location of the grave, but apart from Claudia's car, the small car park was empty, indicating no other parents were there; she would stand out.

He reached the bottom of the hill and looked on the slope towards where he remembered the grave to be. There was only her.

He walked up quietly; she was kneeling with her back to him and sorting out the flowers she had brought.

'I knew you'd come,' he said quietly, when he was about ten feet away.

Heather jumped and turned to face him.

'What the…?' he growled.

'Hello, James. I thought you'd forgotten where the grave was. Do you want me to leave you on your own? I can come back later.'

'You know very well why I'm here. Where's Claudia?'

'Oh, come on, James. I'll leave you to guess why she's not here.' Heather picked up the scissors she had used to shorten the flower stems, and while James had never revealed his nasty side to her, she was aware there was always a first time.

'So where is she?'

'Recovering.'

'Recovering from what?'

'You.'

He took a step back. 'What the hell do you mean, woman?'

'Don't woman me, you sanctimonious git. I've known what's been going on for years, and I've supported Claudia through all the beatings, but rape, James? That's a whole new ball game.'

'Rape? What the hell do you mean?'

'You don't know what rape is? It's when sex is forced upon somebody who has clearly said no, or when someone has been hit prior to the act, after they've said no. The operative word is no.' She held the scissors tighter.

He blanched. Christ, had Claudia told this bloody woman everything? 'I've never raped anybody. She's my wife.'

'You think there can't be rape in marriage? You raped her two weeks ago. And don't forget I know, and both Zoe and David saw the red mark on her cheek from where you'd hit her. And we've got the blouse where you ripped off the buttons. Put all that together, with Claudia's story, and you've got rape, pal. Now back off, 'cos I'm not telling you where we are. And I don't want to see you at Owen's funeral, not anywhere near it. Make your excuses to your kids as soon as you like – you're good at making excuses for not coming home, aren't you?' She raised the scissors. 'Piss off to Marilyn. Maybe she wants you, but Claudia doesn't.'

James took another backwards step, and without saying another word, turned and walked down the slope heading for the road.

Five minutes later she saw his car go past, and she dropped to the edge of the grave and sobbed.

Heather finished off making the flowers look pretty, gathered up all the rubbish and knelt by the graveside. She told Ella about her mummy, explaining she wasn't well and for the next few weeks Aunty Heather would be visiting, but it wouldn't be long before Mummy was well again. Heather quickly wiped down the headstone, finger-kissed it, and headed back down to the car, disposing of all the rubbish in the wire crate.

She knew she couldn't take the risk of going home. He could be anywhere, preparing even now to follow her. She sat and thought for a moment, then took out her phone.

'Michelle? You got a couple of hours spare? I need to talk to you. There's a problem. Don't worry if you're going out, I am aware it's Saturday night,' she laughed.

'I'm not going out, but Steve's going for a game of snooker. You're very welcome. You know where I live?'

'I know the road. What number is it?'

'Seventy-two. You coming now?'

'If that's okay? I can't go home at the moment.'

'Then you'll be in time for spag bol. Is it both of you?'

'No, just me. And thank you, that will be lovely. Claudia's in hospital. I'll explain when I see you. I'll be there in about ten minutes.'

Heather put the little Fiesta into drive and left the cemetery, looking all around for the larger Kia. She didn't see him but knew of old just how devious James Bell was. She looked into her rear-view mirror far more than she looked through the windscreen on the drive to Michelle's, cursing James all the way.

Michelle came out of her front door, accompanied by Steve, as Heather pulled up. Steve walked around to the driver door and opened it.

'You okay?'

'I'm fine.' She smiled. 'I didn't see any sign of the car I was worried might be following me, but he's that bloody clever…'

'Then let's get you inside, and you can relax,' Michelle joined in.

'What car is it?' Steve asked.

'Kia Sportage, same colour as this Fiesta.'

Steve nodded. 'I'll look out for it later.'

The spag bol was delicious and Michelle had already insisted that Heather stay there for the night.

'If he has followed you to here, and hidden the car, it'll be a long night for him. We'll sort you out in the morning, get you back home. And you might want to give thought to using the garage, instead of leaving the car out on the road. He's less likely to spot it by accident then.'

'I'd decided that on the way here. We need to be a lot more careful. I suspect Claudia isn't going to be physically capable of handling him for a few weeks at least. He was pretty scary in the cemetery, and I made it obvious I'd a pair of scissors in my hand. Whether I could have used them is another matter, but he didn't know that.'

Steve came through to them and bent to kiss his wife. 'Won't be in late. And ring if there's a problem. There are a couple of bottles of wine in the fridge if you're thirsty.' He grinned.

Michelle walked with him to the door and slid on the bolt. She knew he would do their pre-arranged knock when he returned.

'So, Claudia. Is she okay?'

Heather shook her head. 'Far from it. This is in confidence now, Michelle. Just the three of us will know about this.'

And Heather began to talk, and to cry. She left nothing out of the events over the past two weeks, and when she had finished Michelle went to the fridge and brought the wine through.

'We need this,' she said. 'And what you've told me, stays with me. Will you tell Claudia I know?'

'Yes, I'll tell her tomorrow.'

Michelle handed Heather a glass, and then sat down by her side. 'I saw my ex today. George Ullyat he's called, just in case you ever cross swords with him. I thought he was going to come into the shop, but he didn't. He just stared through the window at me, and then pointed. It's such a threatening thing, but I don't worry now as much as I used to. He does it all the time, and he knows Steve would hammer him if he laid a finger on me.'

'What's wrong with men that they feel the need to beat women? Is it just because we're physically weaker and mentally stronger? They know they can't win in the brains department, so they shut us down using fear and pain as starting points. I know Owen wasn't violent, not normally, but his behaviour drove me away, and it was the same with both you and Claudia. Did you once love your ex? I know Claudia loved James until he changed after Ella's death, and I loved Owen. They destroyed that love. Not any of us. It baffles me.'

'Baffles me, too. The first time George hit me was because he was drunk. I used to dread him going out. He made sure he never touched my face, just hit me where the bruises wouldn't show. One day I collapsed in pain in a supermarket and they sent for an ambulance. They took me to hospital. It was appendicitis, needed an urgent operation. Then they saw the bruises all over my body. They got someone to come and see me who could help me and I went straight to a hostel when I got out. The police got involved, and that was when he got the eighteen months stretch. It wasn't his first offence, but I hadn't known that when I met him. He stalks me now, threatens me, but I think he knows better than to approach me.'

'They need to die.' Heather smiled at Michelle, the smile softening her words.

'They certainly do.'

'Claud and I were going to buy a gun till we realised we didn't know anybody who sold them. We were going to bump both of them off.' She paused and sighed. 'Sadly, Owen did it himself, the idiot. But to be fair, the drink would have killed him eventually anyway.'

'I've got a gun.'

'Really? Wow!' Heather didn't know what else to say.

'I did know somebody who sold them, and I got one because I knew George would come for me when he got out of prison. And if he got me, I wouldn't survive. But I met Steve before George was released, so I never needed the gun.'

'You never fired it?'

Michelle shook her head. 'No, it's up in the attic, out of harm's way. I know how to load it and fire it, but I've never done it.'

'Good job it wasn't in my bag this afternoon, because I'd have blown James Bell's head off. What he's done to my best friend is unbelievable. I've watched her deteriorate since the baby died, but he's not supported her in any way. He went the week after the funeral to the grave, and today is the first time since then, the first time in seven years. It's like his grief twisted his brain. He stopped being the affable bloke we all knew and loved and turned really cold and unfeeling. Claudia coped with everything on her own, until two weeks ago.'

'What a mess. Shall we get drunk?'

Heather laughed. 'No thanks, I've an early start tomorrow. I've a desk to build, shopping for a new suite, then off to the hospital for two.'

'You'll give her my best wishes? It must be such a worry for her, let's pray they've got it all in those lymph glands.'

'The consultant was hopeful, Claudia said.'

They sat quietly for a while, occasionally chatting, until Heather asked if Michelle minded if she went to bed.

'Not at all. Emotion and worry exhaust you – I really understand that. I'll show you to your room.'

Heather had a quick shower and was in bed within a quarter of an hour; ten minutes later she heard a strange knock on the front door and guessed Steve had returned home. It was only half past nine; she also guessed he had been concerned for her well-being.

She returned to reading her book on her eBook app on the phone, and slowly felt her eyes closing.

Steve bent and kissed his wife. 'I won,' he announced.

'You're home early?' she said.

'Didn't fancy drinking. I've only had orange juice all night. Perhaps that's why I won, I was the only one who could see the pockets.'

'You didn't drink because you're worrying about the two of us back at home.'

'Guilty.'

'We were fine.'

'I know. I just didn't want there to be any trouble. I've driven all around the area looking for a dark blue Kia, but I've seen nothing. Let's hope he went straight home and didn't hang around to follow Heather. Tomorrow I'll find out where he lives, go up and check his car is there, and then she can get hers home and in that garage. If she rings me when she's safely inside the flat, I'll come back home.'

'You're a good man, Steve Baldwin. I bless the day I met you.'

'I know,' he said. 'I'm an absolute star. Superman Steve, that's me.'

She threw a cushion at him. 'Numpty.'

'You certainly know how to bring a guy back down to earth,' he grumbled. 'Is Heather okay? She gone to bed?'

'She's shattered. I'm hoping she's asleep by now, she looked as though she needed to be. We've had a long chat, and she needs some support at the moment. I don't think she'll mind me telling you that Claudia is ill, in hospital currently, and that, combined with losing her own husband this week, has flattened her. Instead of her friend supporting her and comforting her, she's having to be strong for Claudia.'

'She seems nice.'

'She is, and so is Claudia. They've been neighbours and best friends for twenty-odd years.'

Michelle stood and blew out the candles. 'Let's go to bed. Heather needs an early start in the morning, and I'm tired. It's been quite draining listening to Heather, they've shared a bundle of troubles this past couple of weeks.'

'I'll be up in a bit. I'm going to make myself some toast, missed out on a kebab tonight 'cos I came straight home,' he said with a grin. 'Toast and a glass of milk. Just what every smart young man about town should be eating.'

'Numpty,' she said again, kissed him and headed for the stairs. 'Don't forget to…'

'I know. Bolt the door and set the alarm. Night. God bless, sweetheart.'

12

Steve pulled out of the driveway and drove to James's house. The Kia was on the driveway and there was no sign of the occupant. Steve rang Michelle, and within a minute Heather was on her way to the flat.

She used the key to the garage door for the first time, and drove the Fiesta inside, safely away from eyes that might be looking for it. Before leaving the garage, she rang Steve, told him the car was hidden and he confirmed there had been no movement from inside the house.

She thanked him, and he said he would head off home, but would drive by the flat.

Two minutes later, she was sitting in a sun lounger, breathing a long drawn out sigh of relief.

She rang the hospital and was told that Claudia was a lot brighter and was currently sitting in the chair by her bed.

'Tell her I'll be there for visiting please, and give her my love, will you?'

She disconnected and went for a shower before changing her clothes. And then she went sofa shopping.

She chose a beige suite, on the proviso they could deliver it the following Tuesday. Tuesday morning. Early. The salesman looked shocked and said he would see what he could do. She responded with 'No, you will do it. I can't sit on a sun lounger any longer, I'm paying a fair whack of money for this suite, and I want it early Tuesday morning. Can you do it?' And he said yes.

She went home, put the car back in the garage and built the second desk. The room looked smart. She placed the desks on adjacent walls, then slotted the two office chairs into their bases. She looked around the room now promoted to office and allowed herself a small smile of satisfaction. Job done.

Claudia was back in bed by visiting time, looking pale but considerably brighter.

Heather bent to kiss her, and Claudia clutched her hand. 'Get me out of here,' she whispered.

'What?'

'I can't stand it! If the others aren't talking in their sleep, they're snoring, or falling out of bed. Just take me home, Heather, please.'

'When you're better, sweetie-pie. This'll cheer you up. I've been shopping.'

'Well, thanks. That's really cheered me up. I'm in here, and you're out shopping. What for?'

'A suite.' She took out her phone and showed Claudia a picture. 'It's this one, and the obliging young man volunteered to deliver it Tuesday morning. Early.'

'You bullied him?'

'Only a little. I can't have you coming home and sitting on sun loungers. And we have an office. Sort of – two desks, two chairs, two laptops. We need a bookcase or something, it looks a bit empty.'

'And did you take me some flowers to Ella?'

Heather swallowed, and the pause was noticeable. 'Yes.'

'Is everything okay? Heather?'

'It's fine. I took off the dead ones, and replaced them with one of those mixed bouquets, full of bright colours...'

'Heather? What's wrong?

'James came about two minutes after I arrived. I thought he might try to catch you there, so I went later, after I'd left you. He must have sat waiting for you to arrive, and he saw me drive in with your car.'

'Shit.'

The word was loud enough to cause the other occupants of the ward to look over in their direction.

'He didn't realise it was me. It gave him quite a shock.'

'He wanted me?'

'Oh, he definitely wanted you. I let him know I knew everything; the rape, the beatings, and I even said piss off to Marilyn and get out of Claudia's life, all the time brandishing my scissors like a dagger. I think I was too mad to be scared. Anyway, he took himself off, but I was worried he would be waiting somewhere to follow me, to find out where we lived, so I rang Michelle and went there.'

Claudia couldn't speak.

'And I stayed the night. Steve went out, so I told Michelle everything, including what's happening to you now. She's brilliant, so supportive. This morning, Steve drove to James's house, checked his car was there, and then I drove to the flat. We now park in our garage. No more doing the convenient thing and leaving it on the road.'

Claudia's eyes reflected unshed tears. 'I'm sorry, Heather. You shouldn't have to be going through this, you've enough on your plate.'

'Oh, and that's another thing,' Heather interrupted, 'I told him he couldn't come to Owen's funeral.'

'You didn't hold back, then,' Claudia said drily, then grinned. 'Would you really have stabbed him?'

'I suspect I would, but it didn't come to that. He buggered off when I mentioned Marilyn. I'm going to have a closer look at this Leeds City Council website tonight, see if I can't track this Marilyn down. If I can't find her there, I'll look on the Labour party one.'

'You know what, Heather, I don't really care what he's doing…'

'Neither do I, Claud, but sooner or later he's going to have to hand over half of the value of the house and you might need bargaining chips. Marilyn could be a chip. Let's just get the information and file it in our new office. Then you can use it if it becomes necessary.'

Claudia nodded. 'You're right, I know you are. It's just… this bloody cancer feels as though it's living in my brain. Heather, what if it's spread?'

Heather took hold of Claudia's hand. 'Then we'll deal with it. I won't leave you, not for a minute.'

By four o'clock, Claudia was clearly exhausted, and Heather left her, feeling equally drained. She was trying to be cheerful, upbeat, and yet in two days' time she would be arranging her husband's funeral.

She put the car in the garage, crossed the road and wearily climbed the stairs into the flat. Her bedroom looked enticing as she went down the corridor, and she went in and laid on the bed, just for two minutes she promised herself.

Two hours later she woke, feeling chilled.

'Bugger,' she muttered, 'I'll be awake half the night now.' She made herself a large mug of tea and went into the office. Switching on the laptop, she sat and nursed the mug while the laptop loaded.

She typed in Le and the computer obligingly offered up Leeds City Council, recognising Claudia and Heather's earlier fruitless search for the elusive Marilyn. Clicking on Councillors took her through to the listings, and she began to scrutinise them slowly and carefully.

The men were all mixed in with the women, and so she skipped over the male councillors, perusing the female ones much more closely. It had occurred to her that Marilyn might be her second name, and so she checked every one, but reached the end of the list having achieved no success.

She decided to give it one last go and scrolled backwards up the list. And then she found Marilyn.

Councillor Will Monroe. Aka Marilyn Monroe? She had absolutely no proof that Marilyn was the councillor, but she knew, deep down in her gut she knew. And if bloody James Bell turned up at the cemetery this Saturday he'd know that she knew.

Heather felt sick for Claudia. She clearly had no idea, and yet if James was struggling with his sexuality, it explained his erratic behaviour. So why the hell hadn't he been open and honest with his wife, instead of battering her every time she "transgressed"?

He was obviously struggling with his feelings; he'd raped Claudia two weeks earlier.

Heather clicked on his image; blonde hair, bloody good-looking, fit... just what did he see in a slightly overweight forty-five-year-old?

There was very little information on the website, apart from an email address, so she closed the laptop and moved into the lounge. She put something mindless on television, then switched it off and picked up her book. It was going to be a long night.

Claudia, despite having had a sleeping tablet, was wide awake. The noise provided by her three companions as they proved they could sleep was appalling. She had tried reading, but her arm and shoulder area was too uncomfortable, and she couldn't remember any of what she had read.

'You okay, Claudia?' A night nurse she hadn't seen before, and whose badge proclaimed her to be Jenny Taylor, gently touched her arm. 'You need anything?'

'Ear plugs,' she said with a sigh. 'And something to stop my brain careering along at a hundred miles an hour.'

'You're worrying?' Jenny sat down in the chair.

'Wouldn't you be? If it had spread into the lymph glands, then what's to stop it having spread further? I just keep thinking that two weeks ago all I had was a sore spot on my shoulder. Now I'm potentially dying.'

Claudia felt a tear trickle down her cheek, and she angrily brushed it away.

'Hey, come on.' Jenny reached and grasped Claudia's hand. 'Trust Mr Robson, he'll have removed all of it. And don't go reading anything on the Internet, you'll scare yourself silly.'

Claudia turned her head.

'You already have, haven't you?' Jenny said. 'Honestly, leave it to the experts, Claudia. The Internet shows worse case scenarios, and you can do without reading all that rubbish when you've just had major surgery. You'll be back here in seven years or so, being officially discharged. And that's the best feeling ever. Now, shall we have a quick cuppa? That might help you drop off.'

Claudia smiled. 'Thank you. You've made me feel more settled in my mind. I'd love a tea.'

Jenny stood and walked down the corridor.

She carried two cups back with her, but Claudia was asleep. She smiled and went to the nurse's station. 'Tea, anybody?'

Zoe was trying to control her anger. Her father wasn't giving her answers, and she really didn't believe he knew nothing. Her mother had to have had a reason for walking away, and now seemed to have disappeared.

'So where are you? You're not at home.'

'I'm in Leeds.'

'But it's Sunday. Why would you be in Leeds on a Sunday?'

'I have an early meeting tomorrow morning, sweetheart. It made sense to drive up today and get an early night.'

Will grinned at him and ran his fingers down his back.

'Okay, that's you accounted for. Now where's Mum?'

'I have no idea. She doesn't return any calls or texts, so whatever she thinks I've done, I can't put right.'

'And what does she think you've done?'

'I don't know.'

'Right, here's what's going to happen, Dad. You will come back home tomorrow night, and I will be here at the house waiting for you. If you're not here by seven o'clock, I shall ring the police and report her as missing.'

She disconnected and turned to David. Tears were in her eyes and he pulled her towards him. 'You want to go see Harry and Emma?'

She nodded. 'I do. I want Harry there as well tomorrow night. He's done something, my dad, I know he has. If he's hurt her...'

'If it's any consolation, I don't think he'll have hurt her, I just think she doesn't want to be found. Wherever she is, she's with Heather.'

'Of course!' Zoe slapped her forehead with her hand. 'Heather! I should try her. I've just concentrated on ringing Mum and texting her till my fingers are sore. Why didn't I think of Heather?'

She picked up her mobile phone and texted.

Hi Heather. Can you ask Mum to contact me please? Tell her I'm not with Dad, just David. I need to know she's okay, and well.

She put the phone down and waited. And waited.

'She's not going to answer either. But somebody will sooner or later, because there will have to be a funeral for Owen. We all want to go, Heather can't keep that quiet, surely?'

'Look, sweetheart, text Harry and see if they're in. We'll go over there and talk things through. Maybe they can come up with an idea for finding her.'

She texted and put her phone on the coffee table. From experience, she knew it could be a while before Harry returned the text.

She picked it up when she heard the ping and opened the message. It was from Heather and it simply read: **She's okay. Trust me.**

Zoe couldn't speak. She handed the phone to David and he stared at it.

'Look,' he said finally, 'Heather wouldn't lie to you. She's protecting your mum. And at least you've had some communication even if it's only four words.'

The phone pinged again, and David looked at it. 'Harry and Emma are in. He says come over.'

Zoe grabbed her bag and moved to the door. Once more she felt anger. This was bloody ridiculous. Why couldn't her mother answer the calls herself?

David followed Zoe, and they clicked on seat belts simultaneously. Then he removed his, turned around to his wife and took her in his arms. 'Let me hug you for a minute,' he said.

She nodded and burst out crying. He held her until the tears had subsided, then grabbed the tissues from the glovebox.

'Feel better?'

'Not really, but it helped.'

'Right, let's go and talk to Harry and Emma, see if we can sort this out. People like your mum and Heather don't just disappear. They're keeping quiet, that's all. But I think you're going to have to face the fact that your dad's behaviour is the problem. Owen's behaviour was behind Heather going, and while I know it's not drink with your dad, I believe he does hit your mum.'

She shook her head. 'Don't say that, David. If it's true, why have I never clicked on?'

'She would hide it from you. But now you and Harry have left home, she's decided enough is enough, and she's walked out. It's why I'm not worrying too much that she's gone under the radar, so to speak. I think something serious happened that Saturday when your mum was gardening. I could tell she was upset. You're too close to her to see it, I guess.'

They pulled up outside Harry and Emma's place, and Emma came outside to greet them. 'To what do we owe this honour?' she smiled. 'Lovely to see you, no matter the reason.'

They followed her into the lounge, and Harry switched off the television.

'Sit down,' he said. 'Beer, David?'

'No, I'm good, thanks. I'm driving. Zoe might want something though, she's a little upset.'

Zoe looked at Emma. 'You have wine?'

Emma laughed. 'How many bottles?'

Zoe and David finished speaking, and the silence hung tantalisingly in the room. Emma looked at Harry, and she was the first to speak.

'We guessed.'

'So why didn't I guess?' Zoe had anguish in her voice.

Harry echoed David's words from earlier. 'You're too close to her.'

'I'm obviously not that close, she's said nothing about it to me.'

'Sis, you'll be the first one she contacts when she surfaces,' Harry said gently.

She stared at her brother. 'But if you'd guessed, why haven't you done anything about it?'

'Like what? They would both have denied it, and I didn't want him turning on Mum because I'd said something. It's knowing which path to take that's so bloody hard, Zoe. Go on, tell me what you're going to say to Dad next time you see him.'

Zoe shook her head. 'I don't want to see him. If this is all true, and I'm convinced now that it is, I don't ever want to see him again. The thing is, I've kind of given him an ultimatum. I told him that I want him back in Sheffield by tomorrow night, and if he's not there by seven, I'm reporting Mum as a missing person.'

'Don't do that, Zoe. I think the police will know where she is. They had to go and tell Heather about Owen, and I bet Mum was with her. She wouldn't let Heather go through it on her own.'

'And they would ask the police to keep their address secret.' Zoe was clearly thinking things through. 'I'm glad we came here. I feel better about things now. And we'll see her at the funeral.'

She picked up her glass of wine – the second one – and drank slowly. 'Am I being stupid? She's a woman in her forties, and she can live her life exactly as she wants to live it. She's brought me up to believe that, and yet I'm calling her for doing the same thing.'

Emma, practical Emma, spoke. 'Look, in a year's time all this will seem like a bad dream. Your mum will be settled wherever she chooses to settle, your dad likewise, and things will move on. This is the transition period, and I suspect Claudia just wants time out for a few weeks while she gets her brain into gear. I know this won't stop you worrying, but you've got to give her whatever space she needs. We all agreed on that?' She looked around at the other three, and they nodded.

David and Zoe stood. 'Thank you for listening. We're going to get off now,' David said. 'I've got an early start tomorrow, and I think Zoe needs to think all of this through. Thanks for listening, you two, and if we hear anything, we'll let you know.'

Emma and Harry walked to the car with them and waved as the rear lights disappeared down the road.

'You really not worrying then?' Emma asked.

'What do you think?' Harry replied. 'I've been texting Mum all week trying to find out where she is.'

Before heading off upstairs to bed, Zoe sent a text to her father. She kept it short and to the point.

Don't bother racing back from Leeds. I won't be seeing you.

13

The suite was in situ by nine o'clock; the funeral was organised for May 6th by eleven o'clock and Heather was with Claudia by just after two for visiting.

She leaned over to kiss her friend. 'You look good.'

'Thank you. I feel so much better. I'm probably going home tomorrow.'

'Yeah!' Heather's smile lit up her face. 'It's pretty damn lonely in that flat without you. I've taken to talking to myself, and the answers I'm getting are rubbish.'

'So, what news? Have you got a date for the funeral? How do you feel?'

'Yes, it's 6th May, and I'm okay. Broke down in the funeral directors, and they were lovely with me. I think they were a bit surprised I was on my own, but I could hardly expect Owen's cousin to come over from Norfolk to go with me, and he's the only family left. I've arranged for a small notice to go in the paper a few days before, so his friends will know the date. I don't think it will be a large gathering. I need to organise a wake, but I'll sort that in a few days.'

Claudia nodded. 'Thank you for leaving it a couple of weeks. I should be fine by then. I have an appointment…'

'For Weston Park?'

Claudia nodded again. 'The Monday before the funeral. I've to be there for nine, and it will take all morning because they do loads of tests. Will you be able to go with me?'

'Of course. You don't need to ask. Now, let's forget about bloody cancer, let's talk about what we're going to do when you get home. You won't be sitting on a sun lounger, that's for sure, unless we're out on the patio. I just hope you like the suite.'

'Heather, I'm getting lots of texts…' Claudia's face had clouded over.

'From the kids?'

'And James. I'm ignoring his, bombastic little twerp. But the kids are clearly upset. I may text them tonight now I'm feeling more my normal self, to let them know I'm okay.'

'That would be good. Just don't give them details. Not yet. And don't worry about the cemetery this week, I'll take the flowers. Until you're fit enough to cope with meeting up with him again, I don't want you bumping into James.'

'You think he'll be there again?'

'I think he'll be there every week until he sees you. I won't let you go alone, but this Saturday I don't think you'll be strong enough to handle the evil git. But I am.'

Claudia smiled at her friend. 'What would I do without you?'

Heather left for home just before six; Claudia's evening meal had arrived, and so Heather left her to her hospital life. Claudia was to ring the following morning if they confirmed she could go home, and then hopefully their world would be a little more normal.

She drove past James's house to see if his car was there. She needed to pick up some more things but was wary of making waves by him realising she was next door.

His car wasn't there, and she checked her watch. She couldn't take the risk, it was too close to his normal return time. It made her angry that she was as much a target of his violent tendencies as Claudia was, and Heather drove away at considerable speed.

She put the car into the garage, returning quickly to the flat. Maybe she could call home before going to the hospital the next day, but sooner or later she would have to make decisions about the house. Tenants? Sell it? Whatever her final actions would be, she could never return and live next door to a man who had once been a close friend.

Sleep didn't come easily. She was putting a wash load in by half past six and ironing the dried clothes with the new iron that was stressing her because it didn't have the same feel as her old iron, by ten o'clock. She had decided not to go back to the house – she needed to be ready to go as soon as Claudia called her.

The flat looked really nice, and she couldn't wait to get her friend home. When her phone rang out she snatched at it.

'I can come and get you now?'

'You can. I've got my painkillers, my drain tube has been removed, and I'm good to go. I can't carry anything, so I'll wait on the ward for you.'

'Half an hour,' Heather said and disconnected.

Claudia was sitting chatting to an elderly patient when Heather arrived but said goodbye with some speed. 'Get me out of here,' she whispered. 'I can't take any more.'

There seemed to be a lot of bags, but Heather made no comment. She manhandled all of them, and ten minutes later they were on the road and heading for home.

They were quiet on the journey. Heather helped Claudia into the flat and emptied the car of the bags before taking it across the road to the garage. Heather called into see Michelle as she passed the shop, to tell her of Claudia's return and to pick up some bread.

'I'll leave her a couple of days, then come and have a cuppa with both of you,' Michelle said. 'She'll not be wanting visitors yet.'

Heather walked into the lounge and Claudia was sitting on the sofa. 'It's lovely, Heather, just a tad comfier than the sun loungers.'

'You've seen nothing yet,' Heather said with a grin. She moved to the side of the sofa and pressed a button. The footrest rose, and Claudia sighed.

'Heaven,' she pronounced. She fought sleep for half an hour and then succumbed.

By Saturday things had improved, including the weather, and they sat out on the patio all morning.

'I've been doing some thinking,' Heather said, 'making some decisions. I've decided to sell the house. I had intended renting it out, but that would mean me having to visit it occasionally, and I think it's time to cut the strings with that part of our lives. I hate having to avoid going there in case I bump into James. So, it makes sense to sell it. I'll clear the last part of the mortgage with Owen's insurance money, and I reckon the house is worth around quarter of a million. I'm also going to sell the car. It was always too big for me, so I'm going to get a smaller one.'

'We can only get one car in this garage,' Claudia warned her.

'It won't matter, will it? James won't know I've got a new one. I can park mine on the road with no problems. I'm going up to the house Monday morning, bringing down here some stuff that I need, and I'll make a start on the packing. I'll organise putting everything into storage, then get it on the market when it's empty. I'll hang on to the car until the house is sold, so that James never sees whatever the new car will be. And then we're going on holiday.'

'And if I need treatment?'

'Then we'll postpone the holiday until after the treatment. I've already told Michael I won't be going back to work, I'll look for a new job when I feel ready. I won't be short of money, I can wait for the right position. My main concern now is getting you fit again.'

'And you're going to the cemetery this afternoon?'

'I am, don't worry. And I'll explain to her that you're much better.' Heather crossed her fingers at the lie.

Claudia wasn't looking well at all; her skin was like parchment, and she slept a lot. In addition, the area on her leg that had donated the skin for the graft was also troubling her; she had confessed it was more painful than the entire underarm and shoulder area. Heather assumed it was the major surgery she had had, causing theses issues in her friend; she prayed it wasn't anything more serious.

They had some lunch on the patio and then Heather helped her back inside and made her go for a nap. 'The more you sleep, the quicker you'll heal,' she said. 'I'll wake you when I get home. Your phone's on the bedside table, ring if there's a problem.'

Claudia nodded, and closed her eyes.

Heather pulled up outside the cemetery gates to buy some flowers.

'Afternoon, Clark. Busy day?'

'Nah, think they're all doing their gardens now the weather's picked up.'

'You could be right. I'll have two bunches of those carnations, please – oh, and one of those mixed bunches.'

She handed the money over and walked back to the car. The mixed bunch was for the flat, and they would all have to go in the one vase they had. The pretty pink and white carnations were for Ella. She drove slowly around to the small carpark and walked to the graveside.

The sun passed behind a cloud as she knelt to cut the stems shorter on the fresh flowers, and she sensed someone behind her. She froze. She had allowed her mind to be on other issues, mainly surrounding the complexities of selling her house, and she hadn't kept a watch for anything else. She was still holding the scissors when she whirled around.

'Where the fuck is she, Heather?'

James was standing there, fury evident on his face.

'As if I'd tell you,' she sneered. 'Go back to your Marilyn – or is it Will?'

'You bitch. You absolute bitch. What the fuck have you been saying? The kids won't have anything to do with me and I can't find my wife. Where is she, Heather? I need to see her.'

Heather glanced around – Clark had been right, it was devoid of people. No help for her there.

'Go away, James. She's out of your life now, and if you've lost the kids as well, doesn't that tell you something? That you're just not a very nice person to be around? Go and let Marilyn/Will nurse your bruised ego and let me get on with tending to your daughter's grave, the daughter you haven't bothered with for seven years. And Claudia's fine, she doesn't need you.'

Heather knew she was winding him up but couldn't help herself. Her hatred for him knew no bounds at that point.

'You...!' He launched himself at her and she fell backwards, cracking her head against the headstone. His weight pinned her down and she saw his arm raise to hit her. Her right hand, still clutching the scissors came up to try to stop the onslaught; she felt blood spurt and thought it was her own. He was going to kill her.

The scissors were embedded in James's neck and he collapsed against her. His blood was gushing out, covering her clothes and face. She tried to wriggle out from underneath him, but it wasn't easy. It was all over within a couple of minutes, and she finally sat by his side, stunned in every sense of the word. The crack against the headstone had brought blood and dizziness, but equally shocking to her system was the dead body by her side. She had killed him.

Her first instinct, to ring 999, was being thought through with some care. This would be the second dead man linked to her in a couple of weeks, men that the police knew had treated her badly. They would never believe her version of the events of the last few minutes.

She had to get him away, then make decisions. She searched his pocket for his car keys, took off her bloody jacket and covered his face, then ran up the incline to the top car park. His was the only car there, and she drove it around to within ten feet of Ella's grave.

There was nothing in the boot to help her except a shovel which she guessed he had carried throughout the winter in case of snow. Blood was dripping onto her top from her own head wound, mingling in with the initial spurt of blood from James, and she felt an increase in blood loss as she heaved James down the slope towards his car. She levered him into the boot and slammed it shut.

Parking the Kia alongside her own in the lower car park, Heather staggered painfully back to the grave, clutching the shovel.

She began to dig the large puddle of blood by the headstone into the soil, but when she sat on the grave to rest after managing to blend it in, she saw the streak of blood gleaming wetly on the grass where she had dragged him down to the car.

It took a dozen journeys with the small container from the grave, as she fetched water from the tap and poured it on the blood. The cleaning of the headstone was even more difficult, but at least she could explain that – the wound on her head would show where that was from.

Finally, she was done; a casual observer would see nothing amiss. A policeman would.

A car came through the ornate stone entrance and parked in the small car park, so she decided it was time to move.

'Bye, Ella,' she whispered. 'Mummy will come next week, I promise.'

She finger-kissed the headstone and headed down to the Kia. There was a smear of blood on the bumper, and she took out the baby wipes and cleaned it. Her top had very little blood on it, the jacket had absorbed the bulk. She climbed into the car and left through the cemetery gates.

She reached James's house a quarter of an hour later and parked the Kia on his drive. Once again the high privet hedge was effectively hiding all activity. Using his keys, she went into the house and prayed he hadn't changed the alarm code. The beeping stopped, and she breathed a sigh of relief.

She moved towards the back door and around to her own house, where she spent another quarter of an hour showering and changing her clothes. Her blood-soaked items she put in the washing machine. As she went out of the back door, she could hear it churning all the blood down the drain.

Heading back through James's house felt so wrong; she reset the alarm, made sure the car was locked, pocketed his keys and headed for the bus stop.

Twenty minutes later, she was in Claudia's little car, heading home.

Claudia had slept; she woke to the sound of her bedroom door opening and Heather walking in with a cup of tea.

'Ella sends her love and wants Mummy to visit her next week, if Mummy is well enough,' she said with a smile.

Claudia swung her legs off the bed, and shook her head, trying to clear away the fuzziness in her brain.

'What time is it?'

'Nearly five o'clock. Drink this and we'll decide what to do about food.'

She left Claudia to come around and headed into the lounge. She needed a few minutes of solitude, just to get her head around what had happened. She had covered for today, but knew she had to do something about James very quickly.

With the warmer weather, she reckoned she only had a day at the most before the body started to smell. She had to get rid of him, one way or another.

Her biggest worry was the body being discovered with the wound in the neck; she couldn't put the car in his garage with the engine running to make it look like suicide – and that would have to happen immediately anyway. Her thoughts churned; by the time Claudia joined her in the lounge Heather had decided she had to burn both him and the car, to the point of destruction.

Claudia came up behind her and bent to kiss her head. She winced and felt Claudia touch her head.

'What on earth have you done? There's a gash that I suspect needs stitches in it!'

'It'll be fine,' Heather said. 'I slipped in the cemetery and smashed it on Ella's headstone. It's why I was away for so long. I had to clean up all the blood – you know how much a head wound bleeds. Then I had to clean me up, so I sneaked back home and changed my clothes after I very carefully showered. There was no sign of James, so I was okay. I didn't want to wake you by coming back here and showering.'

'I'll get the first aid box. Let's hope James never needs a plaster, because I brought everything with me,' she said with a smile. 'I think I have some steri strips.' Heather doubted that a plaster would help James.

Nursing accomplished, they sat for a while, Claudia reading and Heather planning.

She soon began to realise that burning the car was impractical, she needed him to disappear completely, and even burnt bodies would give something up forensically. He had to be buried. And the logical place was in the large area of knee-high grassland under their elevated patio. If she dug the grave directly underneath, she would be hidden from the sight of everybody, and secure in the knowledge that the council never cut the area because they couldn't get a grass cutter to it, the supporting uprights for the patio prevented access. But she could get the Fiesta down the side alley leading to it if she pulled in the wing mirrors and drove very carefully.

Swapping James's dead weight from the Kia to the Fiesta wouldn't be easy, but did she have a choice? She stood and moved to the kitchen. Two painkillers would help with the ever-increasing headache, and maybe she should have a sleep. It was going to be a long night.

14

Heather reversed the Fiesta as close to the back door of the Sportage as she could get it, then pressed the button to raise the tailgate of the big car. She stared in horror at James's face, his eyes wide and glassy. In the blackness of midnight, and a moonless midnight because of the heavy cloud cover, his face glowed eerily translucent.

She opened the boot of the Fiesta, glad that she had thought to lay down the back seats and cover everything with a blanket. No way would a man's body fit in the small boot space. His body was stiff, and it took her fifteen minutes to transfer him to the smaller car, then cover him with a second blanket. She removed the plastic sheeting James always had in his car to keep the boot clean and stuffed it into the Fiesta. She intended wrapping him in it before burying him. She checked over the Kia, wiped down everything she had touched when she brought him home from the cemetery, packed the shovel she had last used at the graveside, and then locked the car. It was now out of her hands.

She started the engine, and then sat for a minute while she watched for anyone moving curtains to see who was making the noise. All appeared normal and she put the car in drive and edged slowly out of the driveway. She drove down the road, not switching on her lights until she reached the crossroads, then turned right and headed for home.

It was nerve-wrackingly difficult driving down the tight alleyway leading to the unkempt grassed area around the back of the flat. She had to turn off her lights so that no one in the houses opposite would think it strange that a vehicle was travelling along a route not meant for cars, and she breathed a long sigh of relief when she reversed the little car as close to the spot where she intended digging as she could get it.

Heather sat for five minutes, calming her trembling hands and legs. Reaching into the back of the car, she grabbed hold of the shovel, and then opened the door. Heather chose not to close it; she needed no noise alerting anyone.

The grass sods were removed as solidly as she could keep them and stashed to one side. They had to go back on top of the disturbed earth, even though she knew it was highly unlikely anyone would ever see them.

The ground was solid, and it took her two hours to dig a hole big enough to take James. Her head was throbbing, and she hoped it was stress causing it, and not the head injury from earlier. She quietly laid out the plastic sheet and dragged James from the boot. His head cracked against the bumper and she flinched.

'Silly bugger,' she whispered to herself. 'Don't think he'd feel it.'

Rolling him in the plastic wasn't easy, but finally she got him to the edge of the hole and tipped him over. She immediately went to work filling the hole with the mound of soil stashed by the side of it; after she had flattened it by walking up and down on it, she relaid the grass sods.

To her eyes it was obvious it was disturbed soil, that it was a body-sized area of disturbed soil; there was nothing she could do about that. She was exhausted. She hid the spade in the long grass, quietly closed the boot and started the engine, aware that Claudia was sleeping fifteen to twenty feet above her, fortunately with the help of a sleeping tablet.

Heather once more navigated the alleyway without lights, then drove the few yards necessary to get her to their garage.

The garage door screeched as she raised it, but she didn't care. She was now officially just a neighbour arriving home and parking her car.

She returned the rear seats to their more normal position, gathered up the blankets, and locked the garage door behind her as she walked across the small road to her home.

The flat was in total darkness, and she headed for the kitchen. She put the two blankets in the washer and switched it on. It sounded extra loud in the quietness of the early hours, and she heard Claudia call her name.

Moving across to Claudia's bedroom, she opened the door, just allowing her head to go around it. It wouldn't be good for her friend to see her in jeans and a sweater at that time of night. 'You okay, Claud?'

Claudia struggled to sit up, hampered by the dressing on her shoulder. 'I'm okay. Thought I heard a noise.'

'You did. I've just vomited on a couple of blankets. I was too hot with the duvet, so put blankets on last night, but I couldn't get out of bed fast enough. Everything's okay now, I'm back with the duvet and I've popped them in to wash. You want anything? I'm going to have a cup of tea.'

'Yes, please. I'll have one as well. Sleeping tablets make you really dry.'

'Okay, stay where you are, I'll bring it in to you.'

She closed the door and ran to her own room. Her pyjamas were on inside thirty seconds, and she moved back to the kitchen.

Claudia had put on her lamp and picked up her book. 'I'm a bit concerned that you've been sick,' she said, as she looked up at Heather. 'It's a sign of concussion, and that's a hefty whack you've taken to your head.'

'Honestly, I'm fine. I feel much better now I've been sick.' She handed the cup to Claudia, who smiled at her.

'I don't know how I would have managed without you, Heather. It's a fact James wouldn't have looked after me, he'd have had to check with his bosses first, to make sure it came under Labour party guidelines.'

Heather really did feel sick now. How could she explain to her best friend that she had just buried her husband twenty feet below them? She knew she wouldn't even be able to mention James; sooner or later somebody would report him as a missing person, and the police would arrive to find out what Claudia knew about it. It had to be nothing.

'You've got me, Claud,' Heather eventually said. 'I'm here for you until you're able to manage on your own, and then I'll still be here for you anyway.'

'You're a star, Heather, you really are.' Claudia sipped at her drink. 'And it's not fair you having to look after me, you're going through enough in your own life. I should be the one comforting you. I know I've left James, but I can't begin to imagine how I would feel if he died.'

Pile on the guilt, why don't you? Heather's brain felt on fire. She needed to change the subject, she couldn't handle talking about James, not now, not ever really.

She stood. 'I feel better for having been sick, so I'm going back to bed now. And you need to sleep. I'm sorry I woke you.'

Claudia smiled at her. 'Don't worry about it. I sleep without even realising it at the moment. This has been like a midnight feast.'

Heather went back to her own room, and it was just as she was falling asleep, exhausted by her clandestine activities, that she remembered she hadn't told Claudia about her theories regarding Marilyn. Heather's mind drifted away, and she slept.

By Sunday afternoon, Will was feeling frustrated and angry. His Mr President seemed to have disappeared completely; he'd tried texting and when there had been no joy with that, he had rung. He hoped that stupid bitch of a wife of his hadn't caused him any more grief; Will had been aware for the past week that James had been preoccupied with events at home.

He switched on the television and picked up the menu, figuring he might as well eat while he waited for some sort of communication from James. Will ordered a take-away pizza, picked up a file containing some letters from Leeds voters that needed urgent attention, and settled back on the bed to await delivery.

When he finally turned off his light, he still hadn't heard from James, and his frustration and anger had escalated, followed by disbelief that James would ignore him, having made so many protestations of love.

Will Monroe had kept his homosexuality a secret from his fellow councillors, occasionally mentioning dates he had fictitiously had with assorted girlfriends, but he knew he wasn't interested in women.

He had become deeply interested in James Bell though, and the fact that he was a married man with two children had added to the excitement. Will was now, for the first time in his life, considering going public; they had discussed it at length. It seemed the only way to be together properly, after nearly six years of clandestine meetings. The main drawback had always been James's family.

But it appeared that even that had been taken out of the equation; the wife had gone.

And so had James. For the first time since they had shared a bed, Will had gone thirty-six hours without speaking to him, and he sensed something was wrong. Out of his control.

There was still no message when Will's alarm disturbed his troubled sleep, and he knew he had to go to Sheffield. He'd never been to James's house, but that wasn't going to stop Will finding his man.

The obligatory Monday morning council meeting was non-obligatory for him, on this rainy troublesome day; he needed to see James. He was no longer angry, he was simply worried. He was guessing that James was ill, but to be unable to send a text meant the illness was pretty severe. Will's imagination presented him with a stroke, food poisoning and a number of other things that could prevent James communicating with him. He wouldn't allow himself to think that death might be one reason.

Will's first sight of the house showed him James's Kia Sportage parked on the driveway. He left his own car standing half on the pavement and half on the road, then walked up to the front door. He rang the bell and waited. Pressing the bell for a second time, he said a small *please*.

Bending down to the letterbox, he called James's name. And then he listened. No sounds were evident, so he walked around the side of the house until he came to the back door. He looked through the kitchen window but couldn't see any sign of the missing man, or anybody else.

Will knocked loudly, then stepped away from the door and threw a couple of pebbles at one of the bedroom windows. He had no idea where James slept, he just hoped he could hear that someone was there, if indeed he was ill and unable to get out of bed.

Puzzled and uneasy, he headed around to the front of the house once more. He skirted the high privet hedge and walked up the drive next door. There was a car parked on it at an awkward angle, and he tried to remember all that James had told him about his neighbour, the one he had found dead at the bottom of the stairs. Drunk out of his mind, and possibly unable to park his car properly? Will guessed this was the house. He only knocked once and when there was no answer knew he had guessed correctly.

He walked to the dwelling at the other side of James's, but there was no response there either.

Sitting in his car, Will knew he had a difficult decision to make. Should he compromise both him and James by going to the police, or should he simply drive away and let things happen without his intervention?

His hand grasped the gear lever; he put the car into drive and moved slowly down the road feeling utterly lost.

Heather woke early and showered. She felt she needed to scrub every part of her, get rid of the horror of the previous evening, wash everything away. When did she morph from being a housewife with a husband and a job she loved, to a murderer? Yes, it had been accidental with James, and it was self-defence, but if she was brutally honest she hadn't attempted to hold on to the suitcase that had catapulted Owen down the stairs. She had simply opened her fingers.

She was towelling her hair when she heard Claudia call her.

'Heather? Can I have a shower?'

'No.'

'What? Why not?

'You want me to list the reasons?' Still towelling her hair, she popped her head around Claudia's bedroom door and then moved into the room, sitting on the edge of the bed. 'One, you have a dressing on that very painful area on your leg; two, you have a bloody great dressing on your shoulder and underarm; and three, I'd get wet through trying to help you. Enough reasons?'

Claudia looked disgruntled. 'Don't be so clever. I just feel...' She shrugged.

'Mucky?' Heather offered. 'Then give me ten minutes, and you can have a bed bath. You really can't go in the bath or shower yet. I'll help with your back and your legs and arms, you can do all the other bits. Then I'll wash your hair. You'll feel better after that.'

Heather's head dropped a little as she tried to find the right words for what she needed to say next. 'Claud, we need to talk.'

'What have you done?'

Heather looked up, guilt written all over her face. 'Erm... nothing. Well, I suppose I have really. I went on the Leeds website.'

Claudia waited.

'I found Marilyn.'

'But we didn't find her the other day.'

'I know. We looked in the wrong place. We looked at the women councillors.'

There was a heavy silence, while Claudia digested what she was hearing.

'You mean she's a man?'

Heather nodded. 'I think so. And it would explain so much. James's change of personality, his treatment of you – I suspect he's been struggling with his sexuality for a few years. I think Marilyn is Councillor Will Monroe.'

'As in Marilyn Monroe. No-o-o-o. Tell me you're making this up, Heather.'

'Sorry, Claud, I think I'm right.'

'But he had sex with me on that Saturday morning! Forced me to have sex!'

'I know. As I said, I think he's been struggling. He doesn't know whether he wants you or this Councillor.'

Claudia pulled the pillow up to her face, hiding away from the world while she thought through what Heather was saying. A man? She felt sick at the thought.

Heather waited patiently, without speaking, until Claudia surfaced from her cocoon.

'Show me,' Claudia demanded.

Heather stood and went to get her laptop. She brought up the website on which she had spent so much time, then passed it across to Claudia as Councillor Monroe's face filled the screen.

'If you can't believe it, Claud, ring James's work number and ask to speak to Marilyn. I bet there isn't one.'

She handed Claudia's mobile phone to her. 'Go on, try it. He said she was a staff member who was learning the job, didn't he? Said she rang him to check everything she was doing? Let's either prove it or disprove it. If there's no Marilyn in his office, we'll move on to Councillor Monroe. If Marilyn does answer, just cancel the call.'

Heather watched as Claudia rang James's work number, and then heard her ask for Marilyn. There was a brief pause. 'You're sure you don't have a Marilyn? Somebody who's fairly new?' Again a pause. 'Okay thank you, I must have got it wrong.'

She disconnected and looked at Heather. 'Okay, smart-arse, you're right. No Marilyn. I'm going to have to contact James and ask him. My health could be at risk here.'

Heather looked at her for a moment without speaking, and then they both burst out laughing. Hysterical laughter that only friends can share.

'For pity's sake, Heather, get me locked up, will you? I've probably got cancer, and heaven only knows where, and I'm worrying about where James has had his dick! Kill me now, just kill me now.'

Heather hugged her, careful not to catch any sore parts of her. 'You're a star, Claud, an absolute star. I don't know what I'd do without you. Let's get you washed down, and maybe we can go out somewhere. Fancy a run out into Derbyshire? Feel up to a walk through Bakewell market? Feed the ducks?'

'You don't think I should try to contact James then?'

'No, I don't. We've gone to a lot of trouble to steer clear of him, and to keep him from you. I think you'd be creating issues for yourself if you get in touch now. Let's leave him to stew. He knows we're aware of Marilyn anyway, because I said it that Saturday when he turned up at the cemetery.'

'He wasn't there this Saturday then?'

Heather laughed. To her it sounded forced. 'No, and I could have done with him there to help me when I cracked my head on the headstone. That's James being James, isn't it? Never there when you want him.'

15

During the week Claudia had two texts from Zoe, asking if she knew where her father was, as his car was on the drive, but nobody was at home. The second one sounded as though Zoe was seriously worried. **Car not moved. Dad still not there. Have you heard from him?**

Claudia's response to the second one was brief and to the point. **If his car is at home and he isn't he may have gone away for a break.**

She heard nothing else, and despite sleeping more than normal, she was starting to feel much improved. She took a couple of painkillers in the morning, and then didn't need any more until she went to bed. She attended a check-up appointment and they removed the large padded dressing from her underarm and put a smaller, more comfortable dressing on it, sending her home with fresh ones.

She beamed as she came out to Heather, drinking coffee in the hospital's coffee bar. 'I can have a shower,' she said, triumphantly waving the bag of dressings at her friend.

The Western Park appointment the following Monday was intense. She had tests and scans for every part of her, and by the time they left at just after one, she felt exhausted.

'You want to go for some lunch, or straight home?' Heather asked, trying desperately not to be afraid for Claudia. She looked dreadful.

'I'm sorry, Heather, would you think me a proper wimp if I said I needed to go to bed? And we're back here again on Thursday.'

Heather hugged her. 'We're over the worst. Thursday is simply results day and we can then start to live again. Come on, let's get you home.'

'Claudia Bell?'

Claudia stood and grabbed Heather's arm. They followed the nurse into the consultant's room, and he shook their hands.

'I'm Paul Quentin, your consultant. We've now moved you out of Mr Robson's care as your treatment will be at this hospital.'

'Treatment?' Claudia swivelled her head to look at Heather, and once again clasped her hand.

Heather felt inadequate. Fear was oozing out of Claudia, and as her best friend she should be comforting, soothing her.

'Yes, Mrs Bell. Can I call you Claudia?' He stood and walked to the light boxes on the wall, already loaded with scan pictures. He flicked the switches.

'The cancer, I'm sorry to say, has spread.' He pointed to the first picture. 'This is your liver. There is a mass here.' He outlined the shadow with a small pointer.

'Can it be removed?' Heather could hear the panic in Claudia's voice.

'It's always possible to remove a tumour from the liver, your body can function with only part of one, but there is another issue.' He moved across to the second screen, which was clearly Claudia's upper body. 'There are small tumours, secondary cancers, which are here.' He pointed to dark shadows in both lungs.

He took down the first picture of her liver and replaced it with a third one. 'And this is your pancreas. There is a small shadow here,' he pointed. 'Insignificant at the moment, but you have developed a very aggressive form of cancer, and it will grow quickly.'

He switched off the screens and came back to his desk. 'We need to start a hefty regime of chemo and radiotherapy.' He spoke for a further five minutes, outlining what drugs they would use, how she would feel, how often she would need to come in for the treatment, and Claudia's face was blank. She appeared to have switched off.

Heather sat by her side, devastated. The recovery from the operation had left Claudia feeling so much better, and they had come for this appointment expecting to be discharged back to the care of Mr Robson.

'Do you have any questions, Claudia?'

Paul Quentin leaned forward and stared into her face. He had seen this reaction so many times and knew the questions would happen next time he saw her. He was wrong.

Claudia lifted her head, which was now feeling far too heavy for her to support it and fixed her eyes on him. 'How long do I have?'

It was hospital policy to answer every patient truthfully and openly, and he hated it.

'Without treatment, six months at the most. As I said, it is very aggressive...'

'And with treatment?'

'Nine months to a year.'

Heather gasped and tried to hide it. This couldn't be right! Claud was looking so much better...

'And the treatment will make me ill?'

So she had been listening.

'Yes. We have to use an aggressive cocktail of drugs for such an aggressive cancer.'

Claudia stood and shook his hand. 'Thank you for being honest and not sugar-coating it. Will you write to me with the next appointment?'

He picked up his pen and checked his computer. He scribbled a note and pushed it across to her. 'Ten o'clock tomorrow morning.'

She pushed it back to him. 'I can't. I have a funeral tomorrow.'

'Miss it,' he said, and pushed the note back to her.

'No.' She turned towards Heather. 'It's Heather's husband's funeral.'

Paul stared at Claudia. 'Are you always this difficult?'

'Yes.'

'Then can you be here Saturday morning, or do you have another funeral?'

'I can be here.'

'Good. Same time. And don't be late.'

Claudia sank back into the passenger seat. 'Take me home, Heather. I have to think.'

They drove from the hospital to the flat without speaking.

Claudia climbed the stairs while Heather put the car in the garage, and then, with trepidation hitting her from all angles, she followed her friend up into the flat.

Claudia was standing and staring out of the window in the lounge.

'We have to talk.'

'I'm not ready.'

'Yes, you are. If we don't talk now, we won't do it at all. I have to know where we're going from here.'

Claudia turned to face her. In a quiet voice, she whispered, 'I'm going to die. This time next year I won't be here.'

Seconds later they were holding tightly to each other, both crying, both unable to let go.

Eventually Heather managed to get Claudia seated with her feet elevated; the leg with the patch of skin missing was still the most troublesome part of the whole operation.

'Right,' Heather said. 'We need something stronger than a cuppa. Brandy?'

Claudia nodded, and Heather brought the drinks through, albeit in wine glasses.

'Get this down you quickly, there's plenty more.'

Claudia sipped it slowly at first, but five minutes later they had refilled the glasses.

Heather looked on with approval; there was some colour in Claudia's cheeks.

'Claud, you can't ignore this. You have to speak to Zoe and Harry, tell them what's happening,' she said gently.

'I know. They'll be at the funeral tomorrow. I'll arrange to go to Zoe's place and ask Harry and Emma to meet me there, maybe Monday evening? Will you go with me?'

'I'm wherever you want me to be from now on. Today we tell Raymond and Michael we're quitting. I can support us.'

'I have money,' Claudia smiled. 'And I also have a critical illness clause in my life insurance policy, so money won't be a problem. The real issue is James. I have to tell him. This changes everything as far as he's concerned, I suppose. But I want the truth from him, I need to know if this councillor is his significant other, because when I meet up with the kids, the tone will be honesty.'

Heather nodded, wondering when the honesty needed to start. Somebody, sooner or later, was going to report James as missing. And then everything would implode because there had to be traces of him in his car, and probably traces of her. Being taken into custody scared her but leaving Claudia to face the next few months alone terrified her.

The crematorium was packed. Although Owen had very few family members, he had many friends and they had all turned up to mourn him.

Heather and Claudia had shared the first car, and Claudia spotted Zoe, David, Harry and Emma as soon a she stepped out of it. She acknowledged them with a small hand wave, and she followed the coffin down the short aisle, holding on to Heather's arm.

Once settled, she looked to the right where her family sat, and breathed a sigh of relief. It seemed James had taken notice of the ban from attending. Their next attendance at a funeral would probably be her own, and as this occurred to her, she felt the room spin and she slid to the floor. Harry moved across to help Heather lift his mother to the seat, and the vicar paused for a moment, looking over the top of his glasses at the activity beneath his lectern.

'Is everything okay?' he asked quietly, and Heather nodded.

Claudia was starting to come around and remained seated rather than risk standing again. Harry went back to Emma, but his eyes never left his mother all the time they were in the chapel.

Once outside, he went to his mum. 'What's wrong?' he whispered. 'Why did you faint? And where's Dad?'

'I fainted because I've had a little operation, and I'm still recovering. And I've no idea where your father is. I don't want to know where he is, either. That part of my life is over.'

Zoe arrived to stand with her brother. 'We need to talk with you, Mum.' Unshed tears glistened in her eyes.

'I know you do,' Claudia said, and hugged her with her left arm. The right arm still didn't move too well.

'So, when?'

'I'll come to Harry's after he finishes work on Monday. We can all talk then. But if you find your father, and he turns up, you'll not see me again. Is that clear?'

Harry and Zoe nodded. They'd never seen Claudia like this before; strong, dictatorial, unbending.

'I'm going back to Heather now, she needs me today, and she doesn't need my problems. I'll see you Monday evening. Seven o'clock?'

All four of them nodded. Claudia gave an exasperated shake of her head. 'And don't look so bloody scared. I'm not a monster, I'm your mum. Things have just changed a little bit, that's all. I still love the four of you, unconditionally. So can you put this on the back burner until Monday night?' She stared around at them, and they all nodded again.

She gave them a brief smile, squeezed Zoe's hand and moved towards Heather.

Heather and Claudia had a taxi home. It seemed the best and safest thing to do, despite several offers of a lift, and by seven o'clock they were both in pyjamas, curled up on the sofa with cups of tea.

'It went well,' Heather sighed. 'I know I'd left him, but I feel quite lost now. I think we would always have stayed friends, just not married ones. And it really hurts me to know I couldn't stop the fall.'

'Don't beat yourself up about it. If you had managed to catch him, you could have ended up dead alongside him. He wasn't a small man, you know.'

'I know, it seems so unfair... just like your diagnosis. We need to concentrate on that. No more junk food, we eat healthily from now on. We'll be there bright and early tomorrow, follow instructions, and hope we get good results.' Heather knew she was waffling. She sipped at her tea, holding back tears.

The doorbell pealed out and Heather stood to look out of the window. Carefully. They weren't expecting anyone, and she had to be sure who it was before opening the door.

Michelle waved at the movement of the curtain. Heather put up a thumb, and went down to let her in.

'Just thought I'd check in on everybody,' Michelle said. 'I know it must have been a rough day for you. And how's Claudia? Is she on the mend?'

'Come upstairs,' Heather said. 'We'll fill you in.'

Heather saw the shock flash across Michelle's face as Claudia told her what the various test results meant.

'But you look so well! A lot better than when you first came home.'

'I know, and I feel well. A little tired maybe, but eventually I won't feel like this as the cancer starts to overwhelm my organs.'

'I hope you know that it goes without saying, if I can help in any way, just ask. Heather, you listening to me?'

'I'm listening.' Heather smiled at her. 'And thank you. But I will be with Claud all the time. I've packed in my job, as has Claudia. And who knows, this bundle of drugs they're going to give her may shrink the tumours enough to extend her life considerably. I can't believe it will end in nine months, I can't.' And finally the tears that she had denied all day fell from her eyes.

All three women stood in a circle and hugged each other.

Finally, Heather broke away.

'Brandy?' she asked, and they nodded.

Once again the wine glasses were utilised, and she laughed as she handed them around. 'This is becoming a habit. We need to buy some brandy glasses, Claud.'

'There are plenty in James's house,' Claudia said. 'I could do with sneaking in when he's not there and collecting some stuff. But apparently his car is there, and he's not, so it could be a bit of a dangerous game. I won't know when he's back.'

'Where is he?' Michelle asked.

'No idea. My daughter's been trying to get in touch with him, but he's not answering. She's been in the house and he's not ill in bed or anything, he's just gone. We know he's got somebody else in his life, but I don't think the kids know it. He could be in some little love nest with him.'

'Him?'

'Him.' Claudia confirmed it with a nod.

'Each to their own,' Michelle said with a shrug.

'It kind of explains how he's been with me for the last few years, though. He's obviously been struggling, but now seems to have given in. I mean, we're not completely sure, it's a suspicion, but a big suspicion.'

'What a mess. Between the three of us, things haven't been easy, have they? I saw George Ullyat, my toe-rag of an ex, today. Honestly, if Steve knew…' Michelle held up her hands. 'He'd kill him.'

'Aren't you scared?' Claudia asked.

'Terrified. I try never to be on my own, ever. He was peering through the shop window, but luckily there were two of us working today, because I had two birthday cakes to get out. When he saw my assistant, he walked away. Why on earth does he still want to get me, after all this time? I got Steve to walk me here tonight, and he says I've to ring him when I'm ready for going home, and he'll come and get me. I shouldn't have to live like that.'

'This George bloke's obviously an obsessive.' Claudia spoke quietly. 'Heather says you have a gun. I'd keep it in your bag. Loaded.'

Michelle gave a small laugh. 'Don't really think it's in me to kill anybody. I couldn't stand to be locked up.'

'Does he live near the shop?'

'Yes, too near. And he never seems to be around when Steve is with me, so that makes me feel as though I'm being stalked. It's not a good feeling, I can tell you.'

'I'm sure. What can we do?' Heather frowned, her expressive face registering concern for Michelle.

'I don't think there's anything you can do. Unless we have a connecting doorbell from under my counter straight to up here,' Michelle said with a laugh.

'Why not?' Claudia stared at Michelle. 'I suspect we'll be in here quite a lot over the next few months, and it would give some peace of mind to know you only have to press it and we'll come galloping down. He'll back off if there are three of us, and what's more, he'll think twice about doing it again if he realises you contacted us.'

'We'd have to install it ourselves,' Michelle said, thinking aloud. 'I daren't ask Steve, he can't know George is still on the scene. If I fix the bell part under the counter, then we run the cable over to the window area, straight up the outside wall, the cable will fit through your window without having to drill. The box will sit on your window sill, out of the way.'

'We're up for that,' Heather said. 'If you can pick one up tomorrow, come around Sunday and we'll get it fitted. Claudia's got her first chemo tomorrow, so she may feel a bit rough Saturday afternoon. If she's still not well Sunday morning, I'll ring you, but all being good, we'll sort it Sunday afternoon, give you a bit of security.'

'You two are so good for me,' Michelle said. 'I'm so glad I met you. I'm going to leave you in peace and get Steve to walk across and meet me. Get an early night, Claudia, it's a big day tomorrow.'

She picked up her phone to text Steve.

'You don't have to go,' Claudia said. 'Stay as long as you want.'

'Michelle's right,' Heather interrupted. 'You do need an early night. We don't know what's in front of us tomorrow, but I'm pretty sure you'll be better for having a good night's sleep. We'll have hot chocolate or something equally soporific, and you can take one of the sleeping tablets.'

Claudia looked at them both.

'I'm not having the treatment. No chemo, no radiotherapy. And please don't argue with me, it's my decision, and it's made.'

16

D S Liam Norwood ran up the flight of steps and into the police station foyer. The sun was shining, and the sky was a clear blue with an absence of clouds. A beautiful day; he hated working Saturdays, and especially eight o'clock starts on beautiful days.

Since the divorce, he only got to see the kids at weekends, and he'd had to tell them he would pick them up at three instead of his usual early collection. Danny and Liv hadn't been pleased. It had cost him a promised visit to the cinema for Saturday afternoon, and a walk in the Derbyshire hills for Sunday. He knew he would enjoy both with Danny and Liv; if they wanted a trip to the moon he would do his best to provide it.

'Morning, Ken,' he called to the man behind the glass window. PC Ken Staines had been there forever, or so it seemed. His ready smile for everybody but villains was well known in the station. *Don't like villains*, he was frequently heard to mutter, and that just about summed him up.

Liam Norwood was heading through the door leading to the offices when Ken called to him.

'Liam, something interesting came in a few minutes ago. Not sure where to send it to, it's not run of the mill.'

'Villains?' Liam joked.

'Now don't start, young man. Villains is 'orrible people, as you well know. No, this is something a bit different. A Leeds Councillor has contacted us to report a missing person.'

'A counsellor in what? Anything interesting? Sex therapist?'

'Not a counsellor, a Councillor.'

'From Leeds? Why has he contacted us?'

'The missing person is from here, this area.'

Liam let the door close and moved back to the window. 'I'll have a look at it. I'll get it to whoever needs it, and I'll let you know where it ends up.'

He took the paperwork that was being fed under the edge of the window and ran up the stairs to the open-plan office inhabited by the team. He frowned at the state of his desk, just as he did every morning. He sat in close proximity to DC Rosie Havenhand, and her desk was always immaculate; she even polished it, adding further to his discomfiture.

He shuffled a few files around and thought he might ask Rosie for the loan of her polish and duster later, but then dismissed the idea. He pulled the file towards him that he had carried upstairs and began to read. James Bell. Missing. He knew the name, but…

James Bell! *That rings a bell* was the spark that initially ran through his mind, and then he looked closely at the report. It seemed that James worked for the Labour party, and a Labour Councillor in Leeds had been trying to get in touch with him for over a week, unsuccessfully. It was out of character for James to ignore contact, especially with a politician from his own party.

James Bell was the neighbour who had found the body of the chap who had fallen downstairs. Liam closed his eyes for a moment, and the name came to him. Owen Gower. Closing his eyes also brought to the forefront of his mind the horrific scene that had met him when he walked through the door of the Gower house. James Bell was Owen Gower's best mate. Alarm bells rang that were nothing to do with James's inopportune surname.

Liam rang down to Ken in the foyer. 'Log that missing person report to me, Ken, will you? There's a bit of a tie in with a closed case of mine, so I'll check it out till we get answers.'

'Okay, Liam. No problem. Got to go, need to bash some young lads heads together,' and he put down the phone.

Liam picked up the file and walked into DI Ray's office. 'Boss?'

She looked at him over the top of a coffee cup. 'If you're bringing me a request for leave, the answer is no.'

'As if. It's two years since I've had a holiday, so now you mention it…'

'I didn't.' She put down her cup. 'So what do you want?'

'Two weeks in the Maldives.'

She looked at him without speaking or smiling, and he grinned.

'Okay, maybe just a week, but after I've sorted this.' He handed over the file, and she began to read.

He waited patiently, and eventually she lifted her head. 'You're checking it out, and not mispers?'

'I just want to have a look at it. James Bell, the missing chap, is the one who found his neighbour dead at the bottom of the stairs. There was nothing suspicious, the dead chap had so much alcohol in his blood it was inevitable he would fall. He was on his own in the house, his wife had left him a couple of days earlier, but she'd left him because of the drink. There was nothing that gave me cause for concern. The post-mortem ruled it as accidental death.'

'And?'

'I don't know… I don't want to spend a lot of time on it, just satisfy myself we didn't miss anything. You see, James Bell's wife left him to move into a flat with Gower's wife. Seems they'd both had enough, so decided to go. They specifically asked me not to let Bell know their address, because the Bell breakdown was based on domestic violence that was escalating. Bell's wife, and I can't recall her name at the moment, was scared.'

Philippa Ray handed the file back to her DS. 'I'll give you two days. And you can take Rosie with you when you go see the wives, but the rest is down to you.'

'Thanks, boss. I'm going to start with this Councillor Monroe and take it from there. I'll ring him, see what I can get out of him. I don't think it'll merit a trip up to Leeds.'

'Oh, my Lord,' she groaned. 'Be polite. I know what you're like.'

'Don't worry, I'll be as nice as I always am,' he said laughing, as he closed the door behind him.

He punched his fist in the air and mouthed *yes!* He'd expected a fight over the case, because it really had been a closed one and a very simple one. He hoped it still was; he'd liked the ladies very much and didn't want to bring further grief into their lives.

He stopped off at the coffee machine, punched in the number for a latte and then treated himself to a KitKat. Could life get any better than this, he thought, as he ambled back to his desk. Yes; somebody could tidy his desk for him.

Claudia was trembling. The conversation that had begun with Quentin's secretary, and then had very quickly been passed to Quentin himself, had been difficult. She had refused the treatment scheduled to begin within the hour, and he wasn't happy with her. He tried hard to persuade her to come in; yes, he agreed, there would be side effects, but the benefits far outweighed the sickness that was created by taking the drugs. They had talked for some time but she was adamant. It was her life, her body, her decision.

Heather handed her a mug of tea. 'Well?'

Claudia pressed the mug against her lips. She didn't want to speak.

'Claud, I need to know what he said, and what you've agreed. I need to help you, whatever has just happened.'

Claudia put down the tea without having a drink.

'I'm not extending my life by three months and having no quality in that time. I'd rather do what we said, change our eating habits, no alcohol, no dairy products...' She pointed at the mug of tea. 'That is my last drink with milk in it. We'll do some research on vitamins I can add to my diet, and we'll enjoy the next six months without me being ill due to the treatment. Heather, I'm not going to survive this, we know that, but I'm going to live out the rest exactly as I want to live it.'

'And he didn't try to talk you out of it?'

'Kind of, but he did admit I'm not the only one on his books who has taken this stance. I'll still be seeing him every fortnight to assess what pain relief I might be needing, but really, I think he understood.'

'So what now? Would you like to go away for a few days?'

'Yes, I would. But not for a week or so. This leg is still giving me some grief, and I'd prefer to be walking without pain, because I'd like a couple of days in Paris. I can't believe I've never been, and I'd like to see the Louvre before I die.'

'Consider it done. And we'll go first class all the way.'

They high-fived each other, then grinned.

'Councillor Monroe? My name is DS Liam Norwood, South Yorkshire police. I've been handed a file regarding a missing person you're concerned about. A Mr James Bell?'

'Oh, thank you, DS Norgood.'

'Norwood, sir. DS Norwood. Now, can we go through this report and fill in some details please? When did you last see Mr Bell?'

The reply was prompt. 'Saturday, 23rd April. In the morning. I can't give you an exact time, but he headed back to Sheffield before midday.'

'You had a meeting on a Saturday morning? I'm impressed.'

Norwood detected a brief moment of hesitation. He annotated it with a tick, a habit he'd developed over the years to denote unease or a query.

'I didn't say we'd had a meeting,' Monroe carefully explained. 'I said I'd seen him on the Saturday morning. We had a coffee.'

'Where?'

Again the hesitation. Another tick.

'In the Travelodge in the city centre.'

'In the restaurant?'

'No, just in reception. I'm sure the staff will vouch for us, if you need confirmation, DS Norwood. James stays there regularly when he is in Leeds. They all know him.'

'And you? Do they know you?'

Another pause. A third tick.

'I suppose so. James and I work closely together. He works for the party, and I am a Labour Councillor.'

'Okay. Was Mr Bell going straight back to Sheffield?'

'He said he was. I've been trying to remember what he said he was doing, and it somehow was connected to his wife, although she had left him. He'd no idea where she was, but she did something every Saturday afternoon and he was hoping to see her there. He'd been trying constantly to contact her, but she wasn't replying.'

'And you can't remember what Mrs Bell does every Saturday afternoon?'

'She probably meets up with other witches in the coven.'

And the vague notion forming in Liam's head suddenly crystallised. Wife in the background or not, these two men were in a relationship and it was a serious one. This man was hurting. Liam suspected James Bell's wife knew nothing of any clandestine trysts between the two men; she would have said something when they were asking him to keep their address secret.

'I'm sure she doesn't, Councillor, but I'll ask her when I call to see her.' Liam could detect the sarcasm in his tone and remembered Philippa Ray's comment. 'Can you think of anything else that might help?'

'I went to Sheffield.'

'A bit above and beyond, sir?'

'He's my friend. I went on Monday, the 25th of April. He hadn't responded to any calls or texts the whole weekend and I'll be honest, I thought he must be ill. His car was on the drive, but I got no reaction to knocking, or even throwing stones at the bedroom window. It might not have been his bedroom, of course, I've never been there. I came away and didn't know what to do.'

'You've left it nearly two weeks, sir.'

'I know.' Another hesitation, another tick. 'Look, it's really difficult. I'm a Councillor and I need votes to remain in that position. James is a senior official in the Labour party. You must have guessed we were in a relationship, surely.'

'Yes, sir, I had. And how long have you been with Mr Bell?'

'Six years or so. You must have realised that we needed to keep it quiet, but it's been too long without contact. I need you to find him. Please keep in touch, DS Norwood.'

Liam replaced the receiver and leaned back in his chair, his thinking position. That had been a bit of a surprise, was his initial thought. And now he had to potentially go and break the news to the man's wife. Claudia! A light bulb moment finally revealed the name to him. Claudia Bell.

He typed up the report on the telephone conversation while it was still fresh in his mind and slipped the printed copy into the file. He decided to leave interviewing Claudia Bell until Monday; he had no intentions of being late for his children, just on the off chance that this missing person case was a crime. But he could drive by the house, just check it out, make sure Bell wasn't there. He could, after all, simply be keeping a low profile, trying to escape the clutches of Councillor Monroe. Maybe he'd had a change of heart about giving up his marriage for a man who hadn't yet come out to the world.

'I'm off, boss.'

Philippa looked at him over the top of her glasses. 'Okay. You spoken to that Councillor?'

'I have. Enlightening, shall we say.'

'Never mind enlightening, did you employ sarcasm at any point in that conversation?'

'Definitely not.'

'You sure? I won't be having to deal with an irate Council Leader on Monday morning?'

'Not with what I know about Councillor Monroe, no. He'll not dare complain about anything.'

'Really? Tell me more.'

'He was in a relationship, a very secret one, with the missing James Bell. And I'm certain Mrs Bell knew nothing about it. She walked away from the marriage because of increasing violence, not because he was gay. Neither of the men wanted it to be made public, but if anything has happened to James Bell, it'll be more than public, I would say.'

Philippa stared at him, a thoughtful expression on her face. 'You jump-starting it on Monday?'

'I am. It's not a high priority case, not at the moment anyway, and I'm not clocking up overtime for anybody. Monday is soon enough.'

'Then use Rosie for as long as you need her. I've a tingle in these old bones about this one, Liam. And I can see you have.'

He nodded. 'Monday it is then.'

Liam parked outside James Bell's house and sat for a moment, just looking. He took in everything visible; the car in the driveway, the high privet hedge, curtains that were open, and the absence of any humans.

He got out of the car and walked towards the Sportage. Trying to open the boot was a futile exercise. He peered into every window, but nothing looked amiss.

He knocked twice on the front door, then lifted the letterbox and called James Bell's name. Liam listened carefully but there was no response. Walking around to the back of the property, he peered inside the kitchen window. Everything looked normal, nothing out of place. After trying the back door, he moved along the wall to the dining room window, with just as little success.

The gate that led through to the Gower property was open, and he guessed it had been left open unwittingly by the CSI team; he didn't close it. He wanted nothing disturbed. He passed through the gate and onto the next-door garden. After peering into the windows, he could see nothing that looked disturbed.

The tingle that Philippa Ray had spoken of was increasing. Monday morning would see some action. He would visit Claudia Bell and Mrs Gower – Heather, he thought her name was – and have a general chat with them, find out if they'd seen anything at all of James Bell, then he would come back to this house, and call in a forensic team. He would get keys for both properties from the ladies. Maybe telling them he was going into the houses would elicit some sort of response from them. Or maybe there was no response to be elicited.

James Bell hadn't impressed Liam, the man had been bombastic, and quite rude; maybe he'd picked up a couple of enemies along the way who might wish him harm. He'd liked the ladies, had some admiration for the way they'd walked out on relationships that weren't good for them; Liam honestly couldn't imagine either of them being involved in Bell's disappearance.

Liam sat in his car, lost in thought. Deep down, he felt that James Bell hadn't just walked out of a life that wasn't suiting him anymore; certainly Councillor Monroe had allowed a grief of sorts to be present in his voice. Liam had believed his relationship with James was strong.

Surely Bell would have talked it through with Monroe if he had been having second thoughts about their relationship. Although Liam hadn't liked the man, he had taken away an impression of bluntness and forthrightness; no, James hadn't voluntarily left his lover.

Liam glanced at the clock on his dashboard and saw he had fifteen minutes to get to his children. He would put all thoughts of James Bell and his convoluted life on a back burner until Sunday evening, after he had returned his children to their mother and new stepfather.

For now, he would become Daddy.

17

Claudia was standing at the window, watching the footfall in the street below. It was always busy on Saturdays, and today was no exception. That's when she noticed a man leaning against a fence on the opposite side of the road, staring at the bakery beneath the flat.

'Heather, come and look out here.' Heather walked across to join her. 'Could that be Michelle's stalker?'

Heather watched him for a moment. 'If I had to guess, I'd say it was. Should I ring her?'

Claudia handed her phone to Heather. 'I've taken a photo of him. Send that and ask her. And check she's picked up a bell. We can do that when we get back from the cemetery this afternoon. Tell her we'll be home for two, so if she wants to come up when the shop closes, that's fine.'

She heard Heather tapping out the message, continuing to watch the man.

A couple of minutes later, he straightened himself and began to walk away. He glanced back towards the shop once, and then disappeared around the corner at the end of the road.

Claudia's phone pinged. Heather read the message and looked at her friend. 'It was him. He hasn't approached the shop, but he's been standing there for half an hour. She got the bell last night when she went to the wholesalers for some supplies, so we'll sort that this afternoon. She's telling Steve that she's bringing us some cake and we're having a girlie afternoon, so he doesn't suspect there's a problem. Shall we go to the cemetery now? Then our day is free.'

'But it's not one o'clock yet.'

'Claudia, my love, you've left him. He can't dictate to you what time you visit your baby any longer. We can go when we want.'

Claudia shook her head. 'I'm so stupid, aren't I? Yes, let's go now.' She picked up her bag, and the women burst out laughing.

'It's taking some getting used to, this single life, isn't it?' Heather grinned at Claudia. 'Come on, let's go say hello to Ella.'

They bought flowers outside the cemetery gates as usual and drove through to the small car park. They walked up the incline to Ella's grave, and Claudia immediately knelt.

'Told you I'd bring your mummy this week, didn't I, Ella?' Heather said with a smile, and briefly touched the headstone.

'I've missed you, baby,' Claudia said, 'but it won't be too long before we're together again, for always.'

Heather moved away. She couldn't stand this. She looked around for traces of blood, either hers or James's, but couldn't see any. It seemed that the heavy rainfall over the previous couple of days had washed any last traces away. The headstone was clear of her own blood, but that didn't matter so much as the trail she had left by dragging James to the car.

She turned to watch Claudia, who was replacing the dead flowers with the new ones. Claudia was crying.

'You want a hug, Claud, or shall I wait in the car?'

'Would you mind leaving me on my own?'

'Of course not. Take as long as you need.'

'Just watch for James arriving, will you?'

Heather nodded. 'I will.' She walked to the car park, feeling as down as she'd ever felt in her life.

Michelle arrived bearing gifts. Cakes. In the plural. They had a slice along with a coffee and then went down to the shop. Working with the shutters in place and by electric light rather than daylight, they placed the bell push button under the counter, screwing it in place so that Michelle simply had to lean forward and her finger would find it.

The cable was fed under the edge of the counter and round the back of the bread cabinet, concealed until it reached the window. They then fed it through the tiny ventilation window above the main plate glass shop-front window. Heather went up to the flat and leaned out of the window to grasp the end of the proffered cable, before pulling it up into the lounge. She told them to wait, in a loud stage whisper, then connected it to the bell's speaker.

Two minutes later, they had a fully functioning alarm system. Claudia and Michelle locked the bakery and climbed the stairs into the flat. This time they had a glass of wine with the cake and saluted their ingenuity.

'That will make such a difference,' Michelle said, a wide smile on her face. 'I won't be half as worried now. My two dragons will barrel down the stairs to rescue me if he comes into the shop. However, that bit you do have to understand. If that bell rings, he's in the shop with me and I will be alone. I won't ever ring it if someone else is in there.'

They raised thumbs to indicate they understood.

'Right, I'm going to head off home now, leave you two in peace.'

'Are you ringing Steve to come get you?' Claudia was concerned.

'No, I'll be fine. It's the middle of the afternoon. And let's face it, it's only a two-minute walk.'

'Then we'll walk back with you. Seeing George this morning has made me a bit uneasy.' Claudia was firm. 'No arguing.'

Michelle laughed. 'You're right. We've just done this to protect me and I say I'm okay to walk home. Of course I'm not. Thank you, ladies, if you're absolutely sure.'

She picked up her bag, and they all went downstairs.

They strolled along the front of the shops, enjoying the late afternoon sunshine, then passed through the gennel leading to the doctors, and onwards to the road of new houses where Michelle and Steve lived.

They heard the rev of the car but didn't think anything about it. Stopping at the kerbside before crossing over, they waited patiently for the car to pass them. It mounted the pavement just before it reached them, but Heather had sensed something was happening, and was already pushing the other two backwards. All three landed in a tangled heap and the car screamed off, leaving them to pick themselves up.

Heather was first on her feet. 'Claud…'

'Don't panic. I'm fine. I landed on Michelle.'

'Michelle?'

She looked up at Heather, nursing her arm. 'I landed a bit awkwardly. Think I've done something to my wrist.'

Heather moved quickly towards her and helped her to stand. 'Can you walk?'

'Think so. My ankle hurts, but not as much as my wrist. Was it him?'

'I don't know. I couldn't tell. But this puts a whole new slant on it. If you'd been on your own, he could have killed you.'

Claudia carefully felt all the operation sites and thought nothing had been damaged; her leg was still a problem anyway, and it didn't look as though the fall had made it any worse. She simply felt sick and knew that was shock. She leaned over the wall that they had all hit as they fell to the floor and she vomited. It seemed to go on forever; Heather patted her back, making soothing noises, and eventually she was able to stand up.

'I'm okay,' she said. 'Let's get Michelle home before he comes back. But this can't carry on. The police have to take some action.'

'Unfortunately,' Michelle said drily, 'it's not the police taking action that bothers me, it's more Steve taking action. I know he seems like a lovely man, and he is, but if anybody upsets me, he's lethal. I can't tell him about this. I'm just going to tell him I fell over as we were walking back. Please, don't tell him the truth.'

'If that's what you want. But we need to talk about this. You can't live your life waiting for him to come for you again. And now it's going to affect your business, because that wrist looks broken to me. I think you're going to A and E tonight.'

Michelle nodded. 'I can't move it without feeling sick with the pain. I'll get Steve to take me. Can you just help me home? I can't really put weight on my ankle as well. You're right, we have to do something. But it can't be anything Steve knows about. Promise me.'

She was clearly agitated and the two women both nodded. They delivered her to Steve who immediately went to get the car out of the garage.

'I'll ring you later,' Michelle said, 'and let you know how I've gone on, and how many limbs I have left.'

'As long as you realise I can't bake,' Heather said with a grin. 'Not even under instruction.'

Steve pulled the car towards them, and Michelle climbed in. She put down the window and leaned out. 'You'll be okay walking home?'

'We'll be fine,' Claudia said. 'Go and get that looked at, don't worry about us.'

They waved as the car disappeared down the road and Heather turned to Claudia. 'What's hurting?'

'My leg,' she said. 'Let's go home, Heather. I need to have a look at it.'

The walk back to the flat was much slower than the one they had taken with Michelle. Claudia was limping and holding on to Heather. Both breathed a sigh of relief as they climbed the stairs into the flat.

'Right, trousers off and let's have a look at the wound.'

Claudia dropped her trousers to the floor, stepped out of them, and kicked them to one side. 'I haven't even the strength to pick them up,' she said with a smile.

'Let me get a towel for you to sit on, because the wound's bleeding,' Heather said. 'I think I can deal with it though.'

She covered the armchair seat with a towel and lowered Claudia onto it, then raised the recliner so that her leg was comfortable.

She went for the first aid kit, cleaned the bloody part of the wound, and steri-stripped it closed. Neither spoke.

Claudia closed her eyes, then opened them when she felt Heather putting on her pyjama trousers.

'Thank you,' she said with a grateful smile. 'You must have read my mind.'

Heather laughed. 'I'm putting mine on too. Don't think we'll be going clubbing tonight. Quiet night in, good film on telly, or even an early night, whichever you want.'

'We'll go clubbing next week,' Claudia said with a yawn. 'In Paris. At least we won't get run over in the street.'

Heather laughed. 'There speaks someone who's never crossed the Place de la Concorde before. Believe me, you'll need running shoes. You want me to book everything?'

'Yes. Let's go Wednesday to Sunday. Is that long enough?'

'It's long enough to see the main sights, but it's also long enough for you, you're still not well. You speak French, Claud?'

'Non.'

'That should be fun then. None at all?'

'Non. I can count to ten, and I think I know the days of the week...'

'Then you need to get on that computer and learn some. You've four days. Let's hope it's a quiet four days.'

'Let's hope.'

'I'll do us something to eat, and then I'll get on the Internet and book us a swish Parisian trip. As I said, first class all the way for you from now on, Claudia Bell.'

Claudia laughed. 'I'm not arguing with that. But don't do me anything to eat. I don't feel as if I want anything. I'll build up my appetite for the frog's legs.'

She stood slowly and walked to the window. The street was deserted, no stalkers in view.

She had been frightened; she felt as though her life had been about fear for the past seven years, and it had to stop. Now.

'You know what, Heather, having a terminal diagnosis is… liberating.'

'Liberating?' Heather was just leaving the room, but she stopped. 'What do you mean?'

'I have six months to live. Maximum, I reckon. But it means I have six months in which I can do anything. Absolutely anything. Including murder. By the time anything gets to court, I'll be dead.'

Claudia's remarks bothered Heather. She had made no response other than a very weak smile, but Claudia was normally a gentle person, liked nothing heavier than *Death in Paradise* on television, and to hear such words coming from her, combined with the expression on her face, was unsettling.

She recognised that the problems with James had taken her to the edge, so much so that she had walked out on her marriage, but to have changed that much was troubling. She prayed that the cancer hadn't already sent tendrils into Claudia's brain, because if it had, the six months could be shortened by a considerable amount.

She got up at three, giving up on sleep, and booked their Paris trip. The flight from Robin Hood airport departed at the ungodly hour of seven every morning, so She booked it for Wednesday, returning Sunday. Maybe the sights and sounds of the European capital would lift Claudia's thoughts away from being able to commit murder…

She was back in bed by four and slept until eight, waking only because her phone pinged to say she had received a text message.

It was from Michelle, saying she had indeed broken her wrist, was now in a cast, but nothing broken in her ankle. That just needed rest. She also added that her sister, Jade, would be handling the shop from Monday, for a week, so to introduce themselves to her.

Heather rolled out of bed, not convinced she wanted to surface just yet.

Claudia was already up and looking wide awake. 'Morning, lazy bones. It's not like you to sleep in.'

'Didn't go to bed till four.' Heather's mouth felt like a dry desert. 'Any coffee left in the pot?'

'Sit down. I'll get you one,' Claudia laughed. 'Why on earth did you stay up till four?'

'I didn't. I wasn't asleep at three – that accident certainly fried my brain. So I got up and booked our Paris trip. We fly Wednesday morning at seven. It's an early start so do you want me to book in overnight on Tuesday at the airport hotel? It's only Robin Hood though. If it had been Manchester I wouldn't have hesitated, but...' Heather was aware she was waffling.

'No, we'll leave from here. If we get up half past three-ish, have a drink and then go, we'll be there in plenty of time for check in, and we can have some breakfast in the airport. This is just the boost I needed.'

'Five-star hotel on the Champs-Élysées, first class on the plane. Taxi transfer from Charles de Gaulle, has the girl done good?'

'The girl has done extremely good. Euros?'

'Going on Monday to get them. I'll nip to town if you don't want to go.'

'I'll see how I am when I wake up. I'll make you that coffee for being a good girl.'

Heather smiled as Claudia left the room. She seemed so much brighter this morning.

'By the way,' Heather called, 'Michelle's just texted. Her wrist is broken, but her ankle just needs rest. Her sister's going to be running things in the shop for a while.'

Claudia returned holding two coffees. 'I'll make a fresh pot if you want any more,' she said and handed a cup to Heather. 'What's she called?'

'Jade. We've to go and introduce ourselves to her – and possibly tell her not to press any strange doorbell buttons she finds under the counter.'

Claudia smiled. 'In a way, it's good that Michelle is incapacitated. He's clearly stepped up his campaign, this ex of hers. Michelle out of the way and resting means we can do something about him.'

'Like what? We don't even know where he lives.'

'We can find him.'

Heather felt a shiver like icy water running down her spine.

'And what will you do?'

'Kill him. I told you I can do anything now.'

Heather tried to lighten things. 'Don't think it's allowed. The police get a bit iffy about vigilantes. And just how will you kill him? You're five foot nothing, and he looks a burly chap, quite capable of blowing you over.'

'I'll do what he did, use the car as a weapon. And then James will be next on my list.'

Heather felt sick. She just grinned at Claudia and walked out of the room. 'I'll get biscuits,' she said. She leaned her head against the sink and felt the coolness on her brow. This couldn't be happening. Claudia had sounded sincere, but surely she wouldn't carry it through? She didn't have an evil bone in her body; cancerous growths, yes.

Heather forgot the biscuits; instead she walked down the corridor and showered, letting the water beat on her face as she attempted to forget not only the words Claudia had used, but the way she had delivered them. With resolve.

They remained indoors for the whole of Sunday, did some Internet shopping for things they could potentially need in Paris, checked a couple of times via text on Michelle, and eventually had an early night, both tired by weekend activities.

They walked into the bakery Monday morning, and saw what appeared to be Michelle's double, just a little slimmer.

It was empty of customers and Heather walked to the counter and held out her hand. 'Morning. I'm Heather from upstairs, and this is Claudia.' She shook her hand, followed by Claudia.

'And I'm Jade, Jade Pitman,' she said. 'And please don't tell me I look like Michelle's twin. It's the cross I've had to bear all my life,' she said with a laugh. 'We're not twins, I'm a year younger than she is, but we look the same.'

'You certainly do,' Heather responded with a smile. 'It must be good having a sister so close in age though. I've no siblings at all, and neither has Claudia. I'd have loved a sister.'

'They're okay, but when they're older, they're prone to pulling rank,' was Jade's dry response. 'Can I get you anything?'

'Yes, please. Two vanilla slices and a cob.'

Jade packaged them and handed them over. 'Good to meet you. I'm here for the week, so I'll probably see more of you.'

'We're off to Paris on Wednesday for a few days, but you're very welcome to come and have a coffee with us, any afternoon when you've finished.'

'Aw, thank you. Michelle said you were lovely. I won't take you up on the offer today, I'm doing the school run, but tomorrow would be good. Is that okay?'

'It's fine. We'll look forward to it.'

They walked out of the shop with Claudia still limping slightly; the wound opening up was making her favour the good leg.

Ringing their doorbell was a tall man, and by his side a female police officer. Heather froze. DS... Northroyd? She couldn't remember his name. Claudia could. Heather heard Claudia say quietly, 'Norwood.'

18

'DS Norwood? Can we help?' Claudia held out her hand. He shook it and smiled at her and Heather.

'We just need a little chat. Okay if we go upstairs?'

Claudia unlocked the door, and climbed the stairs, again favouring the bad leg. 'Sorry,' she said, looking back at the three people following her. 'Maybe I should have walked up last.'

They reached the top and Claudia stood for a moment, her full weight on her left leg, raising her right one slightly from the floor.

'Are you okay, Mrs Bell?'

'I will be when I'm sitting down.'

Heather squeezed past the others and took Claudia's arm. 'Come on, you can't be like this on Wednesday. Let's get you to the lounge.' She turned to the policeman. 'You'll be pleased to know we're no longer sitting on sun loungers.'

'Good.' He grinned. 'And take your time. Whatever's wrong with that leg, treat it gently.'

Ten minutes later, cups of tea made, and the two women and their visitors were seated, with more comfort than previously, in the lounge.

Heather carried the tray through to hear Norwood asking Claudia if she had had a fall and injured her leg.

'No. Not a fall, an operation, and it's still a bit tender. They only took skin from my leg to place on the actual operation site, but it's been the worst bit for making me uncomfortable.'

'I'm sorry to hear that.' Norwood looked up. 'Thank you, Mrs Gower. Now you're here, can I introduce DC Havenhand,

Rosie Havenhand. Rosie, this is Heather Gower, and Claudia Bell. Claudia is James Bell's wife.'

Claudia froze. 'You haven't told him where I am, have you?'

'No, we haven't. We're here for something different. When was the last time you saw your husband, Claudia?'

Liam watched her face; it was expressive, and he needed to see signs of lying.

She didn't lie. 'I can tell you exactly. 6.58am, Monday, 11th April. I can't be more precise than that.'

'Thank you.' He smiled at her and turned to Heather. 'And you, Heather? Have you seen him?'

'Yes, a little more recently. As we've said, Claudia has had an operation, and on Saturday...' Heather paused for a moment working out dates. 'Yes, Saturday, 16th April, I took some flowers to the cemetery to Claudia's baby's grave, because Claudia was still in hospital. James arrived. He'd obviously been waiting for Claudia, because I didn't go till about half past four, after I'd left Claudia. Normally she goes to the cemetery around one o'clock. I was driving Claud's car. I can't drive Owen's car anymore, because... I just can't, but I'm doing all the driving at the moment, so we're using Claud's car. He obviously thought I was Claud, because he was blazing as he came up to me. I must tell you, he didn't know about Claudia being in hospital. She didn't, and doesn't, want him to know.'

Heather hesitated a moment, reliving the nightmare of the Saturday. 'He was very abrasive, wanted to know where Claudia was. I was scared. He eventually stomped off, I finished arranging the flowers and then drove by a very roundabout route to a friend of ours, somebody he doesn't know, and spent the night there. I was scared he would follow me here, and then know where we lived. We keep our car in the garage all the time so that he can't track us through that.'

'Just a minute,' Claudia interrupted. 'Why are you asking all of this?'

'James Bell has been reported as a missing person. Basically, we're starting at a logical beginning, with you two. Heather, have you had the funeral for your husband yet?'

Heather nodded. 'Last Friday.'

'And Mr Bell didn't attend?'

'No. I told him he wouldn't be welcome, when he was so horrible to me. I made it very clear, while waving a pair of scissors in his face – I had been shortening flower stems with them when he had crept up on me. Anyway, he didn't attend, and that was the main thing, because he would have hassled Claudia and she's not well enough to deal with problems he's caused. The dickhead.'

Rosie Havenhand continued to take notes, simply letting her boss get on with it. He had established a good rapport with the two ladies, he would pick up on stuff if there was anything not quite right.

'Thank you, ladies.' He placed his empty cup on the upturned plastic box.

'Just a minute,' Claudia said. 'I'm sorry, but he's still my husband. You can't just walk in here and say he's missing, with no further information! How long has he been missing? And who saw him last? In fact, here's the biggy... who reported him missing? Was it the kids?'

Liam took out his notebook. 'He was last seen on 23rd of April in Leeds. A Saturday, in the morning. He had a coffee with a Leeds City Councillor, and then headed back to Sheffield.'

'So the last time he was seen was in Leeds, and you're asking questions in Sheffield?' Claudia looked puzzled. 'Why aren't you asking questions of this Councillor?'

'I have. He's the one who reported James missing. He has had no texts or phone calls, no emails or video chats, since that Saturday morning.'

'And the Councillor's name?'

'I'm sorry...'

'You're sorry, you're not allowed to disclose that.' Claudia's tone had become caustic. 'You don't need to, I think we could make an educated guess.'

'Oh?'

'Councillor Will Monroe? Would it be him? James saw a lot of him when he was in Leeds.'

Oh he saw more than a lot of him, Norwood thought, but said nothing.

He put his notebook away. 'So you can't shed any light on your husband's whereabouts, Claudia?'

'No, sorry, I can't. And to be perfectly honest, DS Norwood, I really couldn't care less where he is. I won't be here in six months, so what does it matter?'

Unsure of what Claudia's words meant, Norwood looked at Heather who had moved to stand by Claudia. He took the easy option.

'Please leave your new address with us, won't you?'

Claudia gave a short bark of laughter, then burst into tears. 'Heaven, hopefully.'

Heather led the police officers down to the bottom door and let them out.

Norwood hesitated. 'Terminal?' He kept his voice low.

'Yes. Malignant melanoma. It's spread. Look, we're going to Paris on Wednesday, back Sunday. We won't be available while we're away but will be from Monday morning. The travel on Sunday will probably exhaust her.'

Norwood nodded. 'Then I'm sorry we've had to disturb you. Enjoy your break, it's a beautiful city.'

Heather locked the door behind her and went back up to Claudia. She was splashing water on her face.

'You okay?'

She nodded and dried her skin. 'I just wanted them to go. Where do you think James is?'

'No idea.'

'I'm going to have to tell Harry and Zoe tonight.'

'Oh God, I'd forgotten you're seeing them. Would you like me to drive you there, and then pick you up when you're ready to come home?'

'Would you mind? I think I'd be okay driving now...'

'No you wouldn't.'

Claudia nodded again. 'You're right. I'll go and have an hour's rest. That okay?'

'You don't have to check with me. I'm not James. Go and rest. I'll give you a call when I get back from getting our euros.'

Heather collected her bag, checked that Claudia was okay, and left. She needed to be on her own. Norwood's arrival had rattled her, and she didn't want Claudia second-guessing what could have happened to her husband. Heather didn't want Claud linking the blood on her scalp to the day James had supposedly disappeared.

Two hours later Heather was back home, splitting the euros into two equal piles, finding the passports and E111s, and generally doing other holiday-related chores.

Claudia wandered through just as Heather finished. Claudia looked sleepy, and vigorously ruffled her hair in an attempt at waking herself up. 'I've slept for ages.'

'You obviously needed it.'

'I did. You have the euros then.'

Heather waved her hand towards the two piles. 'All done and dusted. I'm really looking forward to this, but promise me, Claud, if you need to just rest in the hotel instead of going out, you'll tell me.'

'I promise. But I think you'll know. You seem pretty quick at recognising when I'm out on my feet.'

Heather hugged her friend. 'I've known you many years, Claud. Of course I know when you're beat. Will you be okay on your own tonight?'

'I will. The kids are going to be upset, so I think I'll be better dealing with that on my own. I toyed with asking you to come, but I have to think of them now, and I think they'll want me alone. I'll ring when I'm ready to come home, although one of them might bring me.'

Claudia arrived at Harry's seconds before Zoe and David did, and Emma made them a pot of tea.

'No milk for me, thanks,' Claudia said with a smile.

'Crikey, that's new!' Zoe laughed, clearly happy to see her mum at last.

'I've decided to cut dairy out of my diet,' Claudia said.

David handed her the mug, and she sat back in the chair, comfortable with being with her family.

'So what's new, Mum?' Harry said. 'Divorce?'

'No, but there are a couple of things you need to know.' Claudia paused. She'd spent all afternoon wondering how to tell them and was no nearer knowing. 'The first thing is that your dad appears to be missing. I found out at lunchtime today. The police called to see if either Heather or I had seen him, but I haven't since the day I walked out, and Heather saw him the following Saturday, so neither of us could help. He's been reported missing by a Leeds Councillor. No doubt the police will be contacting you to ask if you've seen him, and when. I've not given them your addresses yet, but they'll be asking, I'm sure.'

Zoe gasped. 'Dad? Missing?'

Claudia nodded. 'And on that, I can't tell you any more. I haven't been in touch at all. I have ignored all texts from him, just deleted them, because most of them were quite nasty.' And then a thought hit her. 'He hasn't texted for a couple of weeks. Maybe I should have told DS Norwood that. So, have any of you seen James since the 23rd of April?'

They all said no, and Zoe turned to her mum. 'So what do we do? Has he gone away? On holiday?'

'I have no idea. He hasn't gone away with his significant other, that's for sure.'

'What?' Zoe's eyes opened wide.

'Your father, it appears, has someone else. The Leeds Councillor who reported him as a missing person.'

'What's her name?'

'His name is Councillor Will Monroe?'

There was a stunned silence in the room.

'I can't take much more.' Zoe spoke very quietly.

'But there is more, sweetheart,' Claudia said. 'I have something to tell you.'

She paused, not sure where to start. In retrospect, it had been easy to talk of James's disappearance.

'About six weeks ago I had a little operation to remove a spot from my shoulder that was situated where my bra strap went, and it was causing me some irritation. They took it off and tested it. It was malignant melanoma. I had to have a much bigger operation, with some pretty major surgery involving having lymph glands removed, and that operation revealed the cancer had spread into the lymph glands. My consultant was optimistic that it wouldn't have spread further, and he referred me to Weston Park for scans and X-rays and stuff.'

She stopped speaking and looked around at the others. Nobody spoke.

'I found out last Thursday that it has spread to my liver and elsewhere.'

'No!' The cry came from Emma, and Zoe rushed towards Claudia, hugging her.

'So now you have chemo and radiotherapy?'

'I should have had my first chemo on Saturday. This is hard to say to you all, but I won't be having any treatment other than palliative. They will keep me as free of pain as possible, but I have turned down the aggressive drugs it entails. I have been given six months, without it, and maybe nine months with. But having any therapies means I will be ill, sick all the time, headaches… I can't do that for the sake of an extra three months with no quality of life. It's my decision, guys, so please don't try to talk me out of it.'

Nobody could speak, initially. And then it seemed as if everyone spoke at once.

'But...'

'How...'

'It can't be right...'

'N-o-o-o...'

The last was from Zoe.

Claudia held up her hand, and tears rolled down her cheeks. 'I'm sorry, my darlings, but it is right. And my decision to have no treatment is right. I'm going to Paris on Wednesday for a few days, because I must see it before I die. When I come back I intend seeing as much of all of you as I can before... well, before.'

Emma moved to kneel by her side, and Zoe laid her head on her mother's knee. 'I can't take this in,' Zoe whispered.

'I've had a few more days to get used to it than you have, and believe me, it doesn't get any easier, the taking in. Heather's been amazing. She does all the driving, all the chores around the flat, and we've sat and worked out a healthy diet. She makes sure I stick to it. We're fighting it in whatever way we can, but don't think there is hope, because there isn't.'

The silence in the room became intense as they tried to absorb what they had just been told. Eventually Harry spoke.

'Mum, let me take you home. I think we need to talk. But we also need to know where you're living. You're not going through this with just Heather for backup, she will need time out as well. We promise, all of us, that Dad won't find out from us.'

'You have no more questions?' Claudia looked at them all.

David sighed. 'Not at the moment, no. We may have some later. Do you feel okay?'

'I'm just a little tired, and I think that's mostly because of the operation. And it could also be because I now have a compromised immune system. I handle it by sleeping, so don't worry. I'm not actually ill.'

'Can we tell Dad when he shows up?' Zoe had red eyes, and she turned them on her mother.

'You can, but I don't want to see him. He must not know where I am. I can't stress that enough.'

'We understand,' Harry said. 'Text Heather and tell her I'm bringing you home.'

Claudia stood and kissed them all. 'I'll be in touch, so don't worry that you can't trace me. I just needed time.'

Harry settled her in the passenger seat, and the other three stood watching as the car disappeared down the street.

'Keep an eye on Zoe for me, Harry. She'll not handle this very well.' Claudia wiped away a tear that was threatening to roll down her cheek.

'Stop worrying, Mum. She's tougher than you think. We're all here for you, for anything you want. You know that.'

'I do. Turn left here, and then second right.'

Harry followed her instructions and pulled up outside the bakery. He saw Heather wave from a window above the shop.

'This looks good. Wish I lived near a bakery.'

'It is good. It's a beautiful flat and we're happy here. When we get back from Paris I'd like the four of you to come over for a meal, see properly where I live.'

He helped her up the stairs, noticing she was climbing them slowly, and with a slight limp. He said nothing. He didn't know what to say.

Harry returned her to Heather's care, and then she followed him back down the stairs.

She kissed him and whispered, 'I'll look after her for you. And I'll contact you if you're ever needed.'

He nodded and went outside to his car. He'd never felt so bad.

19

Liam Norwood picked up the typed reports of the conversations he had had with Will Monroe, Claudia Bell and Heather Gower, and re-read them.

His gut feeling told him James Bell wasn't on holiday, or at a conference to do with his job; instinct said he had disappeared involuntarily. The information that had come from the Councillor had suggested it was a happy relationship, long term, and there had been no reason at all for James to walk away.

Liam couldn't see the blame being laid at the feet of the two ladies; they had enough to handle and getting rid of James wouldn't benefit Claudia. So he had three people on his suspect list and all seemed unlikely candidates. He had to look further afield.

Work colleagues? He would approach them and find out if anyone had seen him since that Saturday morning when he had left Leeds. His children? Liam would need to speak to Claudia and get their addresses. He checked his watch, then dialled Claudia's number.

It was Heather who answered. 'She's in the shower. Can I get her to ring you back?'

He explained that he needed her family addresses, and Heather picked up her mobile. 'That's easy. Hang on while I go into my phone.' She then read out the addresses and full names, explaining that it was Harry and Zoe who were Claudia's children. Heather also gave telephone numbers.

'Be gentle with them,' she said. 'Claudia spoke to them last night about her diagnosis. They're not in a good place at the moment, and it will be very raw today.'

'I understand,' Liam said. 'But I have to check every avenue, try to find what has happened to Mr Bell. I also need to check out Mr Bell's house. Does Claudia have a key?'

'Yes, she does. Do you need us there while you look? Don't forget we're going to Paris very early Wednesday morning and then won't be available until Monday.'

'No, you're fine. If we've not managed to track his movements by the end of today, we'll probably go through the house tomorrow. I can ring you or call down to see you if anything crops up. I am aware that Mrs Bell doesn't need stress in her life, and if it can wait until after your Paris trip, then it will. I'm going to speak to Mr Bell's work colleagues this morning, so will pop around to yours later to get the key.'

'Thank you,' Heather said, and disconnected.

Heather felt sick. She had to pray that she had wiped every scrap of blood from that car; even one smear would be enough for them to take it in for forensic testing.

'Did I hear my phone?' Claudia was towelling her hair with one hand, still having to be careful of using her right arm.

'You did. It was DS Norwood. He wanted your key to check out James's house. Norwood's coming by for it later. I also gave him Harry and Zoe's addresses; the detective wants to check with them to see if they've had any contact.'

'I could have told him they hadn't.'

'I know, but this is a police investigation, Claud. He would still have had to ask them himself.'

She sighed. 'Sorry, this is making me tetchy, isn't it?'

Heather smiled at her. 'Be as tetchy as you like. Now come and sit down and I'll dry your hair for you.'

Liam didn't spend long at the Labour Party Sheffield headquarters. Six members of staff all spoke highly of their colleague, expressing concern at his disappearance, but they all knew his wife had walked out on him and assumed he'd taken himself off for a break.

When being interviewed, they all said virtually the same words, and Liam came away with the distinct impression James was a much-liked friend as well as co-worker. So it was only his wife he abused, Liam reflected. He could imagine the conversation when he had left them.

He went back to the office, looked through the very brief notes he had made from the morning interviews, and knew he needed to take this further. It was seemingly out of character for James Bell to disappear.

It took Liam ten minutes to the get to the flat, and Claudia handed over her bunch of keys. 'You will let me have them back when you've finished, won't you? There are one or two bits I didn't bring with me that I'd like to give to Zoe, and when James comes back I don't think I'll ever be in the house again. If he is on holiday, and I really suspect this is all a storm about nothing and he is on a beach somewhere, this will all seem very silly, don't you think?'

'Yes, I do,' he smiled. 'But he's not left the country, either by boat or plane.' Rosie had handed him confirmation of her check at ports and airports earlier. 'We have a request in with his bank to see if he's used any debit or credit cards since the day he went missing, and we're waiting for those results. If he hasn't used them, then that puts a whole new slant on it. He can't holiday without money.'

Liam looked at the bunch of keys. 'Is this for the front door? And I need the code for the burglar alarm please.'

She took the keys back and went through them. 'Front door, back door, shed, garage, Heather's back door, and the spare key for James's Sportage.' Claudia handed them back to him. 'The code is 0223 for the alarm, unless he's changed it.'

'Thank you,' Liam said. 'You go early tomorrow?'

Claudia and Heather nodded. 'Very early, around half past three.' Heather felt a little uneasy that Norwood had the key to her house.

'Then have a lovely time. Paris is wonderful at this time of the year, and make sure you go on a bateau on the Seine.'

Heather escorted him downstairs.

'Is she okay?' Liam asked.

Heather shrugged. 'So so. All this with James isn't helping, and it maybe would have been better to wait a couple more weeks, but in that time the cancer could start to make her feel ill. I don't know what to do for the best. Anyway, we're off tomorrow, and I'll look after her. Simple as that.'

Liam walked to his car. 'I'll see you when you get back. Have a good time.'

Liam called Rosie over to his desk and shuffled some papers around to make it look a bit tidier. She tutted as she sat down. 'You want some polish?'

'No,' he grinned. 'You can do it later.'

He picked up a sheet of paper and handed it to her. 'This is what we need to know and do. Tomorrow, we're taking a small team to James Bell's house, and going through everything. We're not looking at that location for a body – if there's one there the smell will be obvious by now. No, we're looking for something that will suggest where he is, if he has indeed disappeared of his own free will.'

'You think he has?'

'No. That scenario doesn't feel right. I can only go on how other people see him, but nobody has suggested he would do anything like that. He's either been taken for some reason, or he's dead. I can't think why he would have been taken; I didn't get the impression he was well off, just comfortable. I think we'll find a body at the end of this, but we were off to a bad start with it, because he'd been missing for two weeks before we found out.'

DC Neil Evans walked across to his colleagues and handed them several pieces of paper. 'From the bank, boss. And he hasn't used any cards since he was last seen. The final payment was to the Travelodge where he was staying. Stays there a lot so it's a regular transaction. There's nothing else showing up as untoward, just ordinary stuff. Petrol, restaurants, that sort of thing.'

'Thank you, Neil. Sit down with us, will you?'

Neil carried his chair across and sat next to Rosie.

'Okay,' Liam continued. 'This is what I want to happen tomorrow. I'm going to clear everything with the DI first – she may want to become more involved now we've confirmed he's definitely missing. Neil, I want you to sort out three PCs and head up the door-to-door. I particularly want you to focus on when they last saw James Bell. All the reports from interviews are already done and available to read, so can you make sure you've read them before we go. We'll head out at nine tomorrow, people should be up and about by then. Rosie, I want you to get a couple of PCs for searching the house. I will be with you as well on that one. If there's anything at all suspicious, we move out of the way and get forensics in. Right, go and read the reports, tell me who we're taking, and Rosie, can you organise cars please? I want us to be a visible presence.'

They moved back to their own desks, and began the detailed work Liam had requested.

Heather packed suitcases for both of them. Claudia looked on with some amusement; she had never had someone to do her packing before. Heather had said first class all the way, and it was clearly starting right now.

'I'll set the alarm for three, and we'll just have a cup of tea and a biscuit, take any medication we need to take, and head off by half past three. You okay with doing that, or do we need to get up earlier?'

'That's fine. Stop worrying about me. I'm feeling so much better now that I can talk to the kids openly.' Harry and Zoe had called earlier to wish them bon voyage and had kept the conversations light as if by mutual agreement. 'I'll nip downstairs and remind Jade we're going and won't be around until Sunday. She'll keep an eye on the place. I imagine Michelle will be back next week. I've missed her.'

'Okay. These pjs or this pair?' Claudia indicated the pale green ones, and Heather folded them neatly, then zipped the suitcase.

Jade was at the point of closing the shop when Claudia and Heather went down to see her.

'Hi, you two, everything okay? There's not much left if you're wanting anything.'

'No, we're good thanks,' Claudia said. 'We just want to remind you we're off to Paris early tomorrow morning, so won't be around until Sunday afternoon.'

'Oh.'

'Is everything okay?' Claudia sensed something wasn't right.

'Yes, it's fine.' She gave a slight shrug. 'It's just that dickhead has been hanging around all day, and he must realise I'm not Michelle.'

'Tell the police. Just explain he's your sister's ex, and he's stalking her, but he won't leave you alone either. I'm sure they'll do something, warn him off or whatever.'

'No, he's not my sister's ex, he's his brother, Craig Ullyat. George has been missing for ages, and he's convinced our Michelle knows something about it. She doesn't, obviously, but he's around here constantly.'

Claudia frowned. Michelle had said the man was her ex, she was sure. She had even told them that the man standing opposite the shop was George Ullyat, using his actual name.

'Will you be okay walking home?'

'I'm fine. I've brought my dog Elsa with me. She's not massive, but she'd go for anyone who tried to hurt me. She's fast asleep in the back at the moment.'

'If you're sure you're okay... you here next week?'

'No,' Jade responded. 'And I'm quite glad. Michelle's starting to get around a bit better, so by next Monday she should be good to go.' Jade laughed. 'It's not my natural thing to be polite to people all the time. It's been very stressful this week.'

'Oh, I do understand.' Claudia's tone was heartfelt. 'Don't forget we're not here to help if you have a problem.'

'I've a bit of a problem at the moment,' Jade laughed. 'I had my keys in my hand and now I can't find them. Can you see them? It's a big bunch.'

'Would it be these on the bread stand?' Heather moved across and picked them up. 'Good Lord, these are heavy!' She handed them to Jade.

'It's because the shop keys are always on them, Michelle's backup in case she loses hers. There are two front door keys because it has two locks, and the same for the back door, which I suppose we don't really need now. Michelle boarded it up after she was burgled. They'd got in that way.'

Heather had seen the boarded-up door when she was digging the grave for James. It was a relief to know that access was never used.

Jade walked them to the front door and locked it after the two women had left. She didn't want dickhead forcing his way through while she was doing the last bits of tidying up.

Claudia and Heather were asleep by nine o'clock, but swore at their alarms at three o'clock the next morning. Heather put on the kettle, handed Claudia a breakfast bar and some painkillers, and then a mug of tea.

'I don't think I need the painkillers,' Claudia said.

'They're preventative rather than necessary. It could be a long day, so take them and hope they stop any lurking pain.'

Claudia nodded and swallowed the two tablets.

They left home at exactly half past three and by four thirty were checking in at Robin Hood airport. They moved to the VIP lounge where they enjoyed breakfast and were seated comfortably in first class by quarter to seven.

At almost nine o'clock, three police cars pulled up outside the Bell family home, and police cordon tape was fixed around the property. Neil Evans organised his three-member team, and they began their house-to-house enquiries. He had worked on the questions the night before and handed each of them a clipboard with the relevant questions attached.

'Anything of importance that crops up, bring it straight back here to the boss, don't wait until you've finished your bit of the area.' Neil glanced at each one of them, and they all nodded.

Liam and Rosie, along with PC Mark Hobson and PC Norma Ormond, entered the Bell home. The code was still current for the burglar alarm, and Liam breathed a sigh of relief. First hurdle over.

He sent Mark and Rosie upstairs, Norma to the kitchen, and Liam searched the lounge.

An hour later they gathered in the kitchen, each of them having drawn a blank. The only item of significance was James Bell's passport, discovered in the desk of his small office. They had removed his laptop, but Liam didn't expect anything to come of that either. He held the keys they had used to enter the premises in his hand.

'Okay, Mark and Norma, I need you two to look through the garage and the shed.' He looked at the keys for a moment longer. 'Rosie, we're going in next door.'

He picked up his phone and rang Heather's number. He heard the international dial tone, and she answered. 'DS Norwood?'

'Heather, sorry to interrupt your holiday. I've got to make sure Mr Bell isn't in your house as he had a key for your kitchen door. Is that okay with you?'

'Yes, of course,' she said, although she knew it must have sounded off to him.

'Thank you,' he said. 'Enjoy Paris.'

By half past ten, Claudia and Heather were dropping their suitcases off at their hotel and heading out for a coffee. The telephone call from Norwood had rattled Heather, but she was much too far from Sheffield to do anything about it, so she put it to the back of her mind.

The sunshine was glorious, and they headed for the Champs-Élysées. It was a very short five-minute walk and once on the famous avenue it soon became obvious that there was a heightened sense of security.

At first it troubled Claudia that all the policemen were armed, and there were so many of them. She very quickly accepted it and sipped at the coffee Heather had ordered in French.

'Get you,' Claudia laughed. 'Hid that light under a bushel, didn't you?'

Heather smiled. 'It was my favourite subject at school, partly because I seemed to be a bit of a natural. I must have been because it's all coming back to me, and I haven't used the language for years. Most people speak English, so don't worry.'

They finished their coffee and carried on down to the designer shops; they resisted the urge to go in them, promising themselves a shopping day before heading home on Sunday.

By two o'clock they were back checking in to the hotel, and within minutes, Claudia was asleep. Heather hung up their clothes, then rested on her own bed. Her mind refused to think about Owen and James; it centred totally on losing her best friend. She seemed well enough at the moment, but Heather knew the tendrils of cancer were working their way through Claudia's body, getting stronger, killing her.

Heather brushed away the tears and closed her eyes.

Two hours later they were awake, although still supine on their beds. Decisions had to be made about where they would eat, so Heather suggested they dine in the hotel.

'Good idea,' Claudia concurred. 'We'll have a couple of drinks later, then maybe an early night. Up with the larks tomorrow morning and off to see things. Where shall we go first?'

'I've made a list,' Heather said, and scrabbled around inside her bag for the piece of paper.

Claudia took it and looked at the long list of places to see. 'Crikey! I'll put my trainers on then. There's a fair bit of walking if we're going to see this lot.'

Heather laughed. 'There's an easy way. We get on a tourist bus, and we just hop on and off wherever we fancy. I suggest we start at the Louvre, that will blow you away. And, of course, you'll see the Mona Lisa. That's kind of a mind-numbing moment, knowing who painted it, and that he couldn't possibly have imagined how many people would get to see it. The thing about the Louvre is you could take up residence there for a month and still not see everything in it. So, shall we start there?'

Claudia nodded. 'Definitely. And then we can decide after that? No good making a plan, we might want to spend some time in the Louvre.'

Claudia swung her legs off the bed and winced at the niggling pain she felt in her left-hand side.

'Claud?'

'Just a twinge. I'm fine.'

'You want some painkillers?'

Claudia shook her head. 'No, honestly I'll save them for when I really need them. I'm going to have a shower, get changed and contemplate the frog's legs that are bound to be on the menu.'

It was while she was showering that her thoughts strayed to the events happening back in Sheffield. 'Oh, well,' she whispered to herself, 'no news is good news, I suppose.'

20

Liam Norwood and Rosie Havenhand stood outside the kitchen door of the Gower home; Liam checked in his notebook for the code to the burglar alarm James Bell had given him following the discovery of Owen Gower's body.

He unlocked the door, moved quickly to the beeping alarm, and entered the code.

'Right, you take the upstairs, and I'll do down here. I'm not really expecting to find anything, and there's a faint smell, but I guess that's lingering from Mr Gower's untimely end. It's certainly not a strong enough odour to be coming from a body that's potentially been dead for two weeks.'

Rosie climbed the stairs, and Liam went into the lounge. He looked around but could see nothing out of the ordinary. He picked up all the mail from the hall floor, glanced through it and put it on the coffee table. It was mainly junk, with just a couple of letters from the bank. They were probably confirming the new arrangements the couple had made about their banking; Heather had told him about the issues with her husband using money allocated for payments.

He then moved into the kitchen, but again nothing seemed out of place. He could see Mark in the shed in the adjoining garden, doing a thorough search, but again Liam thought nothing would come of it.

Passing through the kitchen he went into the tidy utility room. He glanced around, moved a couple of laundry baskets and was just about to head out of the door and back to the kitchen when he noticed the green light on the washer indicating the load was finished.

He opened the washer door and the musty smell hit him. These clothes had been inside the drum for quite a while, he reckoned, and he pulled one item out. A woman's jacket.

He straightened up and considered all options. Heather had left three days before her husband fell down the stairs, and he was pretty sure she wouldn't have left washing in the machine. He put the jacket in one of the laundry baskets and bent down to see what else was still in the drum. Trousers, a shirt, a bra and pants. A tiny load to put through a full-wash cycle.

He knew this was significant. He didn't know why or how, but he knew.

He took out his phone and rang the station.

'Ken? Liam Norwood. I'm at the Gower house, the one where the owner fell down the stairs a few weeks ago. I need a forensics team here asap.'

Rosie reported nothing out of the ordinary upstairs, and they waited in the kitchen for the forensics team's arrival. Mark and Norma joined them, reporting they had found nothing, but Neil arrived at a run, taking his own words as gospel – if you get something, the boss wants to know immediately.

'Boss,' he said, breathing heavily, 'I've been talking to one of the neighbours. Her name's Mrs Irene Patterson. She makes scones.'

Liam leaned forward and brushed a crumb from the front of Neil's jacket. 'So I see,' he said drily.

'The thing is,' Neil said, ignoring Liam's action, 'she saw Mr Bell's car return about five on that Saturday afternoon. She said she was looking out of her window because she doesn't watch television on a Saturday afternoon, it's all football. It's why she can't be more precise about the time.'

'And it was definitely James Bell?'

'She watched the car turn into the drive and park up. She didn't see him because the privet hedge is too high. She was a bit disgruntled about that. Says it needs to be lowered.'

Rosie joined in. 'So, we know he was alive late afternoon. Have the rest of the team reported anything back to you?'

'Nothing, and they're all just about done. Mrs Patterson was my last lady. But I'm not finished telling it all yet. She was at her bedroom window again later that night, looking out because she couldn't sleep, and she saw a smaller car pull onto the drive. She said it drove backwards. Her words, not mine. She thought it was Mrs Bell's car, but she said it couldn't have been because Mrs Bell never drives it backwards onto the drive. Mrs Patterson went to bed just after that. She thought that happened around midnight but again her timing isn't spot on.'

'And Mr Bell's car?'

'Still in the same place, she thinks. She hadn't seen it move and she says when Mrs Bell parks and Mr Bell isn't here she drives it to the top of the drive.'

'This lady is invaluable,' Norwood said with a smile. 'Can we recruit her?'

He thought for a moment. 'And she never actually saw James Bell? She merely saw his car. He wasn't necessarily in that car at five o'clock.'

There was a bang on the front door and Rosie stood to let the forensics team in. They were in white suits and ready to go.

Liam explained the situation, then stood aside while one person entered the utility room.

He sat at the kitchen table, deep in thought. Were the ladies up to their pretty necks in this? Was that even possible, given the severity of Claudia's illness? His feelings were that he needed to rule them out, rather than rule them in.

He took out his phone once more. 'Ken – sort me a cadaver dog, will you? I want the dog to go over two adjoining gardens. Thanks.'

Bruce, the Alsatian, was thorough. He found nothing and was truly grateful for the drink of water provided by his handler. He didn't know while he was drinking it that his handler was being asked to transport him to a second location.

The forensics team had taken swabs of the work surface immediately above the washer – the presence of blood had been detected. Liam didn't know whether to feel justified or sad.

'You need comparison stuff for DNA analysis presumably?'

The white-suited body nodded. 'We do. Hair brushes, toothbrushes, but we need to collect it and bag it correctly. Don't just bring it to us.'

Both houses yielded items suitable for the analysis and Norwood left Neil Evans in charge, while he and Rosie followed Bruce and his handler down to Heather and Claudia's flat.

It caused some consternation on the road when the crime scene tape went across the entrance to the alleyway leading to the spare ground around the back and underneath the flat.

Craig Ullyat, nonchalantly leaning against the wall of the garden immediately opposite the bakery, suddenly came to attention. He thought it best not to hang around if there was a police presence, not with the little packets in his jacket inside pocket, and he waved at Jade as he left the area.

Jade was glad to see him go; he was really starting to unnerve her, and she wished with everything she had that Michelle had never got involved with George Ullyat, wherever he was.

She didn't know why Craig had gone until a customer came in and told her about the dog van and the police car, the crime scene tape and the nice-looking plain-clothes policeman.

Norwood, Rosie and the handler, who they had found out went by the name of PC Phil Jackson, stood for a few moments just surveying the area Bruce had to cover. It was knee high in weeds and grasses interspersed with tall buttercups, with a small area that went under the high-level patio of the flat Heather and Claudia shared. The police could see a boarded-up door directly underneath the patio, presumably a shop back door. On the edge of this grassed area was a brick-built storage facility, quite small and boarded-up. The window had been smashed, rendering the boarded-up door irrelevant.

Rosie walked across to it and looked through the window, carefully avoiding the jagged pieces of glass still left in around the edges. Lying on the ground was the piece of plywood that had originally been used to board it. The hut was empty except for a couple of candles, dozens of cigarette butts and what she thought was a Sheffield Wednesday woolly hat.

'Good taste,' she murmured, and headed back to report to her boss.

'Nothing of any significance except a Sheffield Wednesday hat, boss,' she said. 'We'll need to get through the door properly to double check, but at first sight there's nothing. Don't think it's a priority.'

'Thanks, Rosie. Okay, Phil, are we ready?'

'No. Give it another five minutes or so, he does it in his own time, does Bruce. He's still sitting down. When he stands up, he's ready for work.'

Liam laughed. 'Just like my team. And can we get that fish and chip shop closed down? All I can smell is that delicious aroma wafting over everything, and I'm starting to crave some.'

Bruce stood. Phil took off the dog's lead and let the Alsatian go. He followed behind him, not too closely but clearly knowing how his dog worked best.

Liam realised it was a pleasure to watch the dog; he worked almost in a grid pattern, not distracted by other smells such as empty crisp packets, cans of lager with dregs still in them and an assortment of other rubbish that would have been of interest to any other dog. He was focused.

Bruce worked his way methodically around, with Phil never more than a few feet away. The dog approached the area at the rear of the brick storage building and barked, then sat down. Phil darted forward and clipped on the lead, then waved a hand towards Norwood and Rosie. They walked across, stumbling occasionally in the long grass.

'He's detected decomposed remains here, sir,' Phil said, suddenly becoming formal.

'Thank you, PC Jackson. I'll get the team on site. You can get Bruce home now, we'll take it from here. It's definitely decomposed remains?'

'Yes, sir. No doubt. He reacts in the same way every time, and he's never been wrong. Did you know we'd find something?'

'Strongly suspected but didn't want to is the best way of putting it.'

Rosie and Liam watched as Phil walked Bruce through the deep grass towards the alleyway. They heard a brief couple of barks as they disappeared, and Liam took out his phone.

'Ken...'

There was a pause while Liam took his 'what do you want now?' barrage from his friend, and then explained exactly what he did want.

Within ten minutes a full team had arrived, a tent erected ready for putting over the spot once they had found what they were looking for, and Rosie and Liam were eating fish and chips.

The digging and scraping began, painstaking work with the sun beating down on the backs of their necks. Nobody said much, and Liam and Rosie watched as they went deeper and deeper, piling the excavated soil against the wall of the brick building.

DI Ray joined them. 'You knew something was amiss, didn't you? Good instincts, Liam. I'm leaving this one with you, not muscling in unless you need me on call.'

'Thank you. I expected you to take over now it looks like murder.'

'You can handle it?'

'Of course. I'll stay here until we get James Bell out of there and despatched to the morgue. I'm calling in the refreshment vehicle though, they're working in intolerable heat.'

'I'll see to it,' Philippa Ray said. She took out her phone and organised it.

It took twenty minutes for the van to arrive, and a grateful forensics team took a drink break before going back to scraping the soil.

DI Ray left them to it, and Liam and Rosie sat on their jackets on the grass. Neil Evans joined them, telling them all his team had completed their reports and uploaded them, along with his own detailed report of the information from Mrs Patterson.

He dropped to the grass alongside them. 'At least it's not raining and washing evidence away with it,' Neil said, wiping the back of his neck with a tissue.

'This is England, Neil. It could be raining in ten minutes,' Rosie said with a laugh. She turned to smile at Neil, and Liam saw the brief eye contact.

Oh, my giddy aunt, he thought, *there's something going on. Who would have guessed?*

He was stopped from making any sort of comment by a shout from the team excavating the large area. Three people immediately began to move the tent to cover the more specific ground and it was finally pegged down.

The three police officers scrambled to their feet and dusted the grass from their clothes before moving across to the tented zone. There was a general hush from the people in the tent, as they continued to scrape away soil from the hole, but now using much finer implements.

'A body?' Norwood asked.

'Yes, we've uncovered what looks to be a skull. We'll know more in half an hour. Go and grab a cuppa, I'll give you a shout when there's something to look at.'

Liam nodded, and the three of them headed across to the refreshment van. They all settled for coffee and carried their drinks back to where they had originally been sitting. Rosie stumbled, and immediately Neil's arm shot out to catch her and steady her; again there was a smile and eye contact.

Liam shook his head and tried to hide his smile. He could have some fun with this one, once they were back in the station.

They didn't speak much while they drank, all of them keen to know the results of the dig. It was the better part of an hour before they were called over. They ducked their heads and went inside the tent.

Liam couldn't contain his surprise. 'Any ID on him?'

'No, none that we've come across yet. This isn't what you were expecting, DS Norwood?' The pathologist's voice was low, respectful of the dead man in the grave.

Liam shook his head. 'No, this poor chap's been dead a lot longer than two weeks, I'm guessing. It's a man?'

'The clothing suggests it is. We can tell you more when we get him out of this hole and back to the morgue. Will you be attending the post-mortem?'

'I will. I'm struggling to accept this, I'm looking for a missing person from a couple of weeks ago, and I end up with a dead body from... you have any idea?'

'Maybe three years. The clothes are still recognisable, so I don't think it's any longer than that. Shall we say ten o'clock tomorrow morning for the PM?'

'Thank you. I'll be there. If there's anything that shows up in the meantime...' Liam handed over his card.

The three officers returned to the cars, and once back at the station, he spent five minutes filling Philippa Ray in on the afternoon's activities.

'Do you make a habit of collecting bodies?'

'No, boss. I don't know where this one came from. It's nothing to do with me.'

'Maybe it wasn't, but it is now. So basically we're no closer to finding James Bell, but we've found somebody else who could be anybody. Is that right?'

Liam nodded. 'It is. But don't worry. I'll sort it.'

Philippa couldn't hide the smile. 'Get out of here, Liam Norwood. And don't find any more. We've got enough corpses now.'

He headed back to his own desk. Neil and Rosie had been deep in conversation, taking advantage of the empty room. They moved apart as he came through the door.

'Does everybody know but me?' he said conversationally, struggling to keep his face straight.

'What?' Neil looked guilty.

'You two. You are an item, aren't you?'

'No...'

'Yes...'

'So which is it?'

Rosie dropped her head. 'You're not supposed to know.'

'Rosie, love, it's obvious. Does everybody know?'

'Nobody knows,' Rosie said quietly.

'Wait while tomorrow. You'll need armour plating.' Liam laughed. 'This is the most fun I've had in ages. I can't believe you didn't tell me, but you'll pay for that now.'

'I resign,' Rosie said.

'And me,' Neil said with a groan. 'Don't do this to us, boss. You'll make life impossible.'

'See you in the morning,' Liam said with a smirk, and walked out of the office. He heard the stapler hit the door with a thud.

21

The Louvre, with the sunshine glistening on the panes of the pyramid turning it into a magical vista, was busy as always. Claudia and Heather joined the queue and went through the security checks before descending down into the great atrium beneath.

'I can't believe I've never been,' Claudia breathed, her voice hushed as she tried to take in everything at once.

'We need to sit down for a while,' Heather insisted. 'That was a heck of a time standing up, and it's going to be a long day. Come on, let's grab a table and I'll go get us a drink.'

They chatted about inconsequential things, Claudia took a couple of painkillers, and they set off on the great journey that is the Louvre.

By the time they reached the Mona Lisa area, Claudia was spellbound. She stood in front of the masterpiece and felt tears prick her eyes. She brushed them away as they rolled down her cheeks and she turned to Heather.

'Thank you so much. I never expected to feel emotions like this, it's just a painting, but oh my word…'

'Stay as long as you want. I'm going to sit on that bench over there, and I'll wait for you. There's absolutely no rush.'

Heather sat and watched her friend, knowing she was totally overawed by the picture, but just as much by the fact that she was there seeing it.

Ten minutes later, Claudia joined her, and they wandered into various other rooms, looking at the great sculptures, the intriguingly massive paintings, taking in the splendour of everything.

They bought a few souvenirs, then made their way back out, heading towards where they had got off the tourist bus.

Heather suggested they go to l'Opera, and the Galleries Lafayette, shop a little, have a meal at one of the small restaurants, then head back to the hotel.

Claudia responded with a grin. 'You almost sounded French then,' she said. 'That seems a perfect plan.'

By eight o'clock, Claudia was in bed, asleep. She had tried so hard to hide her exhaustion from Heather, but the signs were clear. The walking would have to be minimal for the rest of the holiday.

DS Norwood was at the post-mortem, feeling out of sorts. He didn't know why, put it down to his instinct being off kilter, but even so, he was a little bit pissed off.

He had dispatched a trio of officers to the crime scene, with little hope of them finding anything, but he had to make the effort. He didn't expect the post-mortem to reveal anything significant, but in that he was wrong.

It revealed a bus ticket in one of the jeans' pockets, dated 3rd of June 2014. Whoever the young man was, he had gone missing some three years earlier.

He listened to all the clinical information, picking out and remembering the bits he needed, discovering that the young man was healthy apart from the bullet hole in his back, that the DNA was already in the process of being checked, and results would be back on that within twenty-four hours, and that he was around 5'10" tall.

Liam left the building and walked back to his office, deep in thought. Where exactly was James Bell? He decided he would contact Councillor Monroe again, see if anything had occurred to him, or if he had had any contact. He recognised it was a bit of wishful thinking on his part; if Bell had contacted Monroe, he would have notified the station.

Liam sat down at his desk and stared around him in astonishment. It was tidy, and what's more it was polished. Even his filing tray was filed.

Rosie's head was down, working on God knows what, Neil was over by the filing cabinets, and Mark was doing something on his computer. The room was silent.

'What's going on?' Liam asked loudly.

Nobody answered.

'Rosie?'

'Yes, boss?'

'Have you cleaned my desk?'

'Yes, boss.'

'So where is everything?'

'On your desk, boss, just tidy instead of all over the place,' she responded, still looking down at her own desk.

'Are you creeping, Rosie Havenhand?'

'Yes, boss.'

Neil exploded with laughter. 'I'm sorry, boss, I told her it doesn't matter who knows about us, but she's desperately trying to stop you blowing the lid on us.'

Mark lifted his head. 'What are you talking about?'

'Rosie and me. We're... seeing each other.'

'Oh that. Is that all? We all know anyway.' Mark went back to his computer.

That made Rosie lift her head. 'Am I worrying for nothing? Have I polished that desk for nothing?'

Liam burst out laughing, his bad mood instantly dispelled. 'Look, it's absolutely fine. Do what you want with him, but if it ever impinges on what we do, I'll split you up at work. Understood?'

They both nodded, looking sheepish, then returned to what they had been working on.

Liam went into his emails, and saw he had one from the forensics team who had been at the Gower house. They had expedited the tests and the results showed two different blood types on the work surface above the washer, indicating that the clothes they had removed from the washer had been placed there before being added to the drum. One of the bloods belonged to the owner of the pink toothbrush and silver-backed hairbrush taken from the Gower bathroom and bedroom, the other blood belonged to the owner of the blue toothbrush removed from the Bell bathroom.

Heather Gower and James Bell.

Liam rang through to forensics and ordered a vehicle recovery truck to be sent to the Bell address to collect the Sportage parked on the drive. He wanted full forensics on it, and he needed the driver to drop by the station and collect the car key.

He just happened to have it on him.

Friday morning saw Claudia and Heather climbing on board the tourist bus and disembarking at the Eiffel Tower. Once again they went through massive security checks, all the time aware of armed police everywhere they looked. Paris didn't take kindly to attacks on its citizens and visitors.

They finally shuffled their way to the front of the queue and got into the first lift. Lift by lift, they reached almost to the top, walking the final level.

They stepped out onto the viewing area and gasped at the sight before them. Glorious sunshine lit up the whole of Paris, dazzling them from so high above everything. They stayed for some time, drinking it in, both knowing they would never return to see the vista.

Deflation set in when they reached the bottom; the trip to the top had been worth every euro.

'Lunch?' Heather asked.

'Plat du jour?' Claudia laughed, attempting the French accent.

They linked arms, and walked for a short distance, settling themselves in at a pavement table. The lunch was delicious, although Heather took note of the minuscule amounts Claudia was eating.

They jumped in a taxi and asked to be taken to the Seine bateau rides, and once again Claudia was overwhelmed. She listened closely to the headphone commentary, and her head swivelled as she took in whatever the commentator was telling her to view.

As they embarked, Claudia stumbled. 'I'm tired,' she whispered.

'Let me help you up the steps so that we're actually on the road. I'll get us another taxi, we'll head back to the hotel.'

Claudia sat on a wall for half an hour while Heather frantically tried to get a taxi. In the end, she had to walk to find a taxi rank, gave them instructions to where Claudia was waiting, and half an hour later they were back in the foyer of their hotel.

Claudia looked grey, and Heather got her in the room, pulled down the bedding on Claudia's bed, and made her lie down. Within seconds she was sleeping.

Heather was worried. She felt relieved there was just Saturday to get through, and Sunday they would be on their way home.

It had to be a quiet day, Saturday. Visiting Versailles was out of the question, and she didn't think Claudia would be strong enough for the shopping trip they had talked about.

Heather picked up the room service menu and ordered a croque monsieur, not wanting anything too hefty. When Claudia woke up, they could order something for her.

The meal, trimmed with salad and French fries as only the French can do it, was delicious, and Heather ate it while reading, thankful she had slipped her e-reader into her hand luggage as a last-minute thought.

She finally turned off her bedside light and went to sleep about ten o'clock, without Claudia having stirred. Heather was vaguely aware of Claudia getting up during the night to use the bathroom, but when they both stirred around eight, it was obvious the sleep had helped.

They went down to breakfast, and when Heather asked what Claudia wanted to do, she was surprised by her answer, and relieved.

'What I would really like to do is go to the Jardin des Tuileries,' she hesitated waiting for an explosion of laughter from Heather at her accent, 'and just sit and watch the day go by. It's beautiful sunshine again, and if we get bored of just sitting and drinking coffee and eating cakes and watching people, then we can go buy a little painting from one of the street artists.'

'That sounds idyllic. That's exactly what we'll do. We didn't really have time to enjoy it when we went to the Louvre, so I think that will be an excellent way of spending our last day.'

Friday was a good day for DS Norwood. The forensics team working on the car had reported blood in the boot and on the rear bumper, and it had been sent for profiling. They would forward the results as soon as they were available.

Liam put his coffee cup down on the desk and noticed a couple of rings left from earlier movement of the said coffee cup. He licked his finger and attempted to remove them; maybe he might have to buy a can of spray polish and a duster. Or steal Rosie's stuff.

He turned to his computer and read all the reports his team had filed. He stopped at the one Neil had filed, with Mrs Patterson's testimony. With the information on the blood in the utility room in the Gower home, this was starting to make more sense. Heather Gower herself had said she was doing all the driving at the moment, because Claudia wasn't well enough. And he had seen that she wasn't, she had looked very fragile the last time he had seen her.

The small car Mrs Patterson had seen, and thought it couldn't be Claudia's because she never reversed onto the drive, could quite easily have been Claudia's car, reversed onto the drive for a reason – to load a body from the boot of the Sportage into the smaller car.

But where had that smaller car gone after that?

Sheffield, for all that it had an industrial heritage with its mighty steel works, was also the greenest city in the country, and that meant woodlands, many many woodlands dotted all over the city. They couldn't possibly check them all, not even with the awesome Bruce at the end of a lead.

'We need a briefing,' he stated. 'We need to put our heads together, try to track down what I'm missing.'

They looked up at him; he'd been quiet all morning. Rosie, Neil and Mark stood and moved over to the corner with the whiteboard displaying pictures, scrawled words and lines connecting the pictures, and question marks everywhere.

Liam stood by the board. The others sat on the chairs round the small desk, commandeered to make life easier, automatically picking up a pen and paper.

'Right,' Liam began. 'We need to get rid of some of these question marks. Heather Gower. It's looking increasingly as though she's our main suspect, her blood and James Bell's blood were both on that worktop in the Gower utility room. Thoughts?'

Rosie tapped her cheek with her pencil. 'It's all circumstantial, boss. Without a body, we know nothing. He could be away somewhere, licking his wounds from the break-up of his marriage, trying to decide what to do with his future. Both the families are really close, best friends for a number of years, and just to add fuel to the fire, both had started doing their gardens to get them ready for the summer. Gardening means injuries...' She held up her bandaged left hand. 'And that's where any solicitor will go.'

'You think that's it? That I'm clutching at straws? That there is a reason for that blood being there, her clothes being in the washer?'

'No, of course I don't. I think that what you're seeing is absolutely spot on, but someone has to play devil's advocate before you race out to Robin Hood airport and arrest them as they return from Paris.'

'So the question marks stay?'

'I think so. We need a body before we can take this much further. Do we have the results of the forensics on the Sportage yet?'

'Mark?'

'Not as of five minutes ago. Give me a sec, and I'll check.' He stood and moved to his computer, clicking swiftly on his emails. He pressed print, then headed across the room to pick up the printed copy.

He rejoined his colleagues and handed the sheet to Liam.

Liam scanned it quickly. 'Both bloods found in the car, and blood from Heather found on the driving seat and steering wheel. No fingerprints, she must have cleaned it, but she couldn't remove all the blood.'

'Why her blood?' Neil spoke for the first time.

'What?' Liam turned to face him.

'Why her blood? If she's killed him, I can understand his blood being everywhere, but why is hers all over the place as well? Could he have attacked her first, making it self-defence? None of this makes sense.'

'We need to bring her in. Just for a chat, I reckon. I don't want to alert her to the fact we have some pretty damning evidence, even if we don't have a body, because it will give her time to come up with a reason for her being in that car. The evidence can be mentioned once this body surfaces. I'm convinced there is one, somewhere.'

'Then where was he killed?' Rosie threw into the discussion. 'Was there enough blood in the car to prove the exsanguination happened in it, or did he die somewhere else and she put him in the car? Would she have been physically capable of that?'

'If you're scared enough, you can do anything,' Liam responded. 'And no, it says on here the blood was minimal, so he was already dead when he went in that car boot. If he is dead...'

'We're not removing many question marks, boss,' Neil said. 'We seem to be adding them.'

Liam groaned. 'Don't I know it. Okay, here's a plan of action. We have our own reports, witness statements and other stuff. I suggest we all read through them once again. Every single one. No skim-reading, get all the details into your mind. Somewhere in there could be one tiny piece of information that will tell us something that we're not recognising.'

He paused for a moment to look at the whiteboard. 'And let's double-check every damn thing on this board. Make notes if something occurs to you, follow it up. We'll have another briefing Monday morning unless anything happens before then. Claudia

Bell and Heather Gower fly back Sunday, but whatever else might arise, we have to remember Claudia Bell is terminally ill, with very limited time left. I don't believe she's guilty of anything unless she's covering for her friend, and she needs our consideration.'

They moved back to their desks; the briefing had been good for them, and they felt rejuvenated as they pulled the different documents up onto their screens.

Liam began with the earliest; the missing person report from Councillor Monroe. Liam read through that, then read the report on the telephone conversation Monroe had had with him. It was, at first, somewhat sketchy, but it opened up a little as he began to talk of his relationship with Bell. It was clear there was a lot of feelings between the two men, the emotion was evident in the Councillor's words and tone of his voice.

Liam sat back in his chair and allowed his thoughts to roam a little. James Bell was the third man he had known who had changed from being a loving husband and father of several years, to wanting to share his life with a member of his own sex. He wondered if things would have turned out differently for the man if he hadn't made that decision to be true to himself.

22

The Jardin des Tuileries was busy but they found seats at a table at one of the small cafes, ordered coffee and a piece of cake each, and settled back to watch the world wander by. 'Do you think they will have tracked James down by now?'

The question was sudden and surprising, and made Heather stop and think.

'I don't know,' she said cautiously. *I hope not,* she thought.

'I think,' said Claudia thoughtfully, 'that if they had found him, DS Norwood would have rung me, even though he knows we're in Paris. I wonder if he's spoken with Harry and Zoe yet.'

'If he had, I'm sure they would have texted you to let you know.' Heather moved her chair slightly so that she was in the shade of the umbrella. 'Let's forget about James for a while. Time enough to get back into all that when we get home tomorrow. So, tell me what you think to Paris?'

'I've loved every tiring minute of it. What I think we should do to round today off is walk down and get a tourist bus, and go all the way around until we're back here. There must be so much I haven't been able to see, and I really would like to see as much as possible before...'

'Of course we can.' Heather leaned across and squeezed Claudia's hand. 'Whatever you want to do. And at least we won't be walking. Shall we eat in the hotel tonight? We can either go down to the restaurant or have room service. You decide when we get back.'

Heather had felt sick ever since Norwood had rung to ask her if he could go in her house, but she knew there was nothing there that could possibly connect her to James Bell's disappearance.

Her biggest fear was if he should happen to link cemetery visits with James; she was convinced there would still be traces of both his blood on the ground and her own blood on the headstone, and if that was discovered, she would be in serious difficulties. There had been some rain since she had sunk the scissors into his neck, but it would need a torrential downpour to wash the last traces away. So much blood out of one man…

She shivered.

'Are you cold?' Claudia frowned.

'No. I was just thinking about Owen. I miss him. I didn't stop loving him, you know, I just stopped being able to live with him and his drinking. It's an awful position to be in.'

'I stopped loving James.' The statement was flat, emotionless.

'I know. He made you stop loving him. I watched your relationship dissolve, and yet you still didn't leave him.'

'It was that Saturday morning… that caused the complete breakdown in my mind. It was rape, Heather, it really was, and he didn't see it. He thought it was his right. But if he was with another man, why did he want me?'

'Maybe he was planning on leaving you. He just wanted you one last time.'

'You think?' Claudia looked puzzled.

Heather shrugged. 'Not really. I actually think he was a lying, cheating conniving bastard, who held the title rapist as well. He's not worth thinking about, Claud. You finished your coffee?'

Claudia nodded.

'Then let's go catch a bus. We can come back here if you want when we get off the bus. See how you feel at the end of the journey.'

Liam picked up Olivia and Danny, making the swimming pool their first stop of the day. Liam loved his time with them, hated the fact that he hadn't had the strength to make his marriage work. They swam until they were exhausted, then went for a full English breakfast.

Olivia, at seven, bubbled over with an energy he prayed would never leave her.

Danny, two years older than his sister, was the quiet one of the pair, although with a wicked sense of humour. He shovelled sausage tomatoes and some egg into his mouth, then attempted to speak.

'Not with your mouth full, Dan,' his father admonished. 'Swallow it and then speak.' Later he reflected he shouldn't have given him permission to talk.

Dan swallowed the mouthful, and said, 'Did you dig up the body, Dad?'

'What?'

'What was it like? Was it just a skeleton?'

Liam felt panicked. What sort of conversation was this to have over a full English, with your seven and nine-year-old kids?

'Erm... no, I didn't dig it up, as you so crudely put it. We have special forensic people to do that. Now get on with your breakfast.'

'But I need to know. Was it a skeleton, or did it have skin and stuff on it?'

Olivia carried on eating, oblivious to the gory question and answer session happening in front of her.

'Why do you need to know?' Liam knew as soon as he spoke the words that he shouldn't have. Really, he should have just changed the subject, possibly to the Disney film they were planning on seeing that afternoon, something safe and gentle.

'The kids at school want to know.'

Shit. This couldn't be happening! He'd never thought about telling the kids that anything they heard about his job wasn't to be taken to school and discussed.

'The kids at school can't know. Tell them it will be in the papers, and they'll have to read it for themselves.'

'Aw, but Dad, why can't you tell me?'

'No. You know I can't talk about my job.'

'You used to talk about it with Mum. I heard you.'

This was getting worse.

'You didn't tell them at school?'

'Sometimes. They gave me sweets to tell them.'

'Oh my life, Daniel, you can't do that!' He felt the use of the boy's full name was justified. 'That can get me into so much trouble...'

'It can't now, can it,' the young boy responded. 'You don't talk to her at all.'

Liam felt a tightness in his throat. He placed his knife and fork on his plate and looked at his children.

'Hey, can I talk to both of you for a minute?'

Two pairs of matching blue eyes lifted and looked at his face.

'Just because your mum and I aren't together, doesn't mean we've stopped talking. We talk all the time, usually about you two. We just stopped being able to live together, we didn't stop loving each other, and especially we love you two.'

Neither child said anything. Liam ploughed on.

'Promise me you will never repeat anything at school that you hear at home. It's not done, Dan. I still talk to your mum a lot about my work, and I would hate to have to stop talking to her because you might say something to your mates.'

'Sorry, Dad.' Dan's voice had dropped an octave. 'I just never thought.'

'I know.' Liam reached across and ruffled his hair. 'I love you both so much.'

He held his daughter's hand. 'And you, Liv, did you understand?'

She shook her head. 'Nope. Can I eat my sausage now?'

He dropped the children off just after ten next morning; they were going to a summer fayre with their mum, and he handed over a fiver to each child, telling them to spend it wisely, and not on alcohol. They had both giggled and dashed up the path. He waited until they were safely indoors before driving away.

Instead of going home he went to the station. It was quiet; Sundays carried only a skeleton staff, and he sat down at his desk and looked around him. The white board still held the same number of question marks; nothing was any clearer.

Where the hell was James Bell? Liam would dearly love to see Heather's face if he asked her that question.

He powered his computer, and heard the pings denoting incoming mail. The first email he checked was from Councillor Monroe, asking if there were any updates on James.

Liam answered very briefly, keeping everything from him that really couldn't be passed on. Basically, his answer was no, no updates. We don't know where he is. What should have been said was we know where his blood is.

The next email was from the forensics team. He read through it quickly, and then went back to the beginning and studied it thoughtfully.

The body discovered almost by accident proved to be a local youth by the name of George Ullyat, tentatively reported as missing but never really followed up because he was known to disappear if he thought the police were starting to look at him too closely. It seemed that three years prior to the discovery of his body, his brother had come in to the station demanding to know if they were holding the said George. The officer had checked, confirmed they weren't holding him for anything, and asked him if he wanted to make it an official missing person's report. The use of the word official had sent Craig Ullyat running for cover.

And that was the last time George Ullyat had come onto their radar. He was definitely on it now.

The email confirmed they already held Ullyat's DNA on their database from 2012 when he had attacked his then girlfriend, Michelle Samuels. They had been able to successfully match it to DNA removed from the skeletal remains found buried on the spare land.

Liam breathed a huge sigh. He now knew what the first job for the morning was going to be, the one he hated most of all. He would have to tell a family they had lost a loved one. He went into the computer once again and typed in the name Craig Ullyat. It threw up an address, along with a list of offences, none of which had resulted in imprisonment.

He stayed for another hour, re-reading everything, making a few notes, adding a few more question marks; he still felt he knew what had happened to James Bell, and who had done it, but it was so unbelievable he wanted to start back at the beginning and find a different suspect.

And so the week drew to a close. Claudia and Heather were back in their flat, Claudia feeling a little under the weather and Heather feeling worried. It had been an outstanding trip.

Claudia would treasure the memories they had created. If she had to pinpoint the one thing that had given her a feeling of deepest satisfaction, it would be her first sight of the Mona Lisa, and the emotions that picture had engendered.

She rang Zoe and Harry to tell them they were home, and she had some little touristy gifts for them, then sank into the bath Heather had run for her.

Heather went out onto the patio while Claudia was bathing, taking a cup of tea with her. She sat down, then saw the fluttering ribbon. She stood and walked to the railing that surrounded the patio and looked over.

She went icily cold. She began to shiver, and swiftly took a drink of the hot tea. It was crime scene tape that had fluttered into her eyeline. Crime scene tape? What had happened that could necessitate the use of the area being cordoned with the blue and white tape? She could just see the edge of the excavated area around the back of the brick shed, and she sat down again. She picked up her phone and rang Michelle.

'Do you know what's been happening on the spare land out back?' she asked, a little peremptorily. 'Sorry... I didn't mean to sound so bullish. I'm tired.'

'What do you mean?'

'There's crime scene tape, and an excavated area round the back of that brick storage place. I thought you might know what had gone off.'

There was a long pause, and then Michelle said, 'Sorry,' and disconnected.

Heather stared at her phone, bewildered. Sorry? What did that mean? What was she sorry about?

Claudia came out onto the patio wrapped in a huge white towel, with a smaller one around her hair.

'That was lovely,' she said, and bent to kiss the top of Heather's head. 'Thank you.'

'You're very welcome. Want a cup of tea?'

'I'd love one. What's that?' She too walked over to the edge of the patio.

'It's crime scene tape. Don't know why though. I'll get you that drink.'

Heather headed back inside, and into the kitchen. She leaned against the worktop for a while, fighting the fear that was threatening to overwhelm her.

The tea was quickly made, minus the milk, and she went back outside, to see Claudia with her eyes closed. She stood for a moment, and then Claudia said, 'I'm not asleep, just resting my eyes. Come and sit down, you don't have to wait on me.'

'Yes, I do,' Heather said, and the tears came, tears she had been holding back for a couple of weeks.

'Please, please, Claudia, change your mind about the chemo. I can't bear to think of being without you.'

'I won't change my mind,' Claudia said gently. 'When the time comes I want to go to St. Luke's Hospice, where they'll keep me pain free. I can make all my decisions now, while my brain is working properly, so tomorrow I'm going to write my wishes for the end of my life in a book. I'm relying on you to carry them out.'

'You know I will, but this is the hardest thing I've ever had to do, even harder than burying my husband.'

Claudia squeezed her hand. 'I know. I hope you find a good friend who will be with you at your end, but make no mistake, Heather Gower, I'll be up there waiting for you, with a big pot of tea in my hand.'

And then the laughter came.

Rosie and Neil sat closely together on her sofa. It felt strange; she had lived on her own for a long time, and although Neil hadn't officially moved in, he seemed to spend most nights with her.

They finished watching Countryfile and switched off the television. Neil kissed the top of her head.

'Been a long week, hasn't it,' Rosie said. 'The boss is convinced it's Mrs Gower, isn't he?'

'Aren't you?'

'I suppose so. I just don't think it's that cut and dried. Where's the body to prove she's done anything? And to be honest, I'd have wanted to kill him myself.'

Neil laughed. 'Not the right attitude, my love, for a serving officer of the law.'

'Really? Do I have to think sweet thoughts, then, all the time? Not going to happen.'

'Shall we go to bed?'

'What? It's only eight o'clock.'

'Early start tomorrow.'

'Is that the only reason?' Rosie asked with a laugh.

'Nope. That was a lie. I want to kiss you and, you know, we'll see what develops.'

She stood and held out her hand to him. 'Let's go develop.'

It was the fastest he'd moved all week.

Liam stood at his bedroom window, staring out at the starry sky. No clouds but it felt chilly. His thoughts were chaotic.

He knew by the end of the week they would have answers, and somebody would be in custody, body or no body. But first he had to deal with the murder of George Ullyat. It wasn't simply a matter of telling his family, he also had to track down a gun, find out whose hand the gun had been in when it had pointed at George's back, and gather enough evidence to put that person away for life.

He hoped the elusive Craig Ullyat wouldn't clam up; he probably held the key to his brother's murder without realising it. And he needed to track down the ex-girlfriend George had assaulted that had resulted in his prison sentence back in 2012. At the very least she could give background information on George. Liam thought she was called Michelle, but he couldn't remember her surname. He'd put Mark on to tracking her down.

Liam had rung his ex some two hours earlier and told her of his conversation with the kids about the necessity of keeping quiet at school about any of Daddy's work. She had laughed and said she would have a chat with them and make sure they understood. They had chatted comfortably for a quarter of an hour, sorted out issues surrounding money needing to be sent to school for organised trips, and then said goodnight. He knew he still loved her, and he was almost certain she still loved him; it was the job that stopped the perfection.

Almost certain.

Dan had spoken of someone called Martin. He didn't ask about him, didn't want to know, but he recognised that if indeed there was a Martin, it would kill his own hopes of one day reconciling their differences, forever. He wasn't sure if he could bear the thought of losing her completely, not to Martin or any other Tom, Dick or Harry.

He leaned his head against the coolness of the window and sighed. Was the job worth it? The more he thought about it, the more it made sense to do what Rosie and Neil had done; find someone in the same job.

He reached up and closed the curtains, then headed for the shower. It had been a long and muggy day, he needed a cool shower before climbing into bed. He turned the temperature up slightly when he realised it was maybe a little too cool, splashed on the shower gel and shampooed his hair. It hit him with the force of a thunderbolt.

James Bell had been heading back to Sheffield to track his wife down at a place she went to every Saturday. What had Heather Gower said? 'I saw him at the cemetery.'

Liam dried himself and headed back to the bedroom. Attempting sleep, he knew that the jobs for Monday were stacking up; notify a family their son was dead, track down the ex-girlfriend, check in with Heather Gower and Claudia Bell, find a gun, and, last but not least, visit a cemetery.

He was awake at four, with the list going around and around his head. Not a good night's sleep, but hopefully a good day's work. He picked up a book and began to read. *Just another couple of hours might be a good idea*, he thought.

23

'Mrs Ullyat? DS Norwood, and this is DC Havenhand. May we come in for a moment, please?'

She had the look of a startled rabbit. Her blonde hair was in a tangled halo around her head, her pink dressing gown was tied loosely around her waist revealing a cream nightie, stained with multiple breakfasts, and she had clearly clambered out of bed to answer the knock at the door.

'Why?' Her voice was guttural, and suggestive of a long-term smoker.

'If we can come in…' Liam said again.

'Craig!' she yelled. 'Cops for you.'

Liam pushed the door wider, and she stepped back, slightly shocked. There had been no intention to let him in.

'Rosie, can you put the kettle on, please. I'm sure Mrs Ullyatt would like one.'

Rosie nodded and went in search of the kitchen. It was surprisingly clean, and she switched on the kettle before rooting through cupboards for mugs.

'Is this the lounge?'

Agnes Ullyat nodded. 'What do you want?' Liam thought he detected a slight Irish accent.

'Is Craig here, Mrs Ullyat?'

'What's he done?'

'Mrs Ullyat, we're going to get nowhere if all you do is answer my questions with another question. Now can we get Craig downstairs, please. And as far as I am aware, he hasn't done anything, so he doesn't need to do a runner out the bedroom window.'

She stared at him and headed for the bottom of the stairs.

'Craig!' It was a bellow, so much more than a shout. 'Craig!'

There was a muffled groan in answer.

'Get down here. I need you.'

A discernible thud followed as Craig Ullyat must have realised his mother wasn't going to let this drop. Footsteps were heard padding across the room immediately above the lounge.

'Need a piss,' he called.

She shook her head and rejoined Liam.

Craig joined them as Rosie reached the lounge door with the tray of drinks. He stared at her for a moment, then removed one of the cups. She hoped he'd washed his hands.

'Ta.'

'You're welcome.'

She placed the tray on the coffee table and left the drinks there.

'Mrs Ullyat, Craig, I have some news for you regarding George.'

'George? Where is he?' Craig was instantly alert. He replaced his cup on the tray.

'I'm sorry,' Liam continued, 'but Friday we found the buried remains of a man. We have now managed to confirm it is George. We believe he died around three years ago. Would that be about the time he went missing?'

Craig reached for his mother's hand. She had lost all her colour.

'But I thought he was in London,' she whispered.

'Why did you think that, Mrs Ullyat?'

'He said that's where he was going. When he got out of prison he said we'd get up one day and he'd have gone. I always thought that's what happened. I know Craig didn't, said he knew his brother and he wouldn't just leave us, but I knew what he'd said.'

'Craig?'

The lad shook his head. 'This is something to do with that Michelle, isn't it? How did he die?' He wiped away a tear.

'He was shot.'

Mother and brother inhaled sharply.

'Shot?' Craig repeated.

'I'm afraid so. Do you know where his ex-girlfriend lives now?'

'Yes. It's Summerdene Close. Seventy something. Can't remember the exact number. She owns the bakery on the shops, that one with the daft name. Breadline.'

Breadline. The bakery underneath Heather and Claudia's flat. Liam wrote the information in his book, playing for time while he gathered his thoughts.

'She's not there this week, though,' Craig said, sounding sullen.

'Oh?'

'I watch her.' Again the sullen tone.

'Why? What has she done to deserve that?' Liam knew his own voice held sharpness. He didn't like stalkers, knew they could do permanent damage to someone's life, just by getting into their mind.

'I knew she had summat to do with our George disappearing. Bet she's got a gun that matches the bullet that killed our George.'

'We will, of course, be checking all of this out,' Liam said. 'Can you remember the exact date you last saw him?'

'The 4th of June 2014,' Craig said promptly.

'That's pretty precise,' Norwood responded.

'It was my birthday. He bought me two games for my Xbox, said he'd been to town to get them. I never saw him again.'

'He did go to town for you,' Liam said gently. This lad had clearly worshipped his older brother. 'We found a bus ticket in the jeans pocket, dated 3rd of June 2014.'

This time Craig didn't wipe the tears away. He held on to his mother, and Agnes stroked his hair.

Rosie stood and handed the drinks out. 'Here,' she said softly, 'I know it seems daft, but this will help.'

They took the drinks from her, sipping slowly.

'So what do we do now?' Agnes asked.

'Nothing, until the coroner releases the body to you. We don't need formal identification, it's been done by DNA.' He thought it best not to put it into words that the body was skeletal. 'I'm so sorry we've had to bring you this news, it's not a job we enjoy, believe me. And Craig, I can tell how much you loved your brother. Respect his memory and keep away from that bakery and Michelle's home. If retribution is needed, we'll see to it by going down the legal route.'

Rosie and Liam replaced their mugs on the tray and stood.

'We'll leave you alone. We will be releasing George's name to the press now that you've been informed, so you'll need to be prepared for that.'

'Where did you find him?' It was almost as if a torch had switched on in Craig's head.

'There's a patch of land...'

'Round the back of bloody Breadline!' Craig finished the sentence triumphantly. 'I told you she was involved. I was there when you turned up last Wednesday and started putting tape on the alleyway.'

'Craig, I'll make this official if I have to. You're making unsubstantiated accusations against another member of the public, and if I hear one word of this from anyone else, I'll charge you. Is that understood? You keep away from the lady.'

'Don't worry, DS Norwood, I'll sort him. Just get his killer, will you, and Craig can forget all of this. I always liked Michelle, and what our George did to her was wrong. Her married name is Baldwin, by the way.'

'Thank you, Mrs Ullyat, we'll get out of your way. And I really am sorry for your loss, it's even more painful when it's a son or daughter.'

She gave a slight nod, and stood to escort them to the door, pulling her dressing gown around her tightly. 'Thank you,' she said. 'For explaining everything. And don't worry about Craig, I'll sort him. He'll not turn out like his brother.'

It came as no surprise to Michelle when Norwood and Havenhand turned up at the bakery. Jade had filled her in about the police activity eventually – it had taken a phone call to elicit any information of the forensic team's presence – and the presence of a body on the council land. Jade hadn't known who it was.

Michelle did. She had initially put the body in the brick storage area for a couple of days while she dug what she hoped was his final resting place. It had been backbreaking work, the ground had been baked hard after two weeks of solid sunshine, and she knew it had to be deep. She remembered the old man from across the way asking her if she was burying a body, and she had told him she wanted to put some manure and compost in the hole to make the soil richer. She wanted to grow her own salad crops for the shop. He had been impressed and wished her luck.

She waited until the second night, after midnight, and she had dragged George's body out of the shed and into the hole. It was a lot quicker filling it in than it was digging it.

She planted the seeds two days later and used the resultant harvest in the shop. She never planted seeds after that one year. The old man, the only one to have seen her, she hoped, died the following year.

The officers introduced themselves and asked if she could spare a few minutes.

'No,' she said. 'I can't. It's eleven o'clock, and my busiest time of the day. I close at two, and can wait here for you, if that's any help. What's it about?'

'There's been a body found on your land at the back of the shop. We just need to check a few details with you.' Liam played down the situation.

'It's not my land, it belongs to the council.'

'We know. But your shop backs onto it, and you may have seen something that would be helpful to us. We'll see you at two.' He turned and followed Rosie out of the door.

He glanced up and down the road, pleased to see there was no Craig lurking. Liam knocked on the door next to the shop and waited for one of the ladies to answer. Heather did.

'Hello?'

'Mrs Gower, it's DS Norwood and DC Havenhand. Can we come up, please?'

'Two seconds.'

The door opened, and they went in.

'I need you to be quiet for a couple of minutes,' Heather said. 'Claudia has been having some pain in her side, and she's on the phone with her consultant. We're hoping she can collect a prescription from her doctor, but he may want to see her.'

They nodded and followed Heather through to the lounge.

'You had a good holiday?' Norwood kept his voice low.

'Lovely, thanks, we saw as much as we could but Claudia tires easily. We used the tourist bus and taxis a lot, but it was worth it. She cried when she saw the Mona Lisa.'

'So did I,' Rosie confessed. 'It's just knowing who painted it, and that you're virtually stood in the same position he would have been standing when he created it. I found it very emotional.'

They heard Claudia say goodbye, and seconds later she was in the lounge with them.

'Mrs Bell, I understand you're not well. If you have to go…'

'No, apparently it's to be expected. He's faxing a prescription through to my doctors for strong pain relief, and I can collect it this afternoon, so we're good.' She was holding her arm close to her side and in clear discomfort.

'Then we'll not keep you long. I just wanted to check in and fill you in on what's been happening in your absence. We checked out both of your homes but found no clues as to where James could be. That investigation is still ongoing, obviously, but now we have a second one that happened right outside your patio area. You've probably noticed the crime scene tape. We found a body there, one that had been buried for about three years. We have his identification. His name is George Ullyat.'

Claudia felt herself go cold. Hadn't they just put in a doorbell system to help Michelle if George Ullyat showed up?

Rosie took note of the glance that passed between the two women. 'You know him?'

'Only his name,' Heather volunteered. 'He's the one who beat up a friend of ours and served time for it. Is it connected with that?'

'We have no idea, but we intend finding out. I'm assuming the friend you speak of is Michelle Baldwin?'

They nodded.

'I'm interviewing her after the shop has closed at two o'clock.'

'How did he die?' Claudia asked.

'He was shot.'

Claudia couldn't believe this was happening to her. She knew of the existence of a gun; was she supposed to tell the police officer, or keep quiet to protect her friend? And why had that friend pretended that George was the man stalking her, the man who had tried to run all three of them down? Her mind was working overtime trying to come up with logical answers.

And then she knew. The body could have lain undiscovered forever, and that was why Michelle continued to pretend George was still around. Michelle knew exactly where George Ullyat was.

So what had made them dig in that spot? Dare she ask?

She daren't.

Claudia pulled her arm in closer to her side and groaned.

'I'm so sorry, Mrs Bell. We'll go. You need to get that medication. I won't trouble you again unless we have something to pass on to you.' He turned to Heather. 'We'll see ourselves out. If you have anything to pass on, please ring me.'

Heather nodded. She thought that was a strange thing to say. Did he suspect something that he wasn't mentioning? She was starting to feel paranoid. So many questions running through her brain.

'Claud, you okay? I'll go and get the car and we'll go get this prescription.'

'There's no panic, Heather. The co-codamols are working fine now, just getting the odd twinge. I just wanted them to go, so I played on the pain.'

Heather stared at her. 'You had better never, and I mean never, do that with me. I need to know exactly what you're going through if I'm to help you.'

'I promise,' Claudia said, smiling. 'We'll go out later and get them. I want to talk to Michelle when Norwood's chewed her up and spat her out.' Claudia looked at her watch. 'He's not seeing her for another hour, so I'll give her a ring and ask her to come up for a cuppa after he's gone. Unless he arrests her, of course.'

'What?' Heather whispered. 'You think she killed the feller they've dug up?'

'Don't you?'

'But she's such a lovely person.' Heather closed her eyes momentarily.

'And suppose he'd just attacked her again, despite the prison sentence. Suppose the attack involved rape... just suppose, Heather. We know she's got a gun. She told us that much. And it's in her attic, probably hidden.'

'I'll ring her. You're right, as always. We need to talk to her. And while we're waiting for that to happen, we'll nip out for that prescription. No arguing. I saw the pain you were in before you took your painkillers. Did Mr Quentin want to see you?'

'Yes, I said I would go on Wednesday. He wants blood tests doing. Something about tumour markers. I didn't really understand, but I'll ask when I get there.'

Heather rang Michelle, who said she would be only too happy to come up after Norwood had finished with her, and she would bring some buns. She was having a shit day, and it was time it improved.

Heather could tell that Claudia was still uncomfortable, so she sent her to bed for an hour, and went on her own to collect the prescription.

The receptionist looked serious as she handed over the prescription.

'And how is Mrs Bell doing?'

'She's okay. We've just had a few days in Paris, and that was good, but I think she's maybe paying for that. She's tired. And her pain has increased. She needs these.' She picked up the prescription and headed to the pharmacy.

Half an hour later she was home, and Claudia was still asleep.

'Mrs Baldwin, we are aware of your relationship with George Ullyat. Can you remember when you last saw him?'

'No.'

'Not at all?'

'No, I'm sorry, I can't. I saw him after his release because he stalked me for ages, but then he stopped, and his blasted brother took over. The family won't leave me alone, and the police don't want to know, so don't come here asking daft questions. I've reported Craig Ullyat at least four times, and I don't imagine he's had so much as a visit from you.'

She was angry, and justifiably so, Norwood thought.

'I can only apologise for that,' he said. 'I'm hoping it has stopped now. We have had a word with him. However, if you do feel threatened by him, if he continues to watch you, please ring me direct.' He handed her his card. 'I've warned him there will be consequences if he continues to hassle you, and I mean it.'

'Thank you.' She spoke stiffly.

'Mrs Baldwin, do you own a gun? Or have access to one?'

Michelle laughed. 'Even if I did have one, I wouldn't have a clue how to use it. Sometimes I can't even fathom out the tin opener, so a gun would be way beyond me. No, is the answer.'

'You are aware, however, that we have found a body. It was buried on the land outside the back door of your shop.'

'I am. I wasn't in the shop last week because I had a fall which resulted in a badly sprained ankle and a fracture to my wrist. It's certainly not better, but I can cope with it now. My sister covered the shop for me and she kept me informed. Are you trying to tell me it was George?'

'Yes. We had his DNA on file following his prison sentence for the attack on you.'

'DS Norwood, do you have any idea how many people would be in the queue to bump George Ullyat off? I'm nearly at the end of that queue. He was a drug dealer, just as Craig is – he probably took over George's patch as soon as George was off the scene. In fact he's the first person I would be looking at.'

24

'Double double toil and trouble, fire burn and cauldron bubble. Fillet of a fenny snake in the cauldron boil and bake,' Heather said, as she carried a tray of buns and mugs of tea into the lounge. She placed it on the makeshift coffee table and handed small plates out. 'Eat,' she commanded. 'Let the three-witch coven begin.'

'You got any spells for getting rid of smart-arse policemen?' Michelle asked.

'Not yet, but working on it. Think we need newts and toads for that.'

'He's hassling you?' Claudia asked.

'Kind of. He thinks I killed George Ullyat.'

'Did you?' Both women asked at the same time.

'Depends who's asking.'

Again both women spoke at once. 'Friends.'

'Then yes, I did.'

There was silence for a moment.

'Shit,' Heather said.

'Wow,' responded Claudia.

'Hadn't you guessed?' Michelle turned to both of them.

'Yes, we had,' Heather responded, 'but to hear it confirmed by the person who did the deed is another thing altogether.'

'You need to get rid of that gun in your attic. He will get a search warrant you know, or he'll do it by stealth like he did with us. Get rid, please, Michelle.' Claudia was pleading.

'It's not in my attic.'

'But you said…' Heather looked puzzled.

'I said it was in the attic, not my attic.'

Realisation dawned very slowly.

'It's in our attic, isn't it?'

Michelle nodded. 'I left it there because it's quite a big job to get to it. We had loft insulation done, and then boarded the attic out. The gun is wrapped in loft insulation and is stuffed under a length of boarding the guys had already done. They came back the next day and simply carried on completing the flooring. It's buried under the third board in forever.'

'And what if they come for a search warrant for this place?' Heather spoke in a quite chatty, conversational manner, switched off completely from the gravity of the situation. Claudia just didn't want to say anything.

'They'll not find it. And if they did, you didn't live here three years ago, your fingerprints definitely aren't on it, and I imagine neither of you would know how to fire one!'

'I do.' Claudia finally spoke. 'I can shoot. James and I went away on a bonding weekend with the Sheffield Labour Party and one of the things we did was learn how to shoot.'

'So what now?' Heather asked.

'I intend saying nothing.' Michelle sounded tired. 'I've lived with this for three years, and I never thought for a minute he would be found. Why the hell would they turn up on that patch of land and dig in that place? Has Norwood said anything to you about why that happened?'

'Not a thing. But we did get rid of him pretty quickly. Claud pretended to be in a lot of pain, so he went.'

'Is he coming back?'

'He didn't say he was, but he's a policeman. Doesn't mean anything. If you're worrying about what we'll say, we won't give you up, I promise. Sometimes the only way to move on with your life is to get rid of the bloke who was holding you back. You did that, and he asked for it. Was he running away when you shot him?'

'No. I was working out the back, transferring some stuff into the brick shed. I'd had the gun in my pocket for a few days because

I was really scared he was going to attack me again. I went into the shed and suddenly he was in it as well. I was on the floor pushing some boxes under the workbench, and he held me down and raped me. He had his hand over my mouth and I couldn't scream, wasn't strong enough to fight him off. After it was over, he simply got off me and dropped onto the floor. I took the gun out of my pocket and shot him in the back.'

'And nobody heard?' Claudia took hold of Michelle's hand.

'I'd bought a gun with a silencer.'

'I'm lost for words.' Heather stood and walked to the window. 'But thank you for telling us. Now we know the truth we're not going to accidentally drop you in it.'

'Only the three of us know this. I've never spoken to Steve about it, obviously, not even to Jade. I've just kept it to myself, lived with it, been scared by it, and what's worse, I had to have an abortion. The bastard made me pregnant. I was with Steve, of course, but we were using protection until we felt the time was right to have a baby. And I couldn't have kept that baby and have Steve bring it up thinking it was his. The Durex split is too easy to say when you need to cover up an accidental conception. I aborted it and until now have left it at the back of my mind. It's quite…' She searched for the right word. 'Therapeutic to finally have someone who knows about it. I've never been able to talk about it before.'

'Is that everything?' Claudia needed to absorb the whole story.

'It is, apart from it took me two fucking days to dig that bloody hole. He should have stayed hidden forever, I buried him so deep. And now he's back.'

'Then we'll never speak of this again.' Claudia was firm. 'Not while I'm alive, anyway.'

They looked at each other and all picked up a mug of tea.

'To us, the three witches,' Claudia said, and they drank.

'It's been a lovely sunny day today, hasn't it?' Heather said, and they grinned. Normal talk, that's what they needed.

Norwood was sitting at his desk when Phil Jackson walked in. He didn't realise who he was at first, and then he jumped up, holding out his hand.

'Phil! Good to see you. I didn't recognise you without Bruce.'

'It's Bruce I've come to talk to you about, DS Norwood.'

'Liam. I'm almost off duty.'

'Okay, Liam. Right. First of all let me tell you a little bit about cadaver dogs so you'll understand what I'm saying. They're dogs that are trained to locate and follow the scent of decomposing human flesh.'

Liam nodded.

'Bruce works both on and off the leash, as you saw last week. They're trained to detect the scent of decomposition as it rises from the soil. It's kind of the same thing as when a dog knows where he last buried his bone.'

Liam said nothing, just waited.

'The dogs are trained in two different ways. Trailing dogs follow a scent that has fallen on the ground. An air-scenting dog such as Bruce picks up a decomposing human's scent that is carried on a breeze, and the dog can pick the scent out of that breeze and follow it to its source. You with me so far?'

'I am. You're trying to tell me something?'

'I am, something that's bothered me, and I can't ignore it. We walked away from you after Bruce located that target, and as we walked down that alleyway back to our dog van, he barked two or three times, and tried to pull me back to you. I was a bit short with him; he's never done anything like that before. He does his job and we go, quickly.'

'You're telling me there's another body there?'

'I think so. I think he caught the scent, and he knew it was a different one. He tried to get me to go back, and I thought he was being a daft bugger, because he can be at times. The more I think about it, the more I realise I should have let him have another go. If there's nothing there, he was just being a daft bugger, but if there is something, it's me that was the daft bugger. What do you think?'

'I think I want to kiss you, but I won't.'

'Thank the Lord for that,' Phil responded with a grin. 'Tomorrow?'

'Meet you at nine, at that alleyway. Will Bruce be available then?'

'Yes. I need you to requisition him before you go home.'

They both stood and once again shook hands.

'Thank you, Phil.'

'No problem, boss. See you tomorrow.'

Heather was sitting on the patio enjoying her first drink of the day in the warmth of the early morning sunshine; she saw Norwood and another police officer with a dog on a lead appear below her in the knee-high grass, and her cup tipped. She cursed quietly as the liquid spilled down her dressing gown.

The two men were joined by Rosie Havenhand who glanced up at the patio as if that was the subject of the men's discussion.

Heather didn't move. From their position she didn't think she was visible, and she needed to know what they were doing. It slowly dawned on her that they had found George Ullyat's body by using the dog, and in fact that had been a bonus. They hadn't been looking for George. They suspected her and Claudia of murdering James and burying him somewhere on this plot of land.

She mentally called herself all the names in the world; stupid, brain dead, crazy – her list was endless. How could she have been so thick as to bury him so close to her own home?

Her thoughts escalated, as she realised it probably meant Norwood had further evidence linking her to James's disappearance – could it be his car? Had it been forensically examined? Her blood had to be in it, just as much as James's blood was there.

The dog was sitting down but kept half standing, then sitting down again. He was a beautiful animal, she mused, probably one that was about to send her to prison for life.

She saw the handler bend down and speak to the dog as Norwood and his DC stood and watched.

The Alsatian stood for a moment then began to pull on his lead. The handler slipped the lead and the animal shot towards where she was sitting watching the proceedings. The dog was now underneath the patio, and Heather knew it was all over.

The forensics team unearthed James within five minutes. It was very clear where the earth had been disturbed and Liam and Rosie, along with Neil who had travelled down once he heard it had been a successful search, watched with interest. Just because it was a body, didn't mean it was automatically James Bell. They had thought the last body interred on this patch of land was him, only to be proven wrong.

A white-suited member of the digging team pulled back the plastic cover in which the body was encased. Liam went inside the tent on hearing his name called and looked at the revealed face. Decomposition had started, but it was clearly James. He nodded, thanked the team for their help and left the tent.

'Okay,' he said, keeping his voice muted. 'It's definitely James Bell. I need to tell Mrs Bell, but until there is confirmation that there is something linking Heather Gower to that body, I intend leaving her alone. I want her to think she's safe. I'm a hundred per cent sure she killed him, but I don't know why. I want all my facts in place before I arrest her, so that's what we need to concentrate on. And I need to know where he was killed. I think he must have been dead before he went in the car boot. There was very little blood, so there's a site somewhere that could potentially reveal where his death happened.'

'The cemetery,' Rosie said slowly. 'It's our next port of call.'

'It certainly is,' Norwood confirmed. 'But we have to treat this with some care. This is a baby's grave, and the press would crucify us if we got this wrong. Initially, you and I will go, Rosie. We'll only call the forensics in if we think there's anything to get them in for. I suspect we'll have enough on Heather Gower to convict her anyway, once the post-mortem is done. And to be perfectly honest, I think she'll tell us everything. She's not a criminal, she's a middle-class woman who has had things happen to her.'

'You reckon?' Neil asked.

'Don't you?' Liam countered. 'You've read all the reports. And I have a feeling, intuition, call it what you want, that when we do have the facts on this it will prove to be self-defence. Yes, she's going to prison. She concealed a body, and that's major on its own, but she's not going there for life. I'll stake my job on it.'

'Get this wrong,' Rosie said, 'and you might be doing just that.'

Claudia walked into the lounge rubbing her eyes. 'Look at the time! These new painkillers are absolutely knocking me out. Would hate to take more than two, I might never wake up again.' Her face changed. 'What have I just said, Heather?'

Heather stood. 'Hey, don't let this bloody disease define you. Say what you want, when you want, especially if it's just the two of us.' *Which might not be for much longer.*

'I'm sorry,' Claudia said. 'I've not really come around yet. I'll make myself a coffee, that might help.'

'I'll make it.' Heather headed for the kitchen and switched on the kettle. She felt sick at the thought of what was to come; she had no doubt that Norwood had enough against her to arrest her, and it would happen soon. She made them both a coffee and walked back into the lounge. Claudia wasn't there.

'Claud!' she called.

'Patio,' came back to her, and she groaned.

She stepped outside and handed Claudia her drink.

'What do you think is going off out here?' Claudia asked, pointing to the edge of the tent just visible from where they were standing. Norwood and Rosie Havenhand were standing off to the left, and Neil Evans was walking towards the tent. He looked up and saw the women looking down at him. He acknowledged them with a brief wave of his hand.

'Claud, we have to talk,' Heather said.

Norwood stayed until the body had been removed to the morgue, then he and Rosie left for the cemetery; Neil Evans headed back to the station.

Liam and Rosie went into the office at the main gate, manned by an elderly lady with glasses on a cord around her neck. They were cushioned by her ample bosom.

She smiled as they walked in, then the smile disappeared as she was shown their warrant cards. 'How can I help?' Smiles were reserved for grieving relatives, not policemen going about their business.

'We need to locate the grave of a baby. Not sure of the Christian name but it was a little girl, two days old when she died around seven years ago, and she has the surname of Bell. Can you help us?'

'Yes. One minute please.' The woman moved to her computer, typed in the information she had, clicked on a couple of things and printed off the results. She moved back to the counter and handed over the printed sheet.

'This is a layout of the full cemetery. This area here...' She pointed with a red biro. 'Is the children's area. Please be respectful, there are always parents there, and they grieve forever. This grave here...' She marked over the printed cross with the red biro. 'Is the grave of Ella Mae Bell. Her mother comes every week, Saturday afternoon, brings fresh flowers and cleans the headstone. A much-loved little girl.'

'You see her every week, the mother?' Liam interrupted her flow.

'I do.' The woman lifted the counter hatch. 'Come through and I'll show you where the section is.'

Liam followed her through and she led him to the window. 'There.'

He couldn't miss it. The whole section was a riot of colour, not just from flowers but from toys, ribbons, cards; heartbreakingly beautiful.

'And you see Mrs Bell every week, you say?'

'Oh yes, although this past three or four weeks it's not been the same. Is Mrs Bell okay?'

'She is,' Norwood confirmed. 'Been a little under the weather but on the mend now.'

'Oh good. I can set my clock by her. She's usually here by around one, but if it's later than that I don't see her. The CCTV kicks in at one just before I go home.'

'Does the CCTV cover that area?'

'It does. That's where we have most trouble, because the youths target it to get the toys and stuff the parents leave for their babies.'

'And is it saved?'

'Yes. I come in Monday morning, save the stuff that's on since the last time it was set, and reset it. It's all on here.' She patted her screen.

'You don't look at it?'

'Only if we need to. We haven't had any trouble for a while, not since the police let it be known the CCTV was on the youths. Is there something you want to see?'

'I want to get my man here to download everything from the last six weeks or so. Please allow him access to it when he comes. I won't need to get a warrant, will I?'

She looked flustered. 'No, you won't. Of course I'll cooperate. Oh, I hope nothing's wrong.'

'It isn't,' he said with a smile, trying to placate her. 'When my man gets here, he'll have a password so that you know he's the one entitled to take the download. His name is DC Neil Evans, and the password is Bruce. Thank you for your help. We'll get out of your hair. The officer will be here in about half an hour at the most.'

She nodded, then moved to the window and watched as they headed across to Ella Mae's grave.

Liam rang Neil as they reached the children's area, and gave him the password, then they walked up the slight incline to the tiny grave.

'Dear God,' Rosie said. 'This is bloody awful. How do they cope?' She waved her arm around, indicating the many graves of infants. 'How does anybody handle losing a child?'

Norwood stood and read the inscription on Ella Mae's headstone, and for a moment couldn't speak. Didn't even know what to say. It was the part that read *Our Christmas baby* that floored him.

He turned to Rosie and saw the tears in her eyes. 'Hey. We're not allowed to cry. You okay?'

She nodded. 'It's heart-breaking, that's what it is. Every one of these graves belongs to a child. And that woman, the one whose world we're about to destroy when we take her best friend away from her, has been here every Saturday for seven years. It's a shitty world, sometimes, isn't it?'

25

They met up back at the station, Liam, Rosie and Neil, and waited while Neil downloaded the file to his own computer.

'I started from the 3rd of April,' Neil explained. 'Just to put it in context, this is the Monday before Heather Gower's husband, Owen Gower, dies. She admitted to having seen James Bell at the cemetery on Saturday 16th of April, when he was looking for his wife, but said she didn't see him the Saturday after. On the 16th of April, Mrs Bell was in hospital. She'd had her operation for cancer the day before and obviously was very ill. She arrives home on the 20th of April, still very poorly but recovering at home under Heather Gower's care. Heather said she went to the grave on her own the following Saturday, that's 23rd of April, but she said she didn't see James that time. I think that will be the date we need to look at. Councillor Monroe says this was the last time he saw James. It all ties in.'

'Okay, and thanks for the recap. It's good to refresh the timeline,' Liam said. 'Can you take it to the Friday, the day before, and we'll check it from then?'

'Right, I'll switch it through to the screen on the wall, and we can all see it in much more detail.'

Claudia was shaking. 'You're seriously telling me that the body they're digging up down there is James? And you killed him?'

Heather nodded. She couldn't say any more, she had no words left. Telling the full story of him pushing her backwards onto the headstone, and then her bringing around the scissors that ended up embedded in his neck had been hard, but telling her the full story of getting him in the car boot and finally burying him had left Claudia devoid of any colour, and trembling.

Heather forced herself to speak. 'Norwood must have suspected me from the start, and logic made him bring the dog here. It threw everybody off when they found George Ullyat, but Liam's now realised they stopped looking after finding George. He's come back for a second bite of the cherry, and they've found him. James. Claudia, I wish it hadn't happened, but it did. I was so scared of him, and my arm came up to defend myself. I didn't mean for any of this to happen.'

'Oh, Heather,' Claudia's eyes were brimming with tears, 'I know how scary James was, believe me. What I'm struggling with is why you didn't send for the police at the time. It was self-defence, you were badly injured. Your head was a mess.'

'You want to know why I didn't call them? They would have taken me away from you, and you were still so ill. I couldn't leave you, couldn't tell you, I just had to do what I thought was best. But they're never going to believe the self-defence bit now, too much time has passed, and my head has healed.'

The two women sat and stared at each other, unable to comprehend fully the enormity of what was happening.

'They'll be here later today,' Heather said. 'I've a couple of letters to write, and I could do with some time out. Will you be okay if I take an hour?'

'Of course,' Claudia said. 'I'll bring you through a milky coffee.'

She stood and went to her room, picked up the plastic container of painkillers and diverted to the kitchen to make the drinks. She opened up four of the tablets and tipped the tiny granules into the hot milk. Anger was building inside her so fast it was threatening to overwhelm her. They were supposed to be such close friends, and yet Heather hadn't spoken of the minor fact that she had killed James. It put a different light on Owen's death. Claudia took deep breaths before leaving the kitchen.

'Here,' she said, and handed Heather her drink. 'This will make you feel calmer for facing what we have to face later. And if you want to sleep, just sleep. I'll still be here, I'll make sure you're okay.'

Heather took the mug and smiled. 'You try to sleep, Claud. I'm so so sorry for having brought all this on you. You know I love you, don't you?'

Claudia nodded. 'Of course. Go and do what you have to. I won't disturb you, I promise. And I love you, best friend.' She walked out of the room, giving Heather the time and space she had requested.

Returning to the kitchen, Claudia emptied every tablet into an eggcup. She waited twenty minutes and quietly opened Heather's door. She was sprawled on the bed, asleep. Claudia walked around the bed, picked up the cup using kitchen roll and went back to the kitchen.

Adding milk to the same cup was sensible, and she stirred in the pile of granules created by emptying eighteen tablets. She returned to the bedroom and lifted Heather, supporting her with difficulty and considerable pain.

She held the cup to Heather's lips, and she moaned.

'Just a little drink, Heather,' Claudia said softly. 'Then everything will be okay.'

It took ten minutes to get her to swallow it, and Claudia replaced the mug on the bedside table, along with the empty container. She flushed the split capsules down the toilet, not taking the risk of her fingerprints being discoverable on them.

'It was self-defence beyond any shadow of a doubt,' Liam said, the frustration evident in his voice. 'Why the fuck didn't she just get help? It would have been so clear at the scene, the blood on the headstone, the angle of the scissors... and, although she didn't know it, every second of it is on CCTV!'

'She was scared, boss,' Rosie said. 'She probably assumed she would be locked up, and she has a terminally ill best friend who needs her. These two women have gone through enough to break anybody, and I think this broke Heather Gower.'

'Right, we need a forensics team at that baby's grave, because from the amount of blood from Heather's head, there's bound to be some left, and I bet there's some along the trail she made dragging him to the car. We've already linked them both to the Sportage, and now I'm going to take the Fiesta they use, to have that given the full forensics.'

Liam moved back to his desk and made the arrangements, then returned to his team.

'Good work on this. We may only be a small team, but we've cracked this one. This afternoon Rosie and I will go to arrest Heather and tell Mrs Bell we've found her husband. I'm not going to ask her to identify him, but Harry, their son, seemed a smart enough lad when we went to see him. I'll ask him to do it. I'll check with pathology first, they may not want him to ID his father's face, there was a lot of decomposition, but he had a large tattoo on his arm. He can ID him from that.'

Claudia slept until just after two o'clock and woke still feeling fuzzy. The tablets she'd taken from her second container were definitely too strong, although she was under no illusions about this blessed disease, she would need that tablet strength and more as she drew nearer the end of her life. After holding Heather almost upright, the pain in her side had been intense; co-codamol wouldn't have cut it at all.

She headed down the corridor to the toilet, opening Heather's door slightly as she went past. The room was in semi-darkness as Heather had closed the curtains, and she was still in the same position on the bed. Claudia softly closed the door. Time enough to open it later.

She grabbed a fresh glass of water and headed back to the lounge. She picked up her book but put it down almost immediately. She couldn't concentrate. She really had believed James was still alive and had just taken himself off somewhere to punish her. James, her first love, and now her last.

The knock, combined with the doorbell, shook her in its unexpectedness. She waited a moment, and went to the intercom.

'Hello?'

'DS Norwood and DC Havenhand, Mrs Bell. Can we come up please?'

She felt sick. Holding tightly to the handrail she went down the three sections of the stairs and unlocked the door. There were two police cars outside.

The officers followed her upstairs, Rosie and Liam both aware she wasn't moving at any speed.

'Are you okay, Mrs Bell?' Rosie asked, concerned for the woman's pallor and general demeanour.

'I have terminal cancer, DC Havenhand. I look peaky most of the time,' she said with a smile.

'Is Mrs Gower in?' Norwood knew he sounded brusque, but he had never known a time when he had not wanted to arrest a perpetrator. This was a first for him.

'Yes, she is. She went for a nap. I'll go and wake her.'

'Rosie will go with you, Mrs Bell.'

'Oh... okay.'

Norwood continued down to the lounge, and Claudia quietly opened Heather's door, not wanting to startle her awake.

'Heather,' she whispered. 'Heather!' There was no movement, and Rosie Havenhand walked around the side of the bed. She shook Heather's shoulder, then put her finger on the pulse in Heather's neck.

'No...' Claudia's eyes opened wide in shock. 'No!'

Liam heard her and ran from the lounge back to where the women were.

Rosie shook her head. 'I'm sorry, sir, there's no pulse.' She took out her phone and rang for the ambulance

Claudia couldn't cope. Michelle was blazingly angry.

'The silly cow! She brought the police to my door because she buried the wanker virtually in the same spot George was! I'm glad she's dead, I'd kill her myself if she wasn't. What the fuck...'

Claudia sat, immobile, on the sofa. She wasn't sure she was capable of dealing with Michelle at that moment.

'And I bent over backwards to help you two.'

Finally, Claudia spoke. 'But we didn't know you'd killed George, you told us he was watching you all the time, you said he was the feller across the road. How could she have known?'

Michelle stormed down the corridor. 'The second you die I'm taking back this flat,' she called from the other end of the corridor. She went down the stairs and slammed the bottom door loudly as she exited.

And Claudia cried.

An hour later she stopped crying. She went to the small broom cupboard and took out the long pole that opened the loft hatch. She used it to pull down the loft ladder and climbed the treads, grateful that she still had enough movement to get about without too much pain.

She counted the loft boards and checked the third one. They were screwed down, not nailed, and she was thankful for that break. She wasn't sure she would have had the strength to lever nails out, but screws were manageable. She checked the screw head and went back down the ladder for the necessary tool. She blessed Heather for stocking them up with basic equipment.

There was only one screw that caused her a problem and she persevered until it loosened.

An hour later she had the gun, stored inside a box normally used to place purchased buns, and bullets, all wrapped in loft insulation that was making her itch like nothing had ever done before.

She replaced all the screws, leaving it exactly as it had been, then went back down to the lounge, careful to take everything with her. She checked the gun over in the way she had been taught at the gun range, loaded it, and placed it back in the box Michelle had used.

She raised the reclining footrest on the sofa, pushed the box underneath and lowered the mechanism. Totally concealed.

She spent the next half hour showering and washing her hair, getting rid of the itchy loft insulation.

The office Heather had created for them was a peaceful place, just as Heather had intended. Claudia researched gold bracelets until she found exactly what she wanted, organised the inscription, and paid for it. The site promised seven days delivery; all good.

Everything was in place.

26

18 August 2017

DI Norwood checked over the last report to come in on the Bell case and moved it into the folder on his computer. He then archived it and expelled a long breath.

This was the case that had seen him promoted to DI; he had wondered why he had been allowed such a free hand to run it, and it had been obvious shortly after the end of it. DI Philippa Ray was now DCI, and there had been further changes in his team. DC Rosie Havenhand was now DC Rosie Evans, and DC Neil Evans was now DS Evans. Liam had asked Rosie to stick with her maiden name at work, it made life so much easier.

The George Ullyat case was still ongoing, and he often wondered if they would ever find anything else. The gun had never resurfaced in any other crime, and he feared it would become yet another statistic, a dead case unless something accidentally gave them a result on it. He had read the statements so many times, the reports after the finding of the body, but there was nothing other than a bullet to tell them anything.

Agnes and Craig Ullyat had closure of a sort in that they had a grave they could visit, and it appeared that Craig had turned his life around and was working as a trainee plumber, but the case niggled Norwood. One day…

Claudia smiled as her lunch arrived. She knew she wouldn't eat much of it, and as a result of the loss of appetite she was losing weight, but the meals were beautiful to look at.

She had been in St Luke's Hospice for three days; Mr Quentin had made the arrangements for her, telling her she maybe only had three weeks to a month left to put her affairs in order.

Her will had been sorted, and the children would be sharing the proceeds of the sale of the family home, plus the proceeds from the sale of Heather's home. She felt happy that they would be financially settled. A tear clouded her eye at the reminder of Heather's death. She had been shocked to find Heather had changed her will two days after she had killed James, to make sure Claudia's children would receive the proceeds of the sale of her house.

Harry, Emma, Zoe and David didn't know how little time she had left. She was getting very good at acting in front of them. They thought she had requested a room at St Luke's to make life a little more luxurious for her final few months; they were wrong. There was a final scene to play out.

Yolande placed the tray in front of her and checked Claudia's pulse. 'I'm just going to do your blood pressure, and then you can eat this entire plateful, yes?'

'Of course,' Claudia responded, as she did every meal time.

'Well if you don't,' the pretty nurse said, 'you'll be on the sachets of food supplements, from this afternoon. Just thought I'd give you a heads up on that, because they're vile.'

'I'll eat it, I'll eat it!'

'Good. Now give me your arm.' Claudia held out her left arm, ever mindful of long ago instructions that she must never again use her right arm for blood pressure or blood sample tests.

Yolande seemed satisfied and was just about to go out the door when Claudia spoke again.

'Yolande, do you think I could have a day at home, back at the flat? There are a couple of things I need to sort, and then I can come back here until…'

'Yes, of course, Claudia. Will somebody be picking you up, or will you need a taxi?'

'A taxi please. I don't want my family to know, they'll only fuss, and I do want time on my own, one last day in my home.'

'Many patients do this. It's almost like reverse nesting. When do you want to go?'

'I need to make a phone call first, but possibly tomorrow.' Claudia needed all the plans she had made over the weeks since she had lost Heather to come to fruition, and it would all depend on one phone call.

Yolande nodded. 'Just let me know, and I'll arrange it for you. Do you have any pain?'

'I do.'

'I'll get you some tablets. Now eat that lunch. Remember the meal supplements. Yuck.'

Claudia was eating some potato when Yolande returned with her tablets. 'Good girl,' she said with a grin and left the room.

Claudia climbed painfully out of bed and crossed to the bathroom. She scraped most of the meal down the toilet, and flushed it away, leaving a couple of small carrot pieces on her plate.

Yolande was pleased when she came to collect the tray. 'That's really good. What's wrong with the carrots?'

'Nothing, I've never really liked them. I ate a couple but that was enough.'

'Okay. You had your tablets?'

Claudia waved the little pot at her containing the two capsules of powdered painkiller.

'Just about to take them. They send me to sleep straight away, so thought I'd better eat lunch first.'

Yolande laughed. 'They affect everybody like that. They're strong but they do the job. You made your phone call yet?'

'Doing that now as well. Are you nagging me?'

'Yes, you need your rest, Claudia.'

'Okay, get out of here, woman. Leave me in peace.'

Yolande laughed and left the room.

Claudia took her purse out of the bedside drawer, wrapped the tablets in a scrap of toilet paper and placed them in the zipped coin compartment. She then took the tablet she had saved from an earlier medication and put that on her table ready to take after she had made the phone call. It was only one, but it would take the edge off the pain. She needed to save the other two.

Her phone was fully charged, and she scrolled until she reached Monroe. She pressed and listened to it ringing out.

'Good afternoon. Councillor Monroe.'

'Councillor Will Monroe? My name is Claudia Bell, James's wife. I'm sorry we didn't get to speak at his funeral, I did see you, but I was too ill to speak to anyone. I would, however, like to speak face-to-face, because I have cleared a lot of the house prior to selling it, and I have found a heavy gold bracelet that I believe James bought for you. It is valuable and personal, and you need to have it.'

'Mrs Bell, Claudia… I'm shocked. How do you know it's for me?'

'It has yours and James's names on it. There is no ill feeling, Councillor, I stopped loving James a long time ago. I just think this is something you should have. There's no receipt with it and as it's engraved, no shop would take it back anyway.'

'Thank you. This is so good of you. I can drive to Sheffield…' There was slight hesitation as he checked his diary. 'Next Wednesday?'

'I may not be able to do that. I am in the last couple of weeks of my life, Councillor. I have terminal cancer. I need it to be very soon. Tomorrow if possible.'

'Give me a minute.'

She could hear him mumbling in the background and somebody responding, and then he came back to her.

'Is eleven okay?'

'That would be really good. I'm leaving my hospice for the day so that I can see you, I really would like to meet you. It's clear that James really cared for you and I bear him no animosity for that. I just want to meet the person who became such a large part of his life. You have a pen?' She read out her address, and he repeated it back to her.

'Thank you,' Claudia said quietly. 'This means a lot to me. We'll have a cup of tea and drink a toast to the man we have both loved at different times in our lives.'

They disconnected, and Claudia pressed her assistance bell.

'Claudia. You want something?' Yolande smiled at her.

Claudia waved the little pot containing the one tablet. 'I've taken my first tablet, but thought I'd better tell you I'll need a taxi for nine in the morning please, before I take the second one. Going to my home address if they need to know. I'll be back early afternoon, but I'll ring for a cab from home.'

'Okay. I'll sort out your lunchtime medication to take with you. You may need it before you get back, you seem to be needing it more frequently now.'

'Only to be expected,' Claudia said. 'And I don't feel frightened. I know I will slip into a coma when you have no choice but to keep me sedated for the pain, and I don't want that time to come, but I've accepted it all now. My children haven't, but they're grown up, and will support each other.'

'You're a brave woman, Claudia Bell. Now take that other tablet and go to sleep.'

19 August 2017

The taxi arrived on time, and half an hour later, Claudia was slowly climbing the stairs back up to the flat. She had thought the two of them would be here for a long time; they had loved it on first sight. Now it held bad memories of Heather's death, the horrific row she had had with Michelle, and now the final act of her own life.

She checked her watch and saw she had at least an hour to spare before Will Monroe arrived, so she put the small bottle of milk Yolande had given her into the fridge, took down an egg cup, broke open the two capsules of painkillers and put the egg cup back in the cupboard. Claudia stood two mugs on the side, boiled the kettle, then headed across the corridor to the office.

She had an important letter to write to DI Norwood. He had treated her with respect at all times, and she wanted her actions to be for him.

She began to type.

Will Monroe was five minutes early and Claudia opened the door to him with a smile. He leaned forward and kissed both cheeks, then waited patiently while he followed her slow progress upstairs.

'Are you in pain?' he asked.

'Yes, but it's not good to give in to it. It's the nature of the beast,' Claudia said. 'James didn't know. I hadn't had any sort of cancer diagnosis when I left him. According to St Luke's, I'm in the last three or four weeks of my life, and they've allowed me home for a few hours to tie up any loose ends. While I've been waiting for you I've written a couple of letters to friends, checked with my solicitor that my children won't have any problems with my will, generally put my affairs in order.'

'And now I'm seeing why James wouldn't leave you. You're a strong woman, Claudia.'

She smiled. 'I am. Would you like tea or coffee? I have fresh milk, but no cream.'

'Tea with milk, two sugars please if it's a mug.'

They eventually reached the lounge and she apologised for the suitcase on the sofa. 'I'm taking some bits back with me. Sit anywhere else.'

'Thank you.' He smiled as he saw the upturned plastic box. 'Innovative.'

'Heather, my friend who I moved in here with, devised that. I don't want a real one, that will do for me.'

She went into the kitchen and reboiled the still warm water in the kettle. She put a tea bag in each mug, a small amount of milk in Monroe's along with two spoonfuls of sugar, and the contents of the eggcup.

The drinks made, she carried them through to the lounge.

She handed him the bracelet. 'This is what I found. Had you seen it before?'

He took it out of the box, and looked at it, spending some time staring at the engraving. 'No,' he said eventually. 'It's beautiful. He loved me?'

She nodded. 'I think so. It's why I wanted to see you. I know you must be hurting. But can you just tell me one thing… did you start the affair or did he?'

'It was me. I came on to him, but he never fought it. It was as though he'd always been gay, he was simply waiting for the right person, and that person was me. Right place, right time. We were together over six years, you know. I've been hurting since the day I realised he was missing. And according to DI Norwood, he was killed not long after he left me.'

He picked up his cup and drank, still turning over the bracelet in his other hand. 'I can't believe he bought this for me. I guess it must have been intended for my birthday in May.' He looked up and spoke directly to Claudia. 'I'll always treasure it.'

He put down the cup and picked up the gift box, carefully replacing it inside it.

He lifted the cup again and began to drink. They talked about James, sharing memories, and slowly Will's cup emptied. He placed it on the coffee table and cradled the box again. He opened the lid.

''s lovely,' he slurred. ''s mine. From James…'

He leaned his head back against the sofa and tried to focus his gaze on the woman sitting in the chair. 'Tired,' he mumbled.

'Then rest before you drive home,' she soothed. 'Close your eyes for five minutes, you sanctimonious prick.'

'Need… sleep.' He closed his eyes.

Claudia stood and removed the suitcase, the empty suitcase that she had placed there to prevent him sitting on that seat, and raised the recliner. She knelt, groaning at the pain that flared in her side. She waited a moment, feeling the sweat on her brow as her body tried to contain her pain.

She pulled the box out and lowered the recliner. Monroe never moved.

The gun felt good in her hand. She would have liked to have waited until he stirred, but she knew she was ready for returning to the sanctuary of St Luke's. Time was running out.

She raised the gun, held it close to his chest, and fired. There was very little noise; Michelle had spent well on this little item. The blood splatter was gross, and she looked at the sofa. That would be no good for anybody now, she thought.

She took the cups into the kitchen, put the bracelet in a padded envelope addressed to Craig Ullyat with instructions to sell it, and went for a shower. Monroe's blood had gone everywhere, so she changed all her clothes.

The taxi arrived very quickly, and while she was waiting she walked across the road to the postbox and posted both letters.

By one o'clock she was back in her room at St Luke's, and finally giving in to the cancer that was eating away at her body. The pain was overwhelming her, and they upped her dosage for the last time.

Everything was sorted.

20 August

Liam picked up the mail Rosie had placed tidily on his desk and sorted through it. The pink envelope caught his eye, as Claudia had known it would. He turned it over and saw her name on the back.

He ignored the rest of the mail, and carefully opened the envelope. Years of training had taught him to be careful of anything unusual.

Dear DI Norwood,

I am now finishing my life in St Luke's Hospice, and according to the doctors I have maybe three or four weeks. I suspect only a couple of days in reality. Yesterday, the 19th of August, I went back to my flat for two reasons; I met up with Councillor Will Monroe, or Marilyn as my husband knew him, and I wrote you this letter. I have also sent a gold bracelet to Craig Ullyat for him to sell. This is genuinely from me, if anything should come of it. I hope the boy has turned his life around.

I saved two of the strongest painkillers known to man (that's how they feel to me) and I fed them to Monroe in a cup of tea. He was asleep within about ten minutes, and I shot him through the heart. You don't need to go tearing around there, he is definitely dead.

This man destroyed everything. He started his relationship with my husband over six years ago, and I paid the price for that. James beat me many times, but I kept trying to save our marriage.

Because James couldn't bear that I had taken the initiative and left him, he tried to find me at the cemetery, and attacked my best friend. As a result, she killed him, albeit accidentally. Because of that, and also because she didn't tell me, I killed her. I fed her the tablets that you assumed was an overdose. I hope she is waiting for me to join her. We'll have a ball in heaven. And I'm sure she'll promise that she will never let go of a heavy suitcase at the top of the stairs again, it has a bad effect on the person who is trying to hold on to it.

It's been a funny old five months.

Monroe destroyed my life, and now it is coming to an end. It's strange, DI Norwood, but when you have a terminal diagnosis, it becomes very liberating. I am free to do whatever I want, and what I wanted to do yesterday was kill Monroe, so I did. There's a lot of blood, but I didn't spoil his pretty face, I went for the heart.

Oh, and one other thing. The gun I shot him with belongs to Michelle Baldwin. She hid it in the flat's loft three years ago, under the third board in, as you go up the loft ladder. I went and recovered it. I think when you compare the bullet in Monroe with the bullet in George Ullyat, you'll be able to clear up another crime. I've left the gun on our special coffee table.

Sorry I didn't wash the pots, I couldn't be bothered. Oh, and here's Heather's key, I'm sure she would want you to use it.

Congratulations on your promotion; my son-in-law told me about it. It's well deserved, I'm sure.

Remember me, the quiet one, the liberated one.

Best wishes

Claudia Bell

Liam stared at the letter, read it a second time then yelled at the top of his voice. 'Rosie! Neil! We're going out!'

He handed them the letter to read as they headed down to the flat, and he heard Rosie say, 'Shit.'

He thought that was polite.

They pulled up outside the flat and were inside within thirty seconds. They could smell the iron tang of blood and headed for the lounge.

It was carnage. Monroe was slumped on the sofa, a hole in his chest, his eyes closed. Blood had spattered everywhere, ceiling, walls, carpet, all around.

The forensics team were there quickly, and it didn't take a genius to work out the cause of death.

The gun was bagged, and sent for immediate analysis. He didn't want Michelle Baldwin doing a runner because she heard there had been a shooting. They put crime scene tape across the door, and a PC on guard outside.

Liam and Rosie headed for St Luke's, showed their warrant cards to the receptionist, who went to get Yolande, as Claudia's senior carer, to deal with them.

'I'm sorry,' Yolande said, when she arrived at the front desk. 'You can't see Mrs Bell.'

'I don't think you understand,' Liam said. 'We need to speak with her.'

'In connection with…?'

'We can't discuss that with you.'

'Well, you sure as hell can't discuss it with her,' was Yolande's spirited rejoinder. 'Mrs Bell went out for a few hours yesterday, and had a rapid decline when she arrived back here. As a result, she isn't conscious, and so we sent for her family.'

Liam knew when he was defeated. 'Okay. I give in. One request. If I leave my warrant card with DC Havenhand, can I just see Mrs Bell for one minute? No words, I'd just like to say a goodbye.'

'Wait here,' Yolande said. 'I'll ask the family.'

He handed his warrant card to Rosie, and took a deep breath. He'd admired Claudia Bell from the beginning, and he knew he would remember her.

Yolande rejoined them and nodded. 'Follow me.'

Claudia looked so tiny. Her eyes were closed, and Zoe and Harry were holding her hands. Emma and David were with their respective partners.

Liam stood at the end of the bed for only a few seconds, he didn't want to intrude on the palpable grief. 'Bye, Claudia,' he finally said. 'And thank you.'

'Michelle Baldwin, you are under arrest on suspicion of murder. You do not have to say anything, but it may harm your defence if you do not mention when questioned something which you later rely on in court. Anything you do say may be given in evidence.'

Her blue eyes flashed in temper. 'Fuck Heather Gower and Claudia Bell. I knew they were trouble as soon as I first set eyes on 'em.'

Agnes and Craig Ullyat watched as Michelle was led out to the police car. Craig grinned. It had been worth paying Archie Davis that twenty quid to tell him when a cop car turned up; him and his mum wanted to see that fuckin' murderer carted away.

Michelle had a hand placed on her head to help her into the back seat, and her anger showed as she brushed the hand away. Steve was left standing in the doorway looking helpless as she was driven down the road.

Craig put his hand in his inside pocket and touched the bracelet. 'I'm heading into town, Mum. Sell this little beauty before somebody says I can't.' He kissed her. 'Takeaway tonight?'

THE END

Acknowledgements

My grateful thanks go as always to my publishers, Bloodhound Books. Fred and Betsy Freeman have always been supportive of my work, and I am truly blessed. They have a superb team in Alexina Golding, Sumaira Wilson and Sarah Hardy, who deal with queries and issues as if they didn't exist. It is comforting to know that they can handle anything!

I also want to say thank you to all the bloggers who support authors in the best way possible, by getting our books out there in front of readers. That thank you is a massive one.

I have some fans to thank for allowing me to use their names in the book – Heather Gower, Michelle Baldwin, Jenny Taylor, Jade Pitman (and Elsa!) and Norma Ormond. Thank you all for your unswerving support, and I hope you enjoy the parts you played. Sincere apologies if I've turned you into a corpse, I'm inclined to do that occasionally.

My editor, Morgen Bailey, is also worthy of my thanks. More than worthy. This book would be nothing without her. She has taught me so much, and I am truly grateful.

Thanks also go to my fellow pups in the Bloodhound kennels. If queries occur during the writing of books, there is always a fellow Bloodhound author who will come up with the answer. I myself am now an expert in cadaver dogs…

This book has been difficult to write because of the subject matter. I had very little research to do despite the enormity of the subject, and it has all been written from the heart. Take comfort from the fact that in the main, malignant melanoma is curable, and we have amazing surgeons in our NHS who make the statement a fact. I am testament to that.

And finally, my love goes to Bethan, our own Christmas baby, 17.12.76 – 19.12.76, always with us.

I hope you have enjoyed the book, and please leave a review on Amazon; it only takes a minute and I love reading them. They are so important to every author.

Best wishes,
Anita Waller
Sheffield, May 2018